PRAISE FOR JOHN A. MILLER'S
CUTDOWN

"John Miller's new mystery novel only gets better as it goes along. . . . Much better. . . . An intriguing, complex story [with] an intriguing, complex character in the middle of it."

—*The State* (Columbia, SC)

"Impressive. . . . McCutcheon [shows] ingenuity, knowledge of violence and surprising tenderness in this well-plotted, action-filled first bow."

—*Publishers Weekly*

"Readers who enjoy well-written mysteries involving complicated, intelligent, independent characters such as John Sandford's Lucas Davenport, Patricia Cornwell's Kay Scarpetta, and James Lee Burke's Dave Robichaux can add another book to their list of must-buys: John A. Miller's CUTDOWN. . . . Strong and well-crafted. . . . Miller introduces us to Claude McCutcheon, but wisely leaves us eager to learn more. . . ."

—*BookPage*

Books by John A. Miller

Cutdown
Jackson Street and Other Soldier Stories
Causes of Action

Available from POCKET BOOKS

CUTDOWN

A CLAUDE McCUTCHEON NOVEL

JOHN A. MILLER

POCKET BOOKS

New York London Toronto Sydney Tokyo Singapore

This book is a work of fiction. Names, characters, places and incidents are products of the author's imagination or are used fictitiously. Any resemblance to actual events or locales or persons living or dead is entirely coincidental.

POCKET BOOKS, a division of Simon & Schuster Inc.
1230 Avenue of the Americas, New York, NY 10020

Copyright © 1997 by John Miller

Originally published in hardcover in 1997 by Pocket Books

ISBN: 0-671-56905-8

First Pocket Books paperback printing December 1998

10 9 8 7 6 5 4 3 2 1

POCKET and colophon are registered trademarks of Simon & Schuster Inc.

Cover design by Matt Galemmo

Printed in the U.S.A.

FOR LS

Acknowledgments

Seldom, the author's ego notwithstanding, is a novel an entirely solitary effort. Of the many people who had a hand in making this particular novel a reality two stand out: the late Guy Owen, poet and novelist, first noticed and encouraged; Dave Stern, at Pocket Books, paid far more attention than I had any right to expect, and should get much of the credit.

Cutdown *vt* **1:** the creation of a small incised opening, especially in a vein, to facilitate venipuncture and permit the passage of a needle or cannula for withdrawal of blood or administration of fluids **2:** to strike down and kill or incapacitate.

PROLOGUE

Hopewell, Virginia
August 10, 1943

IN THE PREDAWN DARKNESS THE SWIFTLY FLOWING APPO-
mattox River was an undulating black ribbon, its
smooth surface blending seamlessly with the steep,
heavily overgrown banks on either side. Although the
eastern horizon bore a faint promise of the coming
day, the river and its environs lay shrouded in darkness so complete that even an alert observer would
likely have missed the young man picking his way
carefully down to the water. He was hot, thirsty, and
very tired, but despite the prisoner-of-war uniform,
he was still a soldier and he moved with great
discipline. He had had no idea that a river would be
there but somehow sensed, long before he came upon
it, that one awaited him. His determination was such
that upon reaching it, despite a primordial fear of
what might lie beneath its stygian surface, he scarcely
paused. *Better to drown,* he thought, *better to die.* He
entered the river silently, like some sort of reptilian
predator that had slid off the bank, leaving a sound-

less wake in the black water and a breath of fear on the shore.

To the east a wan, penumbral glow appeared on the horizon, not yet dawn but enough to begin turning formless shadows into almost-distinct objects. The young soldier pulled himself ashore at a particularly overgrown spot where a tangle of vines and bushes actually overhung the river, obscuring any sign of transit from water to land. He slept much of the day, waking occasionally to mentally catalog the rural sounds washing over the area: dogs barking, the occasional lowing of a cow, and once, at a distance, two boys laughing.

He stayed hidden until it was completely dark, two full hours after the sun had set. There was no sign of pursuit, no police or soldiers on foot, nor boats on the river, a fact he found both oddly comforting and not a little disturbing. How could the military and civilian authorities not have aroused the countryside when his escape had been detected? Puzzled and yet willing to accept whatever good fortune came his way, he reentered the river and was swallowed by the night.

The Appomattox swirled in eddies around the concrete abutments of the railroad bridge that crossed the river just west of Hopewell. To the north, less than half a mile from the river, the Taylor Oil & Feed sign, standing alone against the darkened sky, beckoned the hungry soldier, pulling him from the black water like a magnet draws an iron filing. He shook the water from himself like a dog, pleased to have an objective in sight, a *thing* to be reconnoitered and overcome. He crossed a deserted street and, after pausing briefly in the shadows to look and listen, boldly entered the country store through its unlocked rear door.

The soldier wasted little time, quickly selecting a pair of overalls and a denim work shirt from a display near the counter. Next to the massive cast-iron and brass cash register he found a small cabinet with a glass top displaying a variety of knives for sale, ranging from folding clasp knives to larger utility blades and hunting knives. He took two knives and immediately used one to slice open a burlap sack of feed grain. He emptied the grain onto the floor and began filling the sack with canned food from the shelves along one wall. When the bag was half full the man froze, struck suddenly with the feeling that he was being watched. He whirled about, one of his newly stolen knives held low in his right hand. After several heart-pounding seconds he looked up at the rafter above his head. His eyes met those of a calico tom watching his every move, and for several seconds the two predators stared at each other. Finally, with a whistling exhalation of long-held breath the man smiled at the cat.

Southern Railroad's locomotive number 209 sat fretfully waiting just outside the roundhouse, not moving and yet not completely still. The fireman was stoking the boiler as the engineer leaned out to search ahead for the conductor's signal to move forward. The Richmond, Virginia, marshaling yard was a maze of railroad tracks and sidings full of freight cars being herded into trains for destinations south and west. It was almost 1:00 A.M. and a heavy fog muffled the sharp noises of steel on steel. The engineer of number 209 saw his conductor's signal and eased the massive General Motors steam locomotive forward. The conductor swung aboard as 209 passed abreast of him and directed the engineer through the marshaling yard to the waiting train of forty-three cars. There were forty-one cars full of olive-drab combat fatigues and leather boots bound for Fort Benning, in Georgia, and two empty "deadheads" belonging to the Southern Pacific Railroad Company being routed to Dallas.

The fireman and his engineer lit cigarettes and gossiped quietly while the conductor picked up the final manifest documents from the dispatcher's tower.

Unseen by the train's crew, the soldier, in his new coveralls and a denim shirt, slipped across the adjoining tracks in the fog and darkness and quickly climbed into one of the empty deadheads, pulling the large door shut behind him. He leaned against one wall of the empty car and slid slowly down onto his haunches, exhaustion seeping over him like water seeking its own level. He had no idea where the train might be going but knew that each mile, in whatever direction, between him and the place he had escaped from was a mile closer to home. *Home. Is it truly possible? From such a distance?* He sighed and then smiled at the thought of the canned food in the burlap bag he had with him, knowing that the contents of any can he opened in the pitch blackness of the boxcar would be a welcome surprise.

The screech of wood against metal as the boxcar's door was suddenly pulled open startled him out of his reverie. He cursed himself for his carelessness, for giving in to fatigue and hunger before the train was actually under way. Immediately, he rose into a crouch, one of his knives held low in his right hand, his dilated eyes searching frantically for danger. A man pulled himself up into the darkened car with a curse, a flashlight in one hand and a wicked-looking piece of angle iron held menacingly overhead with the other. He was big, with stumplike legs and arms and an air of casual brutality about him.

"All right," he growled, playing the flashlight beam toward the opposite end of the car, "whoever the hell's in here damn well better—"

Without conscious thought the young soldier stepped up silently from behind and threw a rock-hard forearm around the man's neck, pulling him backwards while driving the five-inch knife blade into his lower back and right kidney. The intense, sudden pain completely paralyzed the man in the soldier's unrelenting grasp. The knife was withdrawn and plunged instantly again into his mid-back, where it pierced the left ventricle of his heart. Death came so suddenly and so unexpectedly that the yard bull had no final thought and no fear. Quite simply, he was alive and then almost instantly dead. The pain of the first wound precluded struggle or thought, and the terrible swiftness of the second ended his life before he knew he was in danger.

After carefully lowering the body to the floor, the young soldier quickly reclosed the boxcar's door and stood listening intently for voices or footsteps, keenly and unhappily aware that his hoped-for conveyance to freedom was also potentially a trap with only one exit. Only when the train's departure was announced with a jolt did his heartbeat begin to slow and his muscles relax. *Westward,* he thought, as if by force of will alone he could point the locomotive in the direction he wanted it to go. Half a world away from the forests of his youth and only vaguely aware of the actual geography and landscape, the political and economic boundaries and borders between where he was and where he needed to be, he still urged the train *westward* as slowly it began to move. Inside the darkened boxcar he felt only a disembodied sense of movement as they gradually picked up speed, and later, splitting the night, the dopplered ringing bells of road crossing barricades approached, met, and left behind by the rushing train were the saddest sounds he thought he had ever heard.

A. G. Farrell leaned against the counter in Bud Taylor's general store and casually rolled a cigarette using Bull Durham tobacco. The sheriff of Prince

George County, A. G. was the least likely looking law-man imaginable. Not yet thirty, his slight build and boyish features made him look even younger. He wore his rather long dark blond hair parted high on the right side and combed straight back. Although at first glance his wire-rimmed glasses made him look more like a bookish fraternity brother than a county sheriff, his demeanor projected maturity and authori-ty, and his intense brown eyes had a way of holding the attention of men much older than himself. He had been born and raised in Prince George County and, in addition to coming from a family with an honorable and respected record in the War Between the States (his grandfather Farrell had been decorated for brav-ery by General Lee himself), the fact that he had graduated from the University of Virginia and re-turned to a county where a high school diploma set a man apart meant a great deal.

It was 9:00 A.M. and already over ninety degrees, with not a hint of a breeze in sight. After lighting his cigarette A. G. reached for the bottle of cola sweating on the counter in front of him.

"I swear, that's the darndest thing, Bud, someone going to all the trouble to break in here and then not taking more than some work clothes, canned food, and a couple of knives. Who in the world do you suppose would do such a thing?"

Bud Taylor, a lifelong friend of A. G.'s father, had been instrumental in getting A. G. elected when old Sheriff Johnson had finally died. He shook his head with disgust.

"I'll be damned if I know. No one from around here would have done it so it must have been someone from over near Richmond or else a damned Yankee from out at Camp Lee."

A. G. chuckled. He knew that the world was a simple place for Bud Taylor. Other than an occasional trip to Richmond to visit a sporting house, Bud liked to brag that he had never been out of Prince George County nor met a Yankee that was worth a damn in his entire life. His judgment on the latter, although certainly shared by most everyone A. G. knew, including his own mother, was rather suspect inasmuch as it was doubtful that in his entire life he had met more than one or two actual Yankees, a sample far too small to safely rely upon. Nonetheless, in 1943 almost every adult in the county was closely related to or had known an actual Civil War veteran, and feelings still ran high.

A. G. had already concluded that someone from outside the county was the likely culprit. Trouble was, he had no idea who might have been passing through Hopewell last night. He had telephoned the state police as soon as Bud had notified him of the break-in, but they had no reports of any prison or jail escapees likely to be in the area. The only other possibility that he could think of was a soldier from over at Camp Lee, but given the nature of the articles stolen he didn't think it likely. Still, he made a mental note to call the camp provost marshal as soon as he got back to his office. He finished his RC Cola and reached for his Panama hat.

"Well, I reckon I'd better get back to the office and do a little investigating, Bud. Like as not it was some drifter we'll never see again, but I'll call around and let a few folks know so they can be on the lookout."

Bud Taylor grunted in reply, looking distastefully at A. G.'s pleated civilian slacks and short-sleeved white cotton shirt.

"Boy, why can't you wear a uniform like a proper sheriff? And hell, you don't even carry a gun." He shook his head, having argued unsuccessfully with A. G. about his refusal to wear a uniform ever since he had won the election. "How's your mama doing in this heat?"

"Meaner than a snake." A. G. smiled as he donned

the Panama. "Shoot, Bud, everyone around here knows me. I'd feel silly carrying a gun around. Anyway, I've got one at the office if the Germans or the Japs get too close."

Bud followed A. G. out onto the front porch. "Well, you better keep it handy 'cause with the Yankees running the war there ain't no telling what's going to happen. You tell your mama I said hello and that I'm looking forward to a piece of her pecan pie at the church dinner on Sunday."

Back at his office A. G. said good morning to his part-time secretary, Mildred Tatum. Mildred was the chief clerk in the county recorder's office, but was loaned to the sheriff's office two days a week to help with the paperwork and filing. A fifty-nine-year-old widow, she had worked for the county for over thirty years and knew everything and everyone. A. G. filled her in on the break-in at Bud Taylor's place and asked her what she thought.

"Nobody around here would have done it. The good Lord knows we've got our share of no-count trash in this county, but none of them have the gumption to stage a break-in, especially just to steal work clothes and some canned food. I expect it was a transient of some sort, although we're far enough from Richmond that we don't usually have much of a problem with hobos and the like."

"I declare, Mildred, I believe you're right. Do me a favor and see if you can get Major Zimmerman, the provost marshal out at the camp, on the telephone for me?"

Mildred placed the call as A. G. walked into his small office. "He's on the line," she called out a minute later. A. G. heard her resume her pounding on the county's old Underwood as he picked up the telephone.

"Major Zimmerman? This here is Sheriff Farrell

over in Hopewell. How's everything out at the camp this morning? Fine, fine. Say, listen, the reason I called, we had us a burglary out this way last night that was a little out of the ordinary." A. G. knew that Zimmerman, a reserve officer from Long Island, New York, would have handily matched, on all fours, Bud Taylor's mental image of a damn Yankee. He had met Zimmerman, the commander of the Camp Lee military police detachment, on several occasions, mostly having to do with drunk and disorderly soldiers disturbing the peace in Hopewell. He suspected that Zimmerman thought him a typically shallow, if somewhat unconventional, southerner. "The general store just outside town was broken into and some work clothes and canned food stolen. Oh, yes, and a couple of knives were also taken. I doubt that it was done by anyone local and was wondering if you might have any ideas."

There was a long silence on the line before Zimmerman answered. "Although I seriously doubt there's any connection with your burglary we've had a slight . . ."—he paused—"a slight *situation* here at Camp Lee that I should probably fill you in on."

"A *situation?*" A. G. could not keep a bemused tone out of his voice. "What sort of situation?"

"I don't want to discuss it over the telephone. I suggest you come over to my office here later this morning, say around ten o'clock." Without waiting for a response Zimmerman hung up.

A. G. sat for a moment absently listening to the dial tone emanating from the receiver he held casually in his right hand. *A transient?* he thought. *Maybe Mildred's right. Nothing more than a bum stealing food and a change of clothes on his way through Hopewell. But how would he get out of a county where everyone knows everyone else?*

On a sudden hunch he placed a quick call to the

offices of the Southern Railroad in Richmond and learned that one of their switch engines had pulled a small number of empty freight cars through Hopewell en route to the Richmond marshaling yard at around eleven-thirty last night.

A. G. was surprised when the MP at Camp Lee's main gate demanded to see his identification.

"Why all the security?" he asked, holding up his badge for examination.

"It's them goddamned Italians," the guard, a nineteen-year-old from Des Moines, answered. He shook his head with disgust. "They got in here two days ago and damned if one of them ain't already escaped."

Italians, A. G. mused as he drove past the camp's orderly ranks of buildings, each painted white with olive-drab trim. He suddenly remembered that Camp Lee was a facility for holding Italian POWs captured in North Africa. As a local law-enforcement officer he had been briefed on the matter some six months earlier and had promptly put it out of his mind. *No wonder Zimmerman didn't want to talk about it over an open phone line.* A. G. couldn't help smiling as he pulled up in front of the provost marshal's building. *I'll bet the War Department's got his tit in a wringer over this little snafu.*

"Good morning, Sheriff."

A. G. noted Zimmerman's not-quite-rude tone of voice and reminded himself to be charitable. He nodded, smiling cheerfully, and sat down in the wooden chair opposite Zimmerman's desk without waiting to be asked. While discreetly settling himself in his trousers with one hand he pulled his bag of Bull Durham out of his shirt pocket with the other. "You don't mind if I smoke, do you?"

Zimmerman opened his desk drawer and took out a

pack of Chesterfields. "Would you like a cigarette?" he asked, his tone implying a *real* cigarette.

"Why, no, thank you. I prefer rolling my own, don't you know."

Zimmerman sat stonily silent, looking at A. G. as he rolled and then lit his cigarette.

"Well, sir, tell me about the, um, *situation* I believe you called it, out here at the camp."

"There's little to tell. Our first contingent of POWs arrived day before yesterday and one of them escaped that night. His absence was discovered at the morning roll call."

A. G. nodded and studied the tip of his cigarette. "I'm sort of curious as to why you didn't notify me of the escape yesterday morning."

Zimmerman gave A. G. his most contemptuous look. "What takes place on this camp is none of your concern. Matters having to do with interned prisoners of war are governed by War Department regulations and are not subject to civilian"—Zimmerman spat out the word *civilian* as if it were an insect that had flown into his mouth—"review."

A. G. smiled at the provost marshal. "Well, gosh, Major, I understand that and let me assure you that I have no desire to review anything that the military does. It's just that had I known about the escape I might have been able to alert some folks and possibly give you some help in tracking him down."

"I can assure you that I need no assistance in that regard."

A. G. thought better of pointing out that the ongoing failure of the provost marshal to recapture his prisoner indicated that in fact he clearly did.

"I'm sure you don't. Perhaps you can tell me a little about the prisoner. For instance, his name and any information in your records which might indicate whether or not he could be dangerous."

"His name is Angelo Tavecchio and he is a lieutenant in the Italian army. The military records that accompanied the prisoners from North Africa said that Lieutenant Tavecchio was suffering from some sort of trauma-induced amnesia at the time of his surrender. Some sort of head wound. Because of this disability he was considered even less of an escape threat than his fellow officers. And they were considered far less likely to attempt escape than German prisoners."

"And yet he escaped at the first opportunity. I wonder if he might not have been faking his symptoms in order to lull the military authorities into lowering their guard somewhat." A. G. slowly stubbed his cigarette out in an ashtray made from a 105mm howitzer shell casing. "It seems to me that we're dealing with a very smart man here. I think it's reasonable to assume that he doesn't plan to be recaptured and that he's armed and dangerous."

"Armed?"

A. G. nodded. "You will recall I mentioned that two knives were among the goods stolen from the general store in Hopewell."

Zimmerman ran a hand across his face in a gesture of growing annoyance. "In the first place, Sheriff, the escaped POW did not, I say again, did *not* commit the burglary in Hopewell. His mental condition was confirmed not only by Allied doctors in Algeria where the Italian POWs were put aboard ship for transportation to this country but also by U.S. Navy doctors at Norfolk where they arrived, so he couldn't possibly have gotten from Camp Lee to Hopewell in the time required. He is a confused and no doubt frightened man who is probably hiding in a field no more than a mile or two from where we're sitting this very moment. Furthermore, his fellow officers from North Africa assure me in the strongest possible terms that

Tavecchio, as an Italian officer and gentleman, head wound or not, would never harm one of his captors, much less unarmed noncombatants. Hell, he surrendered voluntarily. We're not dealing with Germans here. Do I make myself clear?"

A. G. stood up and once again smiled at Zimmerman. "I should probably be off now. I'm sure you're quite busy"—he paused for just the slightest of seconds—"reviewing your security measures in the hope of preventing future escapes. You've been a great deal of help." A. G. turned to leave but, with his hand on the doorknob, turned once again to face the major. "One last thing. Do you have any idea why an Italian POW, all of whom have been only too happy to surrender according to the newspapers, would go to all the trouble of escaping as soon as he got to the United States? And where in the world would he be planning to go?"

Zimmerman pointedly refused to respond. A. G. paused at the door for only a second and then turned and walked out of the building. Even though all of the windows were rolled down, his 1937 Hudson felt like the inside of an oven as he got in and slowly drove out of the camp and back to Hopewell. Although he had no facts on which to base such a conclusion, he was certain that Bud Taylor's store had been burglarized by the Italian and just as certain that the man had then managed to jump on the Southern Railroad train to Richmond as it passed through Hopewell. *Who else could it have been?* he asked himself. *Even Mildred, who had advanced the transient theory at the outset, knew that we're too far off the beaten track to be bothered by these kinds of petty break-ins.* He smiled. *Better not let Bud Taylor hear me call it a "petty break-in."* Clearly whoever had done it was gone and no longer a threat to the peace and security of Prince George County, but A. G. was unwilling to just file and forget the matter. His mind kept turning things over like a squirrel chewing on an acorn. The Italian should not have wanted to escape in the first place. *Something queer there, something mighty queer. Richmond,* he thought as he parked the Hudson in front of his office in Hopewell, *maybe there's some profit to be had in Richmond.*

An hour later, A. G. winked as he slid into a booth at his favorite café in Richmond. "Hello, Sarah. I'll bet Spencer here has already ordered for both of us. Brunswick stew and barbecue. Coleslaw and lots of hush puppies."

The waitress tucked her nub of a pencil behind her ear. "Bingo. And two RC Colas." She indelicately wiped the sheen of perspiration off her upper lip with her right forefinger and walked away humming "Softly and Tenderly, Jesus Is Calling."

A. G. shook hands with his friend across the table. "Spencer, how in the world are you? Boy, it's been too long since we got together for lunch."

Spencer Lee represented the last gasp of an old but pretty nearly worn-out Richmond family, an out-at-elbow aristocracy reduced by the twin hammers of the War Between the States and almost willful incompetence. Spencer's great-grandfather had patriotically but foolishly invested the bulk of the family's wealth in Confederate war bonds, an investment from which the family never recovered. Nonetheless, like his father and grandfather before him, Spencer had attended the University of Virginia, although unlike them had undertaken to learn something useful while there and had enrolled in the university's law school upon receiving his undergraduate degree.

"A. G., I know you want something, but let's us enjoy lunch before I find out what it's going to cost me."

As they ate lunch and chatted about inconsequential things, A. G. thought about the different paths he and his friend had chosen. Even as a freshman in Charlottesville Spencer had talked of becoming governor of the state, and after law school chose the Richmond district attorney's office as a springboard from which to enter the political arena. A. G., on the other hand, had no such clear goal in life, so his education had truly been a liberal one, with course work in many different areas that interested him. He had a flair for mathematics that ultimately led him to major in philosophy, the intellectual rigors of which delighted him no end. He had been a brilliant student but, despite the strong encouragement of his professors, declined to consider graduate school, returning instead to Prince George County and, ultimately, the sheriff's office. He knew only that for the present he was sheriff and that at some point in the future he wouldn't be. Beyond that he took one day at a time.

After lunch they both lit cigarettes, A. G. rolling a Bull Durham, and Spencer taking a Lucky Strike out of an onyx cigarette case.

"Spencer, I need some information and some help." A. G. described the break-in at Bud Taylor's place and his visit with Camp Lee's provost marshal. He also told of his telephone conversation with the Southern Railroad people that led to his belief that the Italian had gotten from Hopewell to Richmond the previous night. A. G. paused for a moment before continuing. His friend hadn't said a word. "There's something about this whole thing that I don't like. Why the hell would an Italian POW be trying to escape from a camp ten thousand or however many miles from home? Where does he think he's going to go? How does he think he's going to get there? These people, at least according to the newspapers, are voluntarily surrendering, admitting that they don't want to fight anymore. No," he said, shaking his head, "there's something wrong here, something that doesn't figure."

Spencer looked at his friend. "Interesting. How can I help you?"

"First, I'd like you to have a detective from the police department go down to the rail yard and see if anyone, whether a railroad worker or a bum, might have seen anything or anyone out of the ordinary. While your man from the police department is checking out the rail yard I'm going to go over to Southern's office to get the schedule for all freight trains that left Richmond anytime between midnight last night and dawn this morning. Second, I'd like you to check with the local FBI office and find out what information they might have gotten from the War Department about the escapee. If the local FBI folks don't know anything or haven't been notified of the escape yet, ask them to check it out for you."

Spencer chuckled. "Jesus, anything else you want?"

A. G. ignored the sarcasm. "Just that we have to move fast. I'm betting that our man left Richmond last night. We need to get as much information as we can so we can telephone ahead and have somebody waiting when next he gets off whatever train he's on."

"What about Major Zimmerman and the War Department? Shouldn't they be the ones worrying about this whole thing?"

"Of course they should. Unfortunately, the Italian will be a thousand miles away before the government does anything. Zimmerman's still looking around Camp Lee and Hopewell, for God's sake."

"All right," Spencer said as he reached for the check, "I'll get on it as soon as I get back to the office."

"Good. I'll call you when I've finished over at Southern." A. G. smiled at his friend as he stood up and reached for his Panama. "And thanks for lunch."

"Two freight trains left Richmond this morning between midnight and dawn," the office manager for Southern Railroad told A. G. "The first one at twelve-thirty bound for Atlanta through Raleigh and Columbia, South Carolina; the second at two A.M. bound for Chicago."

"I'm thinking my man would have grabbed the first freight out of Richmond," A. G. mused, as much to himself as to the office manager. "That means the train heading for Raleigh and Columbia, isn't that right?"

"Yes, sir, the first train out after midnight, which was when the switch engine from Hopewell arrived, was the twelve-thirty south-bound." The manager consulted his schedule and looked at his watch. "It's already left Columbia and is due into Atlanta at five o'clock this afternoon."

A. G. swore under his breath as he walked from the office. He was convinced that his man had left Richmond on the south-bound freight. If he hadn't gotten off in Raleigh he was almost certain to have gotten off in Columbia. A. G. sighed as he started the drive back to Hopewell. He would have to get the schedule of all freight trains departing both Raleigh and Columbia for several hours after the Atlanta train passed through. And, just in case his man had not gotten off, he would have to ask Spencer to notify the FBI and Georgia authorities in time to allow them to meet the train when it arrived in Atlanta. He knew that with each passing moment the trail would get colder as the possibility tree began to branch at a logarithmic rate.

It was a little after three o'clock when A. G. finally got back to his office. Mildred was waiting for him.

"You got two phone calls, one from Spencer Lee and the other from the office manager for Southern Railroad in Richmond."

A. G. dialed the Southern Railroad office manager's number. "Mr. Robinson? Sheriff Farrell here, returning your call."

"Oh, Sheriff, thank you for calling back. I don't know if this is something you might be interested in, but that south-bound freight I told you about? The one going to Atlanta through Raleigh and Columbia? Well, shortly after you left here we got a teletype message that a body was discovered in a boxcar while the train laid over in Columbia. We don't know who it is yet, probably just a bum, but . . . what's that? No, the teletype didn't say anything other than that a body was found and removed by the Columbia police. Say what? Wait a minute, let me get a pencil. Okay, I'm ready. The schedule for all departures out of Raleigh and Columbia for six hours after our train passed through? Sure, hold on a minute."

With a growing sense of excitement, A. G. wrote down the information the office manager gave him. "I appreciate it, Mr. Robinson, I declare I do. Yes, I'll let you know if I hear something."

He hung up the telephone and then immediately picked it up again and dialed Spencer's number.

"Spencer—"

"Now, look here A. G.," Spencer, recognizing his friend's voice, interrupted him. "The police didn't uncover anything on your escaped POW on their first pass out at the rail yard. However, much as I hate to admit it, something odd did come up. It seems that the yard detective, a fellow by the name of Martin Braun, disappeared in the middle of his shift last night."

"What do you mean 'disappeared'?"

"Just that. This man Braun has been the yard bull out there for years, never missed a day of work, isn't a drinker, nothing to explain why he just walked off the job and didn't come back. The day supervisor mentioned it to my guy when he asked him if anything unusual happened last night."

Struggling to keep an "I told you so" tone out of his

voice, A. G. relayed the information regarding the discovery of the body in Columbia.

"I have absolutely no doubt that the dead man is the Richmond yard bull, Martin Braun. Now, listen. Our man had to have gotten off that train in either Raleigh or Columbia. I just got the schedules of all trains outbound from those two areas and we're going to have to notify authorities along the line to be on the lookout. Also, you should have the Richmond police get a description of Braun down to Columbia right away so we can get a positive identification of the body."

"Jesus, A. G., that's a hell of a conclusion to jump to. The guy could have had a thousand reasons for leaving work without telling anybody. I've got a police car checking out his rooming house right now."

"He won't be there, Spencer. I'm right about this, I know it. What happened was the Italian POW climbed into a boxcar on a train due out of Richmond at twelve-thirty last night. Sometime before the train pulled out, the yard bull discovered him and was murdered. By the way, what did the FBI tell you when you talked to them earlier?"

"I'm calling them now," Spencer said. "I'll get back to you as soon as I hear something."

Shaking his head, A. G. walked out of his office and over to where Mildred sat writing a letter to her cousin in Bluefield, West Virginia.

"Mildred, honey, would you mind getting me an RC Cola from next door? And, look here, get yourself one too. I declare, it must be a hundred degrees in here."

Back in his office A. G. considered the enormity of the task facing him. Within a six-hour span of time from the passage of the Atlanta train through Raleigh and Columbia there were some fifteen possible "connections" the POW could have made, taking him through forty-odd southeastern cities ranging from Charlotte to New Orleans. Sighing, A. G. picked up the telephone and began making the first of many calls, knowing that the county supervisors would have a fit when the phone bill came in.

Indianola, Mississippi
August 12, 1943

Night had long since fallen across rural Mississippi. Some five miles southeast of the tiny farming community of Indianola the soldier walked quietly down an unpaved county road. A rising quarter moon guided him unerringly down the road, while the night sounds of undisturbed insects assured him that no other men were in his immediate vicinity. He had arrived in western Mississippi late that afternoon and, although quite hungry, having long since eaten the last of the canned goods he had stolen in Hopewell, he felt strong and alert. He walked at a steady, deliberate pace, his footsteps muffled by the thick layer of dust on the little-used gravel road. The stillness of the night, coupled with the utter absence of any sign of human habitation, gave rise to a growing sense of uneasiness. His predicament weighed heavily upon him, and for the first time since his capture in North Africa he wondered if he would ever see his homeland again. With some relief he saw the glow of a lamp in a window, and, surrounding it, the almost invisible outline of a small house perhaps a quarter mile off the road. Although he told himself it was hunger, he actually wasn't sure why he found himself drawn to the light. He walked slowly down the dark lane toward the house, every sense alert. Twenty-five yards from it he stopped, his eyes searching with dilated pupils for any detail that might reveal something about the house's occupants. Although he could detect no animal smells that would indicate a dog, he did catch the distinctive smell of a wood-fired cookstove cooling in the humid night air.

At the screen door he paused for an instant, his eyes quickly taking in the layout of the room. The only occupant was an elderly black man sitting in a rocking chair.

"You might as well come on in," the old man called out. "No use to hidin' out there in the dark."

The soldier flung open the screen door, not bothering to wonder how the old man had detected him. "You are alone?" he asked.

The old man laughed. He was stone bald and had a grizzled white beard. "You not from around here. Folks hereabouts all know that old Percy Christmas lives alone. I done buried all my kinfolk." The old man examined his visitor in the light of the room's solitary kerosene lamp. "You not fixin' to cut me with that knife in your pocket, is you?"

"Do not be afraid. I need food. I will pay you." The soldier reached into his pocket and took out the twelve dollars he had taken from the body of the yard bull.

"Sit down at the table. I done had my supper but you're welcome to the leftovers. I got some collards and some corn bread and molasses." He watched the old man get up from the rocker and shuffle awkwardly to the stove. "I 'spect they's still warm in the pan." After serving his uninvited guest the old man rolled a cigarette and watched him eat. "It's the Lord's blessing to watch a hungry man eat," he observed, pointing with his cigarette at the visitor. "I cooked them collards all afternoon with a good piece of fatback, that's why they's so good. You ain't never had no collards before, has you?"

"Never."

The old man nodded. "I figured not. You from up north." It was a statement of fact rather than a question.

The soldier sat quietly and said nothing.

"I sent my boys up north years ago. To work." The old man walked back to the rocking chair and sat down heavily. "Nothin' round here for young folks 'cep'n trouble. Not with Boss Harris livin' just down the road."

"Boss Harris?" The soldier looked up from his plate. "He is a policeman?"

"Naw, suh, but he might's well be. He owns all the land hereabouts and he don't think nothin' more about the colored folks that work it for him than he do a mule." The old man laughed, a bitter sound. "Less, mos' likely." He looked at his guest, still seated at the table. "I wish I could help you more but you'll have to settle for the collards and corn bread."

The soldier thought for a moment and then shrugged. "It is enough," he said, rising and walking to where the old man sat rocking. He once again withdrew the twelve dollars from his pocket. "Take this," he said, extending several of the bills, "for the food."

"You don't owe me nothing," the old man replied, pleased that the offer had been made. "You're welcome to stay the night."

The intruder shook his head and started to leave.

"Just a minute," the old man called out. "Don't be in such a hurry." He took out his makings and began to roll another smoke. "A man on foot at night won't get very far if the police is looking for him."

"You have an automobile?"

The old man laughed, again a bitter sound. "Boy,

you really are from up north." He shook his head at the wonder of such a question. "Sit down." Percy handed his tobacco to the young man. "Have a smoke. Let me tell you something about Mississippi."

Hopewell, Virginia
August 14, 1943

A. G. was at his desk when the call came in.

"Sheriff Farrell? This is Tom Rabb, assistant director of the Mississippi State Bureau of Investigation. We've got something that we were told might be of some interest to you. The sheriff up in Sunflower County called us for some help with a murder that was committed some thirty-six to forty-eight hours ago. We put the details on the wire and pretty quickly heard from the assistant chief of police in Birmingham, Alabama. He passed on the information you had given him and suggested that we call you."

"A murder?" A. G. sat up in his chair.

"That's right. And an odd one. A farmer out in the county, a white man, was killed. The decedent, a man by the name of Harris, was found in his living room. By one of his sharecropper tenants."

"How was he killed?"

"His throat was cut."

"It certainly sounds like it could be my man, Mr. Rabb. If it was I'd guess that he ransacked the house for food, money, and possibly clothing, and headed back to the rail line to catch himself another freight train."

"Not so fast. I don't think he jumped another train, at least not right away. We believe he stole a pickup truck belonging to the dead man. We've notified all law-enforcement personnel to be on the lookout for the pickup, but since the murder was committed possibly as long as two days ago there's no telling where he or the truck might be."

"If this murder was committed by my man, and my gut instinct tells me that it was, where he is matters a great deal less than where he's going."

"Where do you think that might be?"

"Mexico."

A. G. responded without thinking. Having said it, he was not surprised, although in fact he had not consciously thought of or identified Mexico before uttering the country's name in response to Rabb's question. It had to be Mexico. No matter who or what the escapee was, he was a foreign national, an enemy combatant with few options open to him. Mexico was officially neutral in the ongoing world war, and once in Mexico there was always a chance, no matter how slight, of repatriation. However, as A. G. thought about it he realized that it was extremely unlikely that a consular official in a neutral country like Mexico would have the inclination or even ability to arrange clandestine passage across the Atlantic, possibly by submarine, for an ordinary Italian soldier, whether officer or enlisted man.

Not for an Italian soldier.

The answer was so startling, and yet so obvious, that A. G. momentarily forgot that he still had the assistant director of the Mississippi State Bureau of Investigation on the other end of the line.

"I'm sorry, Mr. Rabb, I was distracted for a moment. I seriously doubt that the man responsible for the murder near Indianola is still in Mississippi. If I'm correct he's headed for the Mexican border and unfortunately may already have reached it. Nevertheless, I can't tell you how much I appreciate your call."

After hanging up, A. G. forced himself to roll a Bull Durham and light it before calling Spencer to ask for his help in setting up a meeting with the FBI man in Richmond. Two hours later, in Spencer's office, A. G.

reassured his friend that there was indeed a good reason for his having asked for the meeting. Spencer's secretary announced the arrival of the special agent and showed him in. Spencer stood up to greet him and introduced him to A. G.

"A. G., this is Special Agent Billings. I know that you two have talked on the telephone, but I don't know whether or not you've been properly introduced."

A. G. extended his hand. "We've visited on the telephone but we've not shaken hands. Mr. Billings, I appreciate your willingness to meet with me this afternoon."

"Not at all, Sheriff. We may not always agree but we're certainly on the same side. What have you got for me?"

A. G. smiled. "First, Mr. Billings, I wonder if you might indulge me, and bring me up to date on your investigation into the escape?"

Billings shifted in his seat. "I have nothing to report. As I'm sure you know, Major Zimmerman's military police haven't been able to recapture the Italian anywhere near Camp Lee, and the Bureau has been unable to turn up any clues as to his whereabouts."

"Thank you. Well, let me begin by startling both of you. I believe that the escapee is not an Italian POW at all, but rather a German prisoner who assumed an Italian identity to help him escape when he arrived in this country. Furthermore, I believe this man to be no ordinary German soldier, but one whose rank or duties or special knowledge are such as to make him desperate to avoid identification upon his capture." A. G. paused momentarily to roll a Bull Durham.

Billings stared at him, open-mouthed.

"Bear with me a moment," A. G. said, amused by Billings's obvious incredulity. "I believe I can demonstrate that the facts, far from making my theory seem far-fetched, support no other conclusion. Consider: The escape itself defies all logic. An Italian POW, one who supposedly voluntarily surrendered, plans and executes an escape on the very night, August eighth, he arrives at his permanent POW camp. He doesn't wait around to gather information about the surrounding countryside, he doesn't include any fellow POWs in his escape, he simply vanishes without a trace. It makes no sense whatever unless we consider that he wasn't an Italian at all. If we take a fresh look, from the very beginning, I believe we get a different picture altogether. Our prisoner, almost certainly a German officer, is about to be captured by the Allies in North Africa. For reasons unknown to us, he cannot allow himself to be captured, identified, and interrogated. Somehow, perhaps off a dead body, prior to capture he manages to obtain an Italian officer's identity and uniform. He probably even speaks some rudimentary Italian, certainly at least enough to understand what's being said around him. Howsomever, he knows that his attempt at subterfuge will never hold up against close inspection by his fellow Italian prisoners and, knowing that there isn't any love lost between the two 'allies,' he must somehow prevent such interaction. So, immediately before capture he inflicts a head wound of some sort on himself. Drastic measure, but he is literally in a life-or-death situation. He's captured, an Italian officer with what appears to be a serious head wound and a trauma-induced mental incapacity. By the time they arrive at Camp Lee our man knows that he has just about played the string out. There will almost certainly be much more extensive medical facilities and personnel available, which meant that his 'trauma' would have been recognized for the sham that it was and, so recognized, would raise the question why. Plus, who knows what was happening in North Africa? He must have been concerned that each passing day increased the risk that his false identity would somehow be discovered back there and communicated to the Americans. No, our man knew that he had to escape at the first opportunity." A. G. ground out his cigarette. "And so he did."

"Jesus," Billings murmured, warming to the story.

"So where is he now?" Spencer asked.

"He's gone from Mississippi now, of course, probably halfway across Arkansas or Louisiana. He's getting close to his destination and we'll have to move quickly to stand any chance at all of intercepting him."

Spencer interrupted. "His destination? You mean you think he's heading for a specific destination?"

A. G. nodded. "There's only one place our man can go and that's south of the border."

Billings suddenly sat up straight and snapped his fingers. "Franz von Werra," he said excitedly.

A. G. smiled. "Exactly. It was staring me in the face all along and I was too simpleminded to see it. Franz von Werra. The German pilot who turned up in New York back in early 1940. He and seven other German POWs escaped off a train taking them to a POW camp in western Canada. The other seven were recaptured but von Werra surfaced in New York and, because the United States was not yet at war with anybody, became the talk of the town while the Canadians and the British tried to pressure our government for his extradition. While the lawyers were dithering von Werra took a powder and made good on his pledge to return to Germany." A. G. nodded at Spencer and Billings. "You'll recall that his escape route took him from New York to Mexico, Mexico to Panama, Panama to Brazil, and Brazil to Spain. So I believe that from the moment our man knew that he was going to be interned in North America he planned an escape via Mexico and South America, just like von Werra. That's why he took on the Italian identity back in

North Africa." A. G. looked at Special Agent Billings. "There you have it. Immigration and border patrol people along the entire border from Texas to California should be notified, as should the local law-enforcement authorities of cities along the most probable routes he could take from Mississippi. Everyone should be made aware of the fact that this man is extremely dangerous and has already committed at least two murders in the space of only two or three days."

Billings shook his head slowly. "Jesus H. Christ. Your theory is based upon some very large presumptions but I must admit that it's a compelling one, particularly given the latest murder in Mississippi. It could all be coincidence, but I'm beginning to feel that we should take some of the actions you recommend." Billings rose to his feet and extended his hand to A. G. "I appreciate your sticking with this despite the earlier discouragement from both the Bureau and the War Department. I'll be talking to you soon."

The FBI agent shook hands and hurried from the office. A. G. and Spencer looked at each other.

"That's the damndest story I ever heard, A. G. I don't know if it'll hold water, but if it does I'll tell you what's the truth: This man, whoever the hell he is, made a big mistake when he committed a burglary in Prince George County."

Indianola, Mississippi
August 14, 1943

Percy Christmas sat in his front yard, rocking back and forth and listening to the crickets. It was a fine night, not too humid, and the old man hummed a Baptist spiritual his wife used to sing. *The good Lord works in powerful strange ways,* he thought. He rolled a cigarette and savored the harsh bite of his home-grown tobacco on his tongue. Man and boy he'd lived in Mississippi all his natural-born life, and he knew he'd never again see a thing like the man who had come to him out of the darkness two nights ago. The glowing end of Percy's cigarette traced a parabolic path through the darkness as the old man smoked and rocked.

"Naw, suh," he had told Sheriff Breen that afternoon, "I ain't see'd nor heard nothin'."

He hadn't been the least bit surprised when the sheriff told him that someone had killed Boss Harris and stolen his pickup truck, nor the least bit inter-ested in going against the clear will of the Lord by helping the sheriff in his investigation. It had taken Percy some time, but he had finally figured out who the man was and why he had come. Some folks might have been frightened, but not Percy, for his faith was strong and he had been too close to Jesus all his life to let a visitor from down below scare him. Once he thought about it, it didn't puzzle him at all that Boss Harris's fate lay in the hands of a man who traveled by night. A lifetime of hearing the Scriptures read every Sunday morning had convinced him that as a man sows so shall he reap. Boss Harris had been a hateful, evil man all his life, and it pleased him that he, Percy Christmas, had been selected to point the Man of Darkness in the proper direction. All he had to do was tell the stranger about Harris's truck, and how Harris lived alone just a mile down the road. Then he told him about the cross burnings, and the terror at night when Harris and his fellow Klansmen, fortified with homemade whiskey, rode the county's roads in Harris's pickup truck. At first Percy had been somewhat confused by the stranger's interest in Boss Harris's truck, but it had finally dawned on him.

Percy Christmas couldn't help smiling as he rocked in the gloam of evening, thinking about the stranger conveying Boss Harris's soul to hell in his own pickup truck.

Aguilares, Texas
August 15, 1943

The sun, rising over the young soldier's left shoulder, filled the rearview mirror of Boss Harris's 1937 Ford pickup with an ocherous light that refracted off the motes of dust dancing from the floorboards and seat cushions. Although the truck's differential had complained almost the entire way, through Arkansas and Louisiana and Texas, states with names no less exotic in his mind than any in Europe or North Africa, there had been not a moment of doubt in the soldier's mind that the stolen truck would get him at least this far, a stone's throw from the Mexican border.

Now, looking down at the Rio Grande, he laughed at the dry, gravel riverbed, his last concern about a possibly difficult-to-cross barrier between himself and freedom gone with the dust that swirled up in the hot air.

Hopewell, Virginia
August 16, 1943

A. G. hung up his telephone and took the time to roll and light a cigarette before walking out to where Mildred Tatum sat pounding on the county's old Underwood.

"He's gone," A. G. informed her. "Probably through

Mexico and halfway to Argentina by now. Billings said he doubted they would ever find the truck he stole in Mississippi much less the man himself."

"I doubt they looked too terribly hard," Mildred opined.

"Damn," A. G. muttered, back in his office with the door closed. *Who was he?* he wondered for the umpteenth time. A. G. paced restlessly around his small office, stopping at his window to look down Hopewell's one commercial street. *What secrets was he so desperate to protect?* He turned from the window and sighed. "One thing is certain," he murmured. "The war won't last forever." *And when it's over, I'll find you. And bring you back.*

CHAPTER 1

Berkeley, California
Monday, March 7, 1994

THE POLICE SERGEANT AT THE FRONT DESK WORE A
simple gold earring in his right earlobe and the look of
a man with little patience for human frailty. Claude
McCutcheon stood in front of him for at least thirty
seconds before he bothered to look up.

"Yeah?"

"I'd like to see Robert Norton," Claude said with
exaggerated politeness. Casually dressed in a linen
shirt and well-worn blue jeans, he could have been
anywhere between thirty-five and fifty, depending on
one's point of view. Too-long, sandy blond hair and a
trim, hard waist further increased the difficulty of
judging his age and station in life. "I understand he's
being questioned with regards to a homicide."

"Who are you?"

"I'm his father," Claude responded sarcastically.

The sergeant ignored Claude and picked up the
telephone. He dialed three numbers and waited until
someone answered. "Norton's mouthpiece is here,"
he said. He listened a second, and then hung up the

receiver. "Room 148," he said, looking back down at his paperwork, refusing to meet Claude's eyes. He gestured over his shoulder with his right thumb. "Down the hall."

"Nice earring," Claude sneered as he walked past the desk. He walked into room 148 without bothering to knock, hoping it would offend someone. The small room was shared by four detectives, their civil-service gray metal desks sitting cheek by jowl. Bobby Norton, a slender African American in his mid-forties, sat next to one of the desks. A slightly older man, also black, wearing blue jeans and a lumberjack shirt sat behind the desk. A detective's badge was clipped to the front of his shirt. He looked at Claude and smiled. "Claude McCutcheon. I didn't know you'd started chasing criminal work."

Claude shook hands with the detective. The two men had known each other, though not well, for a number of years. Jim Malone was a big man, as tall as Claude, and heavyset, with burly shoulders and a gut gone to seed. An army retiree, he had spent twenty years as a military policeman, retiring in 1985 with the rank of major. He joined the Berkeley Police Department in 1986 as head of the department's criminal investigation division.

"I haven't," Claude said, nodding at Bobby. "I'm here strictly as a favor to Mr. Norton. In any event, based on what he told my secretary over the telephone I'm not sure he even needs an attorney. Am I correct in assuming that he is not a suspect in the homicide in question?"

Malone nodded. "He was at the scene, though, and so naturally we're interested in any information he might be able to provide us."

"Do you mind if I speak with Mr. Norton in private for a few minutes?"

"No problem," Malone said. "Use room 152, two

doors down. It's an interrogation room. I'll see that no one bothers you."

"Come on." Claude took Bobby's arm and maneuvered him out of the detectives' office.

"Aren't we going in there?" Bobby asked as the two of them passed room 152 and continued down the hall.

"You should know better than that," Claude said as they exited the police station proper. "There's more microphones hidden in there than in the American embassy in Moscow. We'll talk out here."

Standing on the steps at the side of the building, Claude looked across the street at a man urinating into some bushes in full view of the police station. He tried to remember the last time he'd been to downtown Berkeley and couldn't, itself a testimony to the sad decline of a once-beautiful and dynamic community. Several blocks to the east, over the tops of the low-rise buildings, he could see the towering redwood and eucalyptus trees that dotted the campus of the University of California.

"Man, am I glad to see you," Bobby said as he took one of Claude's cigarettes. He was rather nattily dressed in linen trousers, a silk Italian shirt, and faux-crocodile slip-ons.

"Why? If you were just a witness, what the fuck did you need me to hotfoot it down here for?"

Bobby shook his head. "Listen," he said, his tone of voice implying wonder that anyone would ask such a question, particularly someone who knew enough to know that there's no such thing as a confidential conversation anywhere in a police station, "there ain't no way I'm talking to the police in no murder situation without my attorney present."

"I'm not your attorney." Claude lowered his eyebrows and looked hard at Bobby. "What the fuck's going on here? Who exactly was killed?"

Bobby smiled and briskly rubbed his hands together. "That's what I'm trying to tell you. It was Myron Hirsch who was killed."

"Myron Hirsch? The lawyer?"

"That's the one," Bobby said. "You know him?"

Claude shook his head. "I know enough to know that everyone thought he was an asshole. He's a loose cannon on the lunatic fringe of the environmental movement. Or was. He got a lot of press a year or two ago by advocating the lynching of Interior Department officials for authorizing timber harvesting on federal land." He paused for a second, remembering the business at hand. "Where the hell were you when Hirsch got done?"

"Upstairs. See, I had gone over to the boat to see Hirsch about some business."

"What boat? And what sort of business?"

"He lived on a houseboat out at the Berkeley marina. And the business was about my place in Richmond." Bobby ran a small after-hours nightclub in Richmond, across the bay from San Francisco. "He was wanting to raise my rent and we been arguing over some repairs he was supposed to do."

"You mean Hirsch owned the building your club is in?"

"Yeah. Anyway, I went over to his boat to try and settle things with him." Bobby paused and ground out his cigarette on the pavement. "I could see when I got there that he was nervous about something, wanted me to leave, you know? Anyway, I told him I wasn't leaving until we got some sort of understanding on my rent and the repairs. Right then he heard someone coming down the pier to his boat and he told me to wait upstairs. Said his business with this other person wouldn't take long. I would have left but I could see something big was going on and figured maybe if I stayed around I might pick up on something. To help me out, you know what I'm saying? So I go upstairs and man, no sooner do I get there than the shooting starts. I mean, they don't say more than a couple of words to each other and then it's over." Bobby shook his head at the wonder of it all. "Shot the mother-fucker right in the heart."

"Did you see the killer?"

Bobby laughed, a high-pitched, nervous laugh. "No fucking way. I didn't make a sound. I figured if the killer knew I was upstairs he'd of done me too."

Claude smiled. "Were you scared?"

"Shit." All the mirth left Bobby's face. "Wouldn't you have been? I didn't have no piece or nothing on me. I stayed up there and tried not to breathe too loud."

"Could you make out what the killer and Hirsch said to each other before the shooting?"

Bobby shook his head. "No, I couldn't. I never heard the killer at all, just Hirsch laughing and saying something like *sue me*."

"So what happened next?"

"I heard the killer rootin' around Hirsch's office looking for something, tearing drawers open, throwing papers around, shit like that. Then someone else comes down the pier and onto the boat. Police say it was the harbormaster. Anyway, he comes onto the boat and into Hirsch's office and gets himself whacked on the head. Then the killer leaves."

"What did you do then?"

"I waited awhile to make sure he had really left, you know? Then, when I hear the harbormaster groaning downstairs I figure it's time to call the police."

"That's all? You called the police and that was the end of it? How was the harbormaster?"

"Man, he was bleeding bad," Bobby said. "I almost tried to help him but then I thought about all that AIDS shit with blood and all, so I just waited out in the parking lot until the police came. The medics said he would be okay."

Claude shook his head. "That's the goddamndest story I ever heard. Did you tell all this to the detectives inside?" He nodded toward the police building.

"I told them everything I just told you."

"Well, let's go back inside and see if we can wrap this up."

The two men reentered the building and walked down the hall to room 148. As soon as they walked into the room one of the younger detectives angrily accosted them.

"Why didn't you use room 152 like Detective Malone told you?" he asked.

Claude looked at him for a long second as one might look at a particularly annoying child and then turned to Malone. "Have you finished questioning Mr. Norton for the time being?" he asked, pointedly ignoring the younger detective's question.

Malone smiled and waved his colleague back to his desk. "Yeah, Claude, I guess we have everything we need for now. We know where to reach him if we think of anything else."

Outside the police station Claude and Bobby shook hands next to Claude's truck, a decidedly unrestored 1955 Chevrolet pickup that Claude had owned for some eight years.

"Man, I appreciate you coming down like this." Bobby looked at the truck and shook his head, clearly appalled that his friend would drive such a low-rent vehicle.

Claude shrugged. "I'd say that it was hardly necessary, especially since you'd already told them everything you knew." He looked closely at Bobby. "You *did* tell them everything, didn't you? You're not holding anything back?"

"No way, man. What I know, they know." He looked again at the truck, seemingly unable to take his eyes off it. "Man, what is the deal with this, this . . ."

Bobby paused for a second, unable to summon forth an appropriately descriptive adjective. "This *truck?*"

"Listen," Claude said, ignoring Bobby's question, "call me if anything else comes up. No, wait a minute. Don't call me." Claude jerked a thumb back in the direction of the police station. "Call Malone." He smiled to take some of the edge off his words. "And be careful until Malone bags someone." He climbed into the truck. "You need a lift anywhere?"

Bobby shook his head. "No way, man, not in that thing." He laughed. "I'm surprised it hasn't been towed, you know what I'm saying?"

Claude started the truck. "Be careful," he reminded Bobby.

On University Avenue he picked up the cell phone and hit the auto-dial button.

"Law offices of Claude McCutcheon."

"Hey, Emma, it's me. I'm leaving the police station now."

"Well, what's the story?" Emma Fujikawa, Claude's part-time secretary, sounded pleased no end that something interesting had come up.

"Good question." Claude shrugged as if Emma could see him over the cellular telephone. "Norton apparently *almost* witnessed a murder out on the Berkeley marina earlier today. Myron Hirsch finally pissed off the wrong guy and got himself shot through the heart."

"You think Bobby Norton might have done it?"

"No. I wouldn't trust him any further than I could throw him but I doubt that he's ever actually killed anyone, and in any event there doesn't seem to be any reason for him to have done Hirsch."

"What do the police think?"

"Jim Malone did not feel it necessary to grace me with the benefit of his thinking on this matter." Claude looked at his watch. "I think I'll head over to the gym and then call it a day."

"Do you want me to stick around for a while?" It was only three-thirty, and Emma was used to Claude's irregular working hours.

"No, go ahead and shut it down. If you're there to answer the telephone someone might actually try to refer some work to us."

Claude lived in a compact, stuccoed California bungalow that he had purchased for cash in 1978. Over a number of years he remodeled the interior to suit himself, ending up with an eccentric approximation of his own personality. In order to create a single great room, he removed all of the interior walls, replacing their structural function with three heavy glue-lam beams that ran the length of the house from front to rear. The ceiling was removed, revealing the roof joists. The kitchen occupied one corner at the rear of the great room, and a sleeping alcove the other. The water closet, if such it could be called, was defined by three shoji screens next to the sleeping alcove. The floor was a red-hued Brazilian hardwood, and the kitchen area had been laid with unglazed Mexican paver tiles. Other than the futon and an armoire in the sleeping alcove, the only furniture in the house were two pieces in the front of the great room, a well-worn matching leather sofa and club chair, and an antique plank trestle table in the kitchen area with four Shaker-style chairs. For years Claude had been meaning to install pegs on the wall so the chairs could be hung during the day as their original designers intended.

Upon arriving home from the gym Claude luxuriated in a long, hot bath, his head propped against the sloping rear of the antique cast-iron tub. When he got out of the tub he unconsciously glanced in the mirror, noting the small scar running north to south alongside his right eye. It was an old scar, an inch long and barely visible anymore. He smiled, remembering clearly the words of the medic at Fort Jackson who had rather carelessly stitched it for him—*A day in the army is like a day on the farm*—and still had no idea what he had meant by it. *Not a bad face, all in all,* he thought. His eyes, a deep azure blue, were clear, and his hair, light blond in youth, had darkened agreeably with age. He stepped from behind the futon, towel in hand, and saw Sally Pinter, his next-door neighbor, standing in his kitchen. Looking at him.

"Jesus Christ, Sally," Claude said, not unkindly, "you can't just walk in here any time it strikes your fancy." He wrapped the towel around his waist. "What in the world would your husband think?"

"Shoot." Sally tossed her bangs back from her eyes and put a hand on her hip.

Nice, Claude thought, turning quickly aside so Sally wouldn't see him smile. *Lauren Bacall couldn't have done it better.*

"Bud thinks the world of you."

Claude grunted and stepped behind a shoji screen to dress. "That's as may be, but I doubt he thinks enough of me to want his wife to see me naked." Claude paused while he struggled into a pair of light cotton trousers. "Do you want a cup of coffee, or what?"

"No," Sally said airily as Claude stepped back out from behind the screen. "I just came over to tell you that Bud and I are taking little Pete"—their four-year-old—"to visit his grandparents over in Stockton for a couple of days. Bud wanted to know if you'd mind keeping an eye on the house while we're away."

Claude shook his head. "Hell, you guys don't have anything worth stealing." He walked into his kitchen and opened a bottle of water. "But yes, I'll keep a lookout for you."

"Do you still have the key?" Sally asked as if there were some significance to the fact that he had a key to her house.

"If I haven't lost it," Claude replied, knowing that he hadn't. He leaned against the counter and smiled as Sally let herself out the back door. As she went out a large, chocolate brown cat sauntered in and leapt easily up onto the counter. He nuzzled Claude's arm and then sat back, an insolent expression on his face.

"What do you want?" Claude asked, admiring the cat's battle-scarred ears, one of which looked as if it had been trimmed with pinking shears. The cat, quite unbidden, had wandered in and taken up residence in the house some eight years earlier. Claude named him Thurman and the two settled rather comfortably into a relationship underpinned by a fact pure and simple: The house needed a cat and the cat needed a home. By way of response to Claude's question Thurman yawned, revealing a pink tongue and an impressive pair of immense white canine teeth.

"My sentiments exactly," Claude said, pleased that he had nothing further to do with the murder of Myron Hirsch.

CHAPTER 2

New London, California
Tuesday, March 8, 1994

"Miss Tikkanen, may I see you for a minute?"

"Yes, Walter, what is it?" Margaret's voice conveyed just enough of a hint of impatience that Walter Isley, although the company's chief forester and an employee with over thirty years' continuous service, unconsciously dipped his head slightly.

"If this isn't a good time . . ."

"What *is* it?" she demanded.

"You wanted to know when the timber cruise results on that section of old growth above Redway were collated."

"Let's discuss this at . . ." Margaret paused and looked at her watch. ". . . at five-thirty, shall we?"

Although the workday at the offices of the Northwestern Lumber Company ended officially at four-thirty, Walter knew that other than strictly clerical workers, few senior employees had the courage to leave the office before Margaret, whenever that might be. He also knew that she wasn't asking him to meet her at five-thirty, she was telling him.

43

Margaret Stewart Tikkanen moved through the corridors of her company with the power and muscular grace of an Olympic athlete, and with no less confidence than any CEO on Wall Street. A tall woman, with shoulder-length hair more red than auburn, she would have been considered extremely attractive by any objective standard had her sharply chiseled face had even a hint of softness about it. As it was, she was frankly admired whenever she entered a public room, particularly by those who did not know her. Her eyes were an astonishing blue and her body was hard and fit, both physical attributes directly linked to the Finnish gene pool from which her father had emerged. Margaret attended Stanford, starting in the fall of 1968. She graduated in 1972 with an honors degree in economics and, at Joseph's urging, spent the following two years obtaining an MBA at Harvard. While at Cambridge she took her first lover, an energetic young instructor of constitutional law at Harvard Law School with a taste for radical politics and fast cars. She let him drive her Porsche and used him as one might use a particularly comfortable pair of shoes— rather too often than is good for the long term. At the end of her second and final year she sold the Porsche and had his belongings removed without warning from her luxurious town home on the Charles River.

Like her father and grandfather before her, Margaret considered the greater part of Humboldt County, in northern California, to be hers in the same manner that other men and women might have considered their automobiles, or their dogs, or their power tools to be their personal property. She and her father, Joseph Tikkanen, owned not only the Northwestern Lumber Company and all of its lands in fee simple, but also the Eel River Railroad Company and all of its right-of-way from Eureka,

California, south to San Francisco and north to
Portland. She sometimes considered the men and
women who worked for her to be little more than
another form of chattel property, assets not unlike
the company-owned houses they occupied in New
London, one of California's last company towns.
Margaret's father Joseph had inherited everything—the company, the railroad, the vast real
estate holdings, and the employees—from his
father-in-law, her grandfather, F. M. Stewart, a man
who believed in the divine sanctity of mercantile
power.

F. M. Stewart had started in the lumber business
in 1904 when he was just sixteen years old. The son
of an itinerant Scottish blacksmith, F. M. had few
prospects until, at the age of sixteen, he married the
daughter of a bookkeeper at the Humboldt Sawmill
Company in Fortuna. The bride's father lent him
enough money to purchase two mules, enabling
young F. M. to become a contract logger. The
sawmill was owned by two lawyers in San Francisco
who never ventured into Humboldt County, and
who prospered in the sawmill business by virtue of
their steadfast refusal to pay more for labor than
absolutely necessary, a practice young F. M. observed and clung to all his life. F. M. gradually
drove his own competitors out of business, almost
always by bidding lower on the mill's logging contracts than anyone else in the county, reasoning that
he (and, of course, his wife) could live more inex-
pensively than anyone else he knew. During the four
years he worked as a logger he paid most of his labor
force more than he himself made. By 1908 he had
crews throughout most of Humboldt County's
seemingly endless forests of old-growth redwood
and Douglas fir, many of his former competitors
now working for him as foremen. He worked his
men ten hours a day, six days a week, and provided

no benefits beyond a weekly pay envelope. The lumberjacks provided their own saws and axes, and the teamsters were expected to keep the mules and horses in good health and free from injury. When, in the spring of 1908, the San Francisco owners of the mill, through their mill superintendent, suggested that he cut his rates or lose their business, F. M. responded by taking in a local banker as a silent partner and opening his own mill.

F. M. Stewart learned the sawmill business much as he had the logging, putting in fourteen- to sixteen-hour days and taking no money out of the business for himself other than the bare minimum needed to sustain his small household. Although there was no joy in F. M.'s life, he had not expected there to be, and so he felt not in the least deprived. He had learned from his father that a man worked until he could work no more and then he died. Further, he believed that everything he had was his only by virtue of the fact that he was stronger than the next man, and would remain his only as long as his strength prevailed. The years 1908 through 1914 were extraordinarily harsh ones, with the future of the Northwestern Lumber Company doubtful at best. Only the iron hand of F. M. (his silent partner having jumped ship in 1910, convinced that the enterprise was bound to fail) and the assassination of the Archduke Francis Ferdinand in Sarajevo saved the business. The war in Europe and the rush to profit from it in the United States breathed new life into F. M.'s mill. Within the span of six months he was operating two shifts and plowing every penny of profit into expansion, and more importantly in the long run into the purchase of extensive tracts of timberland throughout the county. Also in late 1914, as if in recognition of the improved fortunes of the business, Rachel Stewart, the only issue of F. M. and the bookkeeper's daughter, was born.

F. M. ran his business in a manner that pushed the expression "sole proprietorship" to the outermost reaches of its definitional envelope. He was quick-tempered, intolerant, paranoid in the extreme in his dealings with others, and hardworking to the exclusion of literally everything else in his life. The years between the two world wars were hard ones, and only F. M.'s monomaniacal aversion to debt and bankers allowed the company to enter the Great Depression debt-free and thus survive it relatively intact. Once again war saved the nation and with it the Northwestern Lumber Company. F. M.'s mills worked three shifts and, as chairman of the county's draft board, he saw to it that his employees, as opposed to those of his competitors, were classified as essential to the civilian war effort.

The end of the war brought even greater prosperity to the company. The housing industry literally exploded, fueled by a new generation of veterans eager for a three-bedroom rancher in the suburbs of Southern California. In order to increase his production capacity F. M. bought out two smaller competitors and scoured the county for employees to operate his round-the-clock enterprise. By late 1948 F. M. had twenty-three hundred employees working three shifts at five separate sawmills. He himself continued to work fourteen to sixteen hours a day, much of his time spent in the mills, constantly haranguing his foremen and supervisors to increase production and cut overhead.

"You are wasting money in this mill."

F. M. stopped in his tracks. Few of the many men who worked for him had the courage to speak to him unbidden. "Who are you?" he demanded, thrusting his head forward aggressively.

The young man who had spoken, standing with an almost military bearing, was unintimidated. "My name is Joseph Tikkanen and I have been working here for almost four months."

F. M., taken aback by the man's demeanor of quiet self-confidence and authority, was instantly on his guard. "Where are you from?" F. M. heard the young man's accent but could not place it.

"I am from Finland. I came here after the war."

"What are you talking about, 'wasting money'?"

Joseph pulled a piece of paper out of the hip pocket of his dungarees. "If you will lay out this machinery"—he pointed to the rows of milling machines that took rough-cut lumber from the band saws—"in this fashion"—he now pointed to the diagram he had drawn—"you will have the same, what do you call it, production, with two fewer men per shift."

F. M. studied the diagram and saw that Joseph was correct. "Why didn't you tell your foreman?" He nodded in the direction of the shift boss, who was listening to their conversation.

Joseph look at the foreman, his immediate superior, and shrugged. "He is a fool."

F. M. pointed to the foreman. "You're fired," he said peremptorily. He looked at Joseph. "You're the new foreman. I want these changes implemented before the end of the day. As soon as it's completed I want the payroll for this mill reduced by six men. Seven," he amended, remembering the foreman, a fifteen-year employee, he had just fired.

As word of the encounter raced through the mill, angry, xenophobic voices demanded that something be done about Tikkanen. Predictably, the next morning, a confrontation took place in the mill.

"We don't like ass-kissers around here, especially foreign ones."

Without a word Joseph leapt forward, smashing the

other man's nose with a straight right. Off balance, the man fell backwards, his broken nose gushing blood. Joseph moved quickly and pummeled the man, smashing his face with sledgehammer blows from both fists. The other men on the shift, aghast, watched their comrade absorb a brutal beating. No one lifted a hand, however, and Joseph stopped just short of killing the man. He looked about him. "He is fired. Two of you men carry him outside. The rest of you get back to work. I am docking everyone's pay one hour to compensate the company for lost production." He glanced about, hoping someone else would challenge him. No one did.

When F. M. heard of the confrontation, he promoted Joseph to mill superintendent, in charge of production for all three shifts. In the weeks and months that followed, Joseph moved swiftly to consolidate his new power, promoting men loyal to him and driving everyone else to new heights of productivity with what could only be called a frenzy. In the spring of 1950, barely a year after first arriving in New London, Joseph married F. M.'s only child, Rachel, a plain, obedient young woman five years his senior. By the time Joseph's first and only child was born in 1951 he was F. M.'s second-in-command, the much-anticipated heir apparent. He named his daughter Margaret Stewart Tikkanen.

Joseph took over as sole owner of the Northwestern Lumber Company rather sooner than anyone had anticipated. On a lovely spring morning in 1952 F. M. had the misfortune to be standing twelve feet from one of the mill's planing machines when the machine's rapidly spinning blade struck a knot in a piece of Douglas fir it was forming into a two-by-four stud. Propelled with enormous energy and speed a tiny sliver of wood, no more than four inches in length and less than the diameter of a pencil's lead, passed completely through the old man's right thigh, cleanly severing the femoral artery in passing. The force of the unexpected blow knocked him down, but he remained on the sawdust-covered wooden floor of the mill for only a few seconds before rising, angrily shaking off the helping hands of the horrified operator of the planing machine. He motioned the man back to work, cursing him for leaving his machine, and stumbled to the foreman's office inside the mill, a cramped, dirty room in which sat the foreman's desk and one wooden chair. Finding the office empty (the foreman was required to do his paperwork after his shift ended, on his own time), F. M. Stewart sat down and in short order bled to death.

"Norton has disappeared," Margaret informed her father as she walked into his office. She handed him a copy of the *Oakland Tribune,* which featured the headline: "Radical Environmentalist Murdered."

Her father looked up from the papers on his desk. Although Margaret had taken over the day-to-day operation of the company, she still looked to Joseph for advice and consent on strategic issues and major capital expenditures. "What does that mean?"

Margaret shook her head. "Impossible to say. Someone may have gotten to him. Or, he could be getting ready to offer something for sale to the highest bidder."

Joseph studied the paper. "What about his lawyer, this McCutcheon?"

"He claims not to represent Norton, though our contact in the Berkeley Police Department says that the detective heading up the investigation isn't so sure. But even if he's not actually representing Norton, my guess is that he's either gotten or he's trying to get his finger into the pie."

"You think McCutcheon's involved?"

"I think he is now. We know from our contact in the police department that Hirsch wasn't expecting Norton to show up when he did." Margaret smiled, a nonhumorous facial expression feared by all who worked at the Northwestern Lumber Company. Father and daughter shared, in addition to an uncanny physical resemblance that transcended X and Y chromosomes, an unconscious bearing of authority that more often than not bordered on threat. "When a two-bit crook needs help selling stolen goods, who better to call than a lawyer?"

"I take it then that you wish to ignore the missing Mr. Norton for the time being and concentrate on this lawyer, McCutcheon."

"That is precisely what I intend to do."

Joseph sat back in his chair. "You might consider calling one of our friends in Sacramento for some assistance. It could be that McCutcheon, like many lawyers, has political aspirations."

Margaret nodded. She knew that from the moment he had taken control of the company, her father had slowly and deliberately developed a political power base not only in Humboldt County but also in Sacramento and Washington, D.C. He taught her that money, and money alone, was the key that unlocked the door to legislative access—it was, as one former Speaker of the House so eloquently put it, the mother's milk of electoral politics. Numerous political careers at the local, state, and federal level were started and maintained with money provided by the Northwestern Lumber Company, most of it in the form of cash and none of it directly traceable back to the company. Joseph's success as a patron of the democratic process was staggering. Over the years Joseph, and later Margaret, counted among their possessions four members of the Congress of the United States (three representatives and one senator), seven assemblymen in Sacramento, including three successive Speakers of California's House, and every governor, Democratic and Republican, elected since 1958. The company demanded relatively little for its money, requiring only that the men (and later women) it bought be unwavering (not to mention successful) in their efforts to turn aside, by whatever means necessary, all attempts to regulate the lumber business or to insert the governmental bureaucracy into the intimate and delicate relationship existing between employer and employee.

Margaret eagerly supported, and in a number of significant ways expanded upon, her father's vision when she took over active management of the company. Locally, she went far beyond the mere clandestine distribution of cash to elected officials and political aspirants. She publicly provided the funds needed for a new county medical center in Eureka, established a scholarship fund for the sons and daughters of all county employees, and fully endowed the School of Forestry at Humboldt State College. She became the patron saint of all the county's law-enforcement and fire-control agencies with the establishment of a trust fund to care for the families of any officer who might die in the line of duty. In all, her careful financial largess created an atmosphere throughout the county wherein one publicly criticized the Northwestern Lumber Company at substantial personal risk.

The first priority, Joseph repeatedly impressed on Margaret when he first revealed to her the nature and extent of the company's illegal political payments, *must always be absolute security regarding the knowledge of these matters.* He showed her how he recorded every name, every payment, every vote purchased on specific legislation of particular interest and importance to the company in a series of journals he kept under tight lock and key in his office safe.

Over the last half-dozen years, as she had gradually taken over responsibility for the day-to-day operations of the company, Margaret also assumed responsibility for making all the necessary entries in the journals.

She'd been the one who had discovered their theft.

"We may in fact need Sacramento's help in this," she agreed. "But right now I want to develop as much background information as I can on McCutcheon. We have to know what sort of leverage we can use against him when the need arises."

Albany, California
Tuesday, March 8, 1994

"Mornin', Emma."

It was just before 11:00 A.M. and Claude yawned as he thumbed through the mail on Emma Fujikawa's desk. His office was a second-story walk-up on Solano Avenue in Albany. Although the stuccoed building, which housed a small real estate office on the ground floor, was exceedingly modest and ordinary in appearance, Claude's second-floor offices, like his home, reflected his eclectic tastes. The outer office and reception area, which Emma occupied, was furnished with a modern, handmade oak desk and credenza together with two oak filing cabinets. The floors in both Emma's and Claude's offices were a dark-hued Brazilian hardwood that Claude and a friend had installed and finished to a satiny, gleaming shine. The furnishings in Claude's office consisted of an antique walnut rolltop desk sitting in one corner, and, more or less in the middle of the room, a leather love seat and, facing the love seat, two leather side chairs. Between the love seat and the chairs, on the hardwood floor, was a Sarouk prayer rug. There were none of the ubiquitous framed diplomas and certificates with which attorneys in general seem compelled to cover their office walls.

"Have you seen the *Oakland Tribune* this morning?" Emma held the paper triumphantly.

"No." Claude eyed the object of Emma's question suspiciously. "Why?"

Emma couldn't keep the delight out of her voice. "They tried to interview Bobby Norton in connection with their story on the Hirsch murder and he referred all questions to, wait a minute"—she fumbled with the paper, finding the section with the offending words—"my attorney, Claude McCutcheon."

Claude stifled a curse and, taking the paper, walked into his office. The story of the murder occupied most of the front page, together with a picture of a smiling Bobby Norton standing in front of his club in Richmond. Claude looked up as Emma walked into his office.

"You look like a man in need of coffee," she said, placing a cup on his desk.

"How old is it?"

Emma smiled and did not respond, knowing that Claude only asked to annoy her. She nodded at the paper Claude was holding. "The newspaper doesn't appear to know a great deal about the murder."

Claude nodded. "Thanks for the coffee." He pointed to Bobby Norton's smiling face. "Would you buy a used car from that man?" He shook his head, amused in spite of himself. "No, it's all mostly speculation and uninformed comments from people who knew Hirsch or at least claim they did. It's true that Bobby was there when the murder was committed but in fact he didn't see or hear anything of significance." Claude paused and sipped his coffee. "Or at least he says he didn't. With Bobby, who the hell knows?"

"What exactly is the deal with you and Bobby Norton anyway?"

"We go back a long ways. Over twenty years. He helped me out a lot when I was doing some pro bono work for a veteran who had gotten himself strung out on drugs. Bobby had an older brother who was badly wounded in Vietnam and was spending a lot of time at the VA hospital over in the City, trying to help him with his rehabilitation."

"Whatever happened to the brother?"

Claude shook his head. "Sad story. He had big problems, both physical and mental, and committed suicide eight or nine years ago. Bobby asked me to be one of the pallbearers at his funeral."

Before either could say anything further the telephone rang. Emma reached across Claude's desk and picked up the receiver.

"Good morning, law offices of Claude McCutcheon." She listened for a second and then covered the mouthpiece with the palm of her hand. "It's for you. Malone at the Berkeley Police Department. Do you want to take it?"

Claude nodded affirmatively. "Yeah, let me have it." He put the receiver to his ear. "Jim? Yeah, Claude here. What can I do for you?" Claude listened silently for a moment. "Well, have you checked his club? Maybe he's over there inventorying the booze or something." Claude placed his hand over the receiver. "Bobby Norton's turned up missing," he told Emma. "What's that?" he said into the receiver. "No, I wouldn't have the faintest idea. Maybe with a girlfriend or something. Listen, Jim, I'm not his lawyer. I don't give a damn what some reporter thinks or says. I don't know where he is and frankly, I don't much care. He told me yesterday that he told you guys everything he knew, and as to whether or not that's the truth, well, your guess is as good as mine." Claude listened for another minute. "Yeah, sure, if he gets in touch with me I'll tell him you're looking for him. No, no, I understand. You bet. Good-bye." Claude hung up and looked at Emma. "If I can get my hands on Bobby Norton I'm going to wring his goddamned neck. He's got everybody thinking I'm his lawyer."

"Where do you suppose he's disappeared to?"

"Who knows?" Claude shrugged. "My guess is that he hasn't told the police everything he knows and he's trying to figure some angle or scheme by which he can turn a profit."

"That might be more dangerous than he thinks. I'd guess that whoever killed Myron Hirsch certainly wouldn't hesitate to kill again if he thought there was a witness."

"No doubt that's why Bobby has decided to drop out of sight. And of course it could be that in fact he doesn't know a damned thing but is trying to appear as if he does in the hope of defrauding the poor, ignorant murderer."

"Do you think he'll get in touch with you?"

Claude shook his head. "Not unless he needs something. As far as I'm concerned he's on his own, and I told him as much yesterday. Meanwhile, if anyone from the Fourth Estate calls, try to make it as clear as you can that we do not now, have never, and do not expect in the future to represent the elusive Mr. Norton."

Claude finished thumbing through the rest of the newspaper and then spent an hour finishing the paperwork on two matters that had recently been closed. At midmorning he walked out of his office.

"I'm going to stroll up to the Café del Sol for a

cappuccino," he said, putting the paperwork he had finished marking up on her desk. "You want me to bring you a croissant?"

Emma thought for a moment and then shook her head. "No, Dolores"—her sister—"is meeting me here for an early lunch."

"Where are you guys going?"

"We haven't decided yet. Any ideas?"

"How about sushi down at the Tokyo Fish Market on San Pablo?"

Emma wrinkled her nose in disgust. "I should have known better than to have asked you." She waved her hand. "Go get your cappuccino."

"Claude McCutcheon, the Melvin Belli of Solano Avenue!"

Claude shook his head as he joined the regular group of espresso drinkers at the Café del Sol. "Somebody must have left a copy of the *Tribune* in here this morning," he said, addressing the small group, "because I know none of you would have actually paid for one." He gave a thumbs-up to the owner of the café. "Double cap, light on the foam."

"What's the deal, Claude?" Winifred Hale asked. Winifred ran a small tax and bookkeeping service a block down Solano from the café. An unreconstructed Leninist, she had come out of the closet as a defiant lesbian in the mid-1950s when Berkeley was a bastion of republicanism and owned, it was rumored, half the commercial real estate in Albany and El Cerrito. A lifetime of Irish whiskey and unfiltered cigarettes had left her with a voice that sounded like gravel sliding around in a cement mixer. "You've never done criminal work before."

"And not fixing to start, either," Claude assured her.

"You think Bobby killed Hirsch?" someone asked.

Claude shook his head. "I think he was just in the wrong place at the wrong time." He took a sip of his cappuccino. "I expect he's lucky he didn't get killed himself."

"I'm surprised it took this long for someone to kill Myron Hirsch," Phil Black said. A retired merchant seaman, Phil owned a small shoe-repair shop that he operated on an irregular and unpredictable schedule. "He's pissed a lot of important people off over the last few years." He looked around as several murmured assent. "Hell, anybody could have done it."

"It's a Mr. Garner Beckett on line three," Emma called out. Claude had been back in his office for about half an hour. "Says he's the managing partner at the law firm of Everhart, Jackson and Jones."

Claude, seated at his desk, smiled. He couldn't see Emma but could hear the sarcasm in her voice as she emphasized the words "managing partner." The Everhart firm was the largest corporate law firm in the City. *She's been hanging around me too long,* he thought approvingly. "What's he want?" he yelled, knowing it would annoy her.

There was a second of silence and then Emma appeared in the doorway to Claude's office. "Why don't you pick up the telephone and ask him?" she inquired with exaggerated politeness.

Claude picked up the receiver. "This is Claude McCutcheon," he said, winking at Emma. "What can I do for you?"

"Mr. McCutcheon, my name is Garner Beckett and I'm the managing partner at the law firm of Everhart, Jackson and Jones."

"So I understand."

"Yes, well, I am calling to discuss your retention as special counsel to an old and valued client of my firm's. My client is prepared to pay you a substantial retainer against your hourly fee for legal services to be rendered."

"And who, if I may be so bold, is your client?"

"I would prefer not to divulge that information until such time as you and I have entered into a preliminary understanding regarding the representation," Beckett said pompously. "Suffice it to say that the client is a closely held corporation with an extremely large and impressive asset portfolio. I rather doubt you would not wish to add them to your client list."

"And how exactly did I come to you or your client's attention?"

"That information, too, I would prefer not to discuss at this time. Really, Mr. McCutcheon, I can assure you that the opportunity and the privilege to represent a client such as the one in question comes along but rarely, particularly to one, such as yourself, in sole practice."

Claude laughed. *What an asshole,* he thought. "Well, I'm sorry to have to disappoint you, Mr. Beckett, but my dance card, or 'client list' as you call it, is rather full at the present time and I'm not taking on any new representations, particularly of the mysterious variety. Nonetheless, I assure you that I am honored beyond all reckoning by the confidence you and your client have shown in me. Good day." Without waiting for a reply Claude hung up. He looked and shrugged at Emma, who was still standing in the doorway to his office. "Who knows how these people get my telephone number?" he asked rhetorically.

"What did he want?"

"Said he wanted to refer a client to me, some hotshot corporation with big bucks."

"Someday you'll wish you had a client like that." Emma, ever the pragmatist, heartily disapproved of Claude's laissez-faire approach to client acquisition.

In fact, he seldom took on new clients, and then generally only to do someone a favor.

Claude shook his head. "I doubt it." He looked at his watch. It was almost eleven-thirty. "I'm outta here."

"Are you going to be back this afternoon?"

"No." Claude stood up and hitched up his blue jeans. "I'm meeting Claire Williams for lunch over in the City. That's why I wore my nice boots." He held up a foot to show off his anteater-hide cowboy boots.

"I can't imagine why she would have anything to do with you, not after the way you treated her."

Claude and Claire Williams, a research attorney with the California Supreme Court and an adjunct professor of law at the University of California's Boalt Hall, had been lovers the prior year, and Emma had hoped that she might be the one woman capable of maneuvering Claude to the altar.

"I treated her like a queen," Claude responded lightly, knowing that Emma had been quite charmed by the soft-spoken, attractive attorney.

"Then why didn't—"

Claude held up his hand, interrupting Emma. "Because, as I've told you a dozen times, she was too old and set in her ways to settle down with a sensitive person such as myself."

"She's younger than you are," Emma pointed out.

"Not enough younger. Besides, she already has a child and doubtless would want more."

"You better be careful," Emma warned. "You're going to wind up old and lonely."

"I should be so lucky." The telephone rang. "Whoever it is," he said, "I've already left."

Emma reached over and picked up the receiver on Claude's desk. "Law offices of Claude McCutcheon," she said. She listened for a moment. "I believe you just missed him. Let me put you on hold and I'll see if

I can catch him on the stairs." She looked at Claude and smiled sweetly. "It's your client, Bobby Norton."

Claude sighed and took the telephone. "What, exactly, did you hope to accomplish by telling everyone that I was your attorney?" he demanded when Emma reconnected the line. "And where are you calling from?"

"Listen," Bobby replied, ignoring Claude's questions, "we need to talk."

"About what?"

"Never mind about what. I'll meet you down at The Last Roundup"—a seedy bar and pool room on San Pablo Avenue in Albany—"in half an hour."

"Sorry. I was just leaving for an appointment in the City." Claude looked at his watch. "And I'm going to be late as it is. Give me a number where I can reach you later this afternoon and I'll try to call you when I get back on this side of the Bay."

"Man, this is more important than any goddamned meeting in the City."

Claude shook his head as if Bobby could see him. "That's the best I can do," he said, his tone of voice conveying a finality that got through to Bobby.

"Okay, okay, here's a number you can call me at, but for Christ's sake don't give it out to anybody." He gave the number to Claude, who repeated it out loud so Emma could copy it down. "Call me as soon as you get back."

"By the way, Jim Malone over at the Berkeley PD is looking for you."

"Let the motherfucker look," Bobby said defiantly. "Besides, he ain't the only one looking."

"Just a reminder: I don't do criminal work," Claude said. "My recommendation is that you get yourself a criminal lawyer lined up before too much longer because it looks like you're going to need one."

"Just call me when you get back. I guarantee you'll be interested in what I've got to tell you."

"I doubt it. And listen, don't wait breathlessly by the telephone. I may be late getting back." He hung up before Bobby could respond.

"What was that all about?" Emma asked as she handed the telephone number she had written down to Claude. He wrote Bobby's name on it and put it in his top drawer.

"Just as I feared. It sounds as if that nitwit heard or found something in Myron Hirsch's office after the murder that he believes he can profit by. Something he neglected to tell the Berkeley PD about. Or me, for that matter."

"What does he want with you?"

"God only knows." He paused and smiled suddenly. "Although on second thought, where Bobby Norton is concerned I doubt even She knows. I suspect he wants help marketing his information to the highest bidder."

"What are you going to do about it?"

"Disabuse him of any such notion as quickly as I conveniently can."

"To what do I owe the honor of your telephone call?" Claude asked, after he and Claire Williams sat down at their table. They were eating at Briscoe's, a small, south of Market Street café that specialized in nothing in particular, the daily menu, and even the question of whether the café would open on any given day, depending entirely on the personal whim of the owner and cook, Briscoe Morgan.

"No particular reason," Claire said. "I hadn't heard from you for a while and didn't want to lose touch."

Claude smiled. "I recall that you told me never to call you again the last time we spoke." He looked up as the owner approached their table. "Hello, Briscoe. I'm surprised you decided to open up today."

Briscoe shrugged. "I probably wouldn't have if you hadn't called," he said. "It's too nice a day to be in here putting up with a bunch of dickheads." He nodded toward Claire. "I thought you two had broken up."

"Just because we're having lunch together doesn't mean we're an item," Claude said. "What are you cooking today?"

"I got some nice fish down at the market this morning. I could either mesquite-grill you a couple of salmon fillets or a piece of swordfish. Which'll it be?"

Claude looked at Claire. "Salmon?" When she nodded affirmatively he gave Briscoe a thumbs-up.

"Salmon it is," Briscoe rumbled. "I steamed up some asparagus about an hour ago and thought I'd serve it cold with a vinaigrette and a diced hard-boiled egg."

"I hope you cut off most of the fibrous stalks," Claude teased. "Nothing I hate worse than tough asparagus."

Briscoe looked down at Claude for several seconds while searching his mind for an appropriately vulgar response. Finally, inhibited by Claire's presence, he turned from the table with a grunt, snapping his fingers at his only employee, a young busboy. He returned from the kitchen a moment later with a bottle of wine, two wineglasses, and a corkscrew.

"Here," he said, placing everything on the table in front of Claude, "I think this wine will go well with the salmon." It was a gewürztraminer, from a winery Claude had never heard of in the Anderson Valley, north of the Bay Area. "The salesman was in here the other day and left a couple of bottles. It's on the house." He walked away, leaving Claude to open the bottle for himself.

"Not exactly the wine service protocol they teach at the Cordon Bleu but it gets the job done," Claude said to Claire as he fumbled with the corkscrew. "And, the price is right." He wrestled the cork out of the bottle and poured two glasses. "A toast to old times," he said, raising his glass. "I'm glad you called."

Claire put her face into her hands and began to cry. *Bad sign*, Claude thought. *I should have known something was queer when her invitation to lunch came out of the blue.* "What in the world is wrong?"

Claire looked up and, in spite of her tears, smiled. "I'm such a fool," she said. She took a handkerchief from her purse and wiped her eyes. "I've been so worried and you're the only one I could think of to call."

"Why don't you back up and start at the beginning?"

Claire nodded and took a sip of her wine. "It's Nina." Nina was Claire's daughter.

"What is she now," Claude asked, "sixteen?"

"Fifteen. And she's started lying to me and cutting classes at school."

Claude smiled, relieved. "If that's all it is I wouldn't worry too much. Jesus, you wouldn't believe the heartache I gave my old man at that age, and look at me now."

"The problem is that she and two of her friends are hanging around with an older man, an ex-convict of all things. He's become something of a Pied Piper to them and it's driving me insane." Claire began to cry again. "It's like they're mesmerized by this man. When I try to discuss it with her she either refuses to talk to me or she lies."

"Have you talked to the police?"

"Yes, and they're no help whatever. I was told that until a crime was committed they could do nothing. In fact, they told me that by just talking to him they could be charged by the ACLU with unwarranted police harassment of a parolee."

Goddamn it, we've turned into a nation of rabbits.
Claude looked away for a minute, trying to rein in his
growing anger. "Have you spoken with the man
himself?" he asked tightly. "What's his name?"

Claire nodded. "I tried. His name is Ralph Martini.
I called him at his apartment and told him that I did
not approve of Nina's visiting him there."

"And what did he say?"

Claire looked away, embarrassed. "He asked me to
meet him for dinner so we could discuss my shortcomings as a single parent."

"What did he serve time for?"

"He was convicted of selling drugs to minors three
years ago and given a five-year sentence, but he
served only eighteen months. Nina met him through
one of her friends, one of the girls who sees him
regularly." Claire shook her head. "How can kids be
so stupid? He's got them believing he's some kind of
guru."

"What about the other girls' parents? Haven't they
done anything?"

"Both girls come from single-parent homes just like
Nina, and their mothers are just as frightened as I am,
and just as helpless."

"Where are *their* fathers?" Claude asked angrily,
knowing the answer. *Another child's life about to be
ruined,* Claude thought, *while the deadbeat father sits
around up at Tahoe sipping white wine with his new
girlfriend. And* I'm *going to be asked to be the thumb
in the dike.* He said nothing and an uncomfortable
silence built between the two of them that was broken
when Briscoe approached with their lunches.

"You two fighting?" he asked impolitely as he
served them.

Claude smiled, pleased in spite of his anger, with
Briscoe's insolence. "Only just a little for old time's
sake." He waited until Briscoe left the table before
speaking again to Claire. "What exactly did you

have in mind me doing?" *As if I didn't know,* he thought.

Claire looked down at her lunch, avoiding Claude's direct gaze. "I thought you could talk to him," she said in a low voice, toying with her asparagus.

Claude nodded. *Another ACLU card-carrying liberal bites the dust,* he thought sardonically, and just as quickly chided himself for being unkind. Even if accurate. "Give me his address. Do you know where he works?"

"He works at an auto body shop on Twenty-fourth just off Valencia." She wrote the address down and gave it to Claude. "I didn't know who else to call."

"I'll talk to him this afternoon."

"I'm looking for Ralph Martini."

Al's Auto Body (*Se Habla Español*) was a grimy little one-bay garage on 24th Street, in the heart of the Mission District. Probably a chop shop, Claude thought cynically as he looked around, although on second thought, noting the almost unbelievable clutter and filth, he doubted that the owner had either the gumption or the intelligence to run one.

"Yeah? And who the hell are you? A cop, or what? Listen, pal, I got a business to run here and my employees ain't invited to receive visitors during working hours. You got that?"

Al himself, by the name on his extraordinarily filthy mechanic's jumpsuit, confronted Claude at the entrance to the shop. Before Claude could respond a short, slightly built young man, dressed in an equally filthy jumpsuit, walked up from the rear of the shop. Al looked at him and jerked a thumb in Claude's direction.

"This guy's looking for you. I think he's a cop. You can use the office but you only got five minutes and it's coming out of your afternoon break, you got that?"

Al walked into the shop, muttering to himself, leaving Claude and Ralph Martini alone.

"Are you from the probation office?" Ralph asked, his voice whiny and shrill. "Jesus, you guys aren't supposed to hassle me at work, I got enough trouble keeping this job as it is."

Claude motioned Ralph into the tiny, cluttered shop office and closed the door behind them.

"I'm here about Nina Williams," he said tautly.

"Are you a cop?" Ralph asked nervously, wiping his hands compulsively on a greasy rag. He unconsciously backed away from Claude, bumping into the office's sole piece of furniture, a battered metal desk covered with crumpled paperwork and an oil-splattered water pump whose bearings had burned out.

Claude shook his head. "I'm what you might call a friend of the family, and the family doesn't want you seeing her anymore."

"Oh, yeah?" Ralph said, emboldened by the news that Claude wasn't a policeman. "Well, fuck you. What makes you think—"

Before he could say anything else Claude's fist slammed into his face, knocking him to the floor.

"What the hell was that for?" Ralph sat on the floor for a second, his hand to his face. Claude's punch had opened a substantial cut on his cheekbone. "Jesus Christ, I'm bleeding all over the goddamn place." He stood up and, seeing the blood on his hand, raised his right arm.

Claude grabbed Ralph by the front of his jumpsuit. "Go ahead, asshole, take a swing." Claude shook him like a terrier shaking a rat.

Ralph, thoroughly cowed by the frightening look on Claude's face, immediately lowered his arm and began whining.

"Shut up," Claude growled, "and listen. You're never going to see Nina Williams again, you understand? If she comes over to your apartment, you don't let her in. If she calls you, you hang up. You don't talk to her, you don't see her, you don't even think about her."

"You can't do this," Ralph whined. "I got rights. I'll call the police on you."

Claude laughed. "You do that, you miserable cocksucker, and by God we'll see who they believe in this matter. Me, or a punk already convicted of selling drugs to children. You'll be back in the slammer so fast you won't know what hit you." He shook Ralph one more time and then leaned in, his voice low and frightening. "But that'll be the least of your worries because if I hear or even suspect that you've seen Nina again, or talked to her on the telephone, I'm going to make you wish you'd never been born."

"Hello, Claire? Yeah, Claude here. I wanted to call and let you know that I spoke with Ralph Martini. Yeah, he's some weasel all right." Claude paused and listened for a moment. "Well, it's hard to say. I think he finally got the impression that I was serious and that there would be unpleasant consequences if he continued to see Nina, but you never know. What's that? No, we'll just have to wait and see. Call me right away if you even suspect that she's still going over there." He listened again and laughed. "I doubt it. Your kid's been nothing but trouble for me. Remember the times you made me sneak out at the crack of dawn so she wouldn't discover that I'd spent the night with you? Yeah, I know you do. Remember, call me if you hear anything."

Claude hung up the telephone with his left hand and lifted his right hand out of the large bowl of ice water in which it had been resting. He examined it carefully, pleased that the swelling appeared to be well under control, a sure sign that no knuckles had been broken. He got a bottle of beer out of the refrigerator and walked to the front of his great room. As he felt the last of the adrenaline from his encounter with Ralph Martini leave his system, he yawned and stretched, relaxing the tension in his back and shoulders. He sat down in the leather easy chair and stretched his legs across the ottoman. Thurman padded quietly into the room.

"We're a pair, you and me," Claude observed, holding a hand out to the large, brown cat. Thurman leapt into Claude's lap and settled down, dreams of slaughtered gophers and old, crippled mice giving rise to a thick, primordial purr that seemed to fill the quiet room. Claude placed his beer bottle on the hardwood floor next to his chair and yawned again, his drowsy eyes drawn to the heavy Rolex on his left wrist as he automatically covered his mouth with his hand. It made him smile, the watch did, and the two of them, man and beast, drifted out of sight of land on a flat, calm sea of memory.

I'm pregnant.

Though almost thirty years had passed, he heard the words as clearly in his mind as the day they had been spoken. An aching sadness came upon him as he thought of young Nina Williams and the child that he and Barbara Curtis had never known. Barbara Curtis was a freshman at Duke University in 1965, back when college girls still dated soldiers. She and her roommate, a girl from Spartanburg who was seeing a squadmate of Claude's named Danny Carter, drove down to Fort Bragg to watch one of the Hollywood jumps the 82nd Airborne Division occasionally put on for visiting dignitaries and the folks back home. After the jump Danny and Claude bigtimed it for the girls, dusty fatigues redolent with the sweet smell of burnt castor oil from the C-130s, Zippo lighters and Lucky Strikes, eyes shining and cheeks flushed. At the end of the day Claude made a date to see Barbara the following Saturday in Durham. They did little more on that first date than sit in the large reception area of her dormitory and talk. Although the conversation was somewhat strained, their lives touching on too few common points to allow shared values or interests, they nonetheless agreed to see each other again the following Saturday, both of them wondering why. Their second date began, as their first had, with small talk in the dormitory reception area, but ended with Barbara sitting on Claude's lap under a sycamore tree not far from the dorm asking him rather urgently not to ejaculate inside her. Afterwards, they sat on the stone wall that guarded the Women's Campus and shared a cigarette as the whistle at the Irwin Cotton Mill across the street signaled the end of the second shift. Claude didn't find out what *ejaculate* meant until the next day when he borrowed the first sergeant's dictionary and looked it up.

Without giving it a great deal of thought Claude became a Saturday-night regular at the Rebel Yell Tourist Court on the Durham–Chapel Hill highway. Barbara and Claude would spend Saturday afternoons and evenings cloistered in one of the tattered and ridiculously out-at-elbow cabins, door locked and shades drawn, cast-iron bed frame noisily protesting their otherwise silent couplings. She was always passive, accepting him with little outward enthusiasm yet never denying, never complaining. (Once, early on, she asked if he would like her to fellate him. Trapped without the first sergeant's dictionary for guidance he cautiously nodded assent. She must not have enjoyed it overmuch for she never asked again.) As much as anything Claude had loved the wonderful silence, the hours spent lying next to each other as the light faded inexorably away, leaving only the filtered neon glow of the VACANCY sign to pierce the gloom, a low-rent aurora borealis dancing over the bed. Back at the dorm at Duke good-byes were mostly limited to a confirmation of the desire to meet again the following weekend. Sunday mornings Claude would get up early and steal away to Fayetteville, unsure of whether or not this was how things were supposed to be. By Monday reveille Saturday was no more than a vaguely titillating memory, as faded and colorless as a lifer's tattoo.

"I'm pregnant."

Claude was not so much surprised as resigned, having grown up knowing that marriages generally got started in roadside tourist courts or the backseats of '49 Fords.

"I asked you not to ejaculate inside me."

Ignoring what he assumed was an essentially rhetorical accusation, Claude stated the obvious: "I guess we'll have to get married."

Like shadow boxers dancing in a darkened ring they began to spar, feinting and jabbing, bobbing and weaving, moving in separate spheres, each unaware of the other's words.

"A girl at the dorm knows an intern at Duke who'll take care of it."

Claude felt a heavy, although not uncomfortable, sense of adultness, of responsibility. "I'll take two weeks' leave and we can drive up to Michigan so I can meet your folks. We could even get married up there if you'd like."

Barbara sighed. "The only problem is money. He wants five hundred dollars to do it."

Claude looked at Barbara. "Or we could get married at Fort Bragg. That way it wouldn't cost us hardly anything."

Barbara sat on the bed and hugged her knees to her chest. "Can you get five hundred dollars?"

Claude shook his head, puzzled. "Five hundred dollars? What in the world for?"

Barbara Curtis, Claude mused, eyes closed as he slipped in and out of sleep, Thurman still nestled in his lap, *I wish we could have done better. Are you happy? Do you ever think about the kid from Fort Bragg and those wonderfully indolent afternoons at the Rebel Yell?* A car door slamming outside woke Claude and Thurman at the same time. The house was dark and a quick look at the Rolex showed that it was nearly ten o'clock. After letting Thurman out Claude stumbled back to the futon and lay down, asleep almost before his head settled onto the pillow. He slept restlessly, troubled by dreams of a child that had never been born, a child that looked like young Nina Williams.

CHAPTER 3

New London, California
Thursday, March 10, 1994

WHAT, EXACTLY, HAVE YOU LEARNED ABOUT MR. MC-
Cutcheon?" Margaret Tikkanen sat behind her desk,
her fingers steepled under her chin. If McCutcheon
was the key to recovering the stolen documents, she
meant to know as much as possible about him. She
had learned well from her father that in business, no
less than in war, superior intelligence gathering usually represented the margin of victory.

"Actually, a great deal given the short amount of
time available." Margaret had had Rod Jackson's
detective agency on an annual retainer since she had
taken over as chief executive of the company. An FBI
alumnus, Jackson was well trained and exceptionally
efficient, and although he had three associates working for him, he always put aside whatever else he
might have been doing to personally handle any
investigations Margaret requested. At five feet eight
inches tall he was slightly shorter than the Bureau
liked its special agents to be, and a thickening waist-
line bore testimony to too much rich food and too

little hard exercise. Still, he had prospered since leaving the Bureau and starting his own detective agency because he *always,* as he liked to put it, delivered the goods. He handed her the original of his preliminary report on Claude McCutcheon, a remarkable achievement on just two days' notice. "As you can see, the Bureau had quite a file on the man from an incident he was involved in last year."

"What sort of incident?"

Jackson shook his head. "Hard to say. Most of McCutcheon's file was classified, including the details of exactly why he had garnered so much official attention. It apparently had much to do with an agent no longer with the Bureau, a woman by the name of Rita Johnson."

"Did you contact her?"

"No. My source in Washington said that she left the country shortly after resigning from the Bureau and hasn't yet returned. I'm sure I could eventually run her to earth, but I seriously doubt it would be worth the time and money it would take. My guess is she wouldn't tell us anything we don't already know or can more easily get from other sources. Whatever it was, though, was big-time because she was one of the top-rated agents in the entire country at her level."

"Um-hmm." Margaret quickly scanned the report. "Quite a military record. Enlisted at nineteen, commissioned at twenty-one, paratrooper with the 82nd Airborne in Vietnam, two Bronze Stars and a Silver Star for valor." She looked up from the report. "Not bad for one so young," she said contemplatively, more to herself than to Jackson. She returned to the business at hand. "You say here that he went to college at Berkeley, in 1972, graduated in 1975 and immediately entered law school there. But I noticed that he got out of the army in . . ." She paused and looked at the report. "Here it is, in 1968. What did he do between 1968 and 1972?"

"Hard to say. Apparently he went back to North Carolina for some period of time, but by and large he dropped out of sight for almost two years, until mid-1970, when he was issued a California driver's license. Where he was and what he was doing nobody seems to know."

Margaret nodded to herself. She knew that it was not unusual for men who had seen a lot of combat to drop out of society while they came to grips with their experiences. Some disappeared forever, living in cabins in the wilderness like hermits.

"McCutcheon comes on-line again in Southern California, in the Santa Monica–Venice Beach area," Jackson continued. "In 1971 he was arrested on a warrant issued by the LA District Attorney's office, although all charges were dropped within six months due to a lack of evidence."

"Arrested? What was the charge?"

Jackson consulted his notes. "The illegal importation from Mexico of bodybuilding steroid drugs. The DA's records indicate that McCutcheon was supplying a number of gyms in Los Angeles County as well as several college and even professional sports teams with the drugs."

"Interesting. And all the charges were dropped?"

"That's correct. I thought it was worth following up on so I made a couple of calls. Turns out he's still well known and highly thought of by not only much of the athletic community but also the law-enforcement people as well." Jackson shook his head. "Nobody knows a damn thing about the man but they all like him. Word is that he helped a number of people out, financially speaking, mostly Vietnam veterans like himself, and made a lot of friends. It appears as if most of whatever money he made from his drug importation business he simply gave away, usually to down-and-out veterans the government wasn't helping. So, when an overzealous assistant DA got on his case over the steroids, the evidence just up and disappeared. And, of course, no one was willing to come forward and testify against him so the whole thing was dismissed."

"If he had so many friends down there, why'd he move north?"

"That I can't answer. All I can report is that in 1972, not long after his case was dismissed, he decided to get off the beach and go to college, San Francisco State. A year later he transferred to UC Berkeley. Graduated in 1975 and entered the law school the next semester." Rod looked up at Margaret. "I've attached copies of both his undergraduate and law school transcripts to the report. He graduated from Boalt Hall in 1978, in the top five percent of his class, incidentally, but never joined a big law firm. He's been a sole practitioner with an office in Albany ever since."

"You've been very thorough. I'm particularly impressed that you thought to get copies of his transcripts. Was that difficult?"

Jackson smiled. "Nothing is too difficult when one has taken the time in his or . . ."—he nodded at Margaret—"or her profession to cultivate the proper contacts."

"Is McCutcheon well-to-do?"

"I think not, at least not in the sense of having a great deal of money. He lives modestly, in a small house he's owned for some sixteen years and drives, of all things, a 1955 Chevrolet pickup truck. No apparent vices and an extraordinarily low-key lifestyle. Again, however, his contacts, his relationships, appear to be of the priceless variety."

"What do you mean?"

"Well, take for example this FBI business. He was clearly involved in something big for the FBI to have devoted so much attention to him in the past year. And yet, the records relating to whatever it was have disappeared and no one with any direct knowledge of the matter is willing to discuss it in even the most circumspect manner. I've never run into that before. Even the local law-enforcement people wouldn't talk to me about him. I can only conclude that they're protecting him out of friendship or fear, and my gut reaction is that it's the former rather than the latter. He still has lots of friends."

"Do you think he knows you've been investigating him?"

"Almost certainly. I'd be astonished if someone that I've talked to hasn't called him with the word that a private detective has been asking around."

"What's your impression of the man?"

Jackson smiled ruefully. "I'll be honest with you. I like him. I've never met him, and I can't get anyone to tell me anything substantive about him, but I like what I've seen. He didn't get those medals in Vietnam by shucking and jiving and he clearly has gotten his life together without anyone's help since then."

"He also seems quite capable of breaking the law when it suits him," Margaret pointed out.

"I won't argue with that other than to point out that most strong, successful people, men and women, ignore the niceties of the law when it suits their purposes."

"Yes, thank you." Margaret rose, indicating that the meeting was over. "You have done your usual exemplary job. If you send in your invoice through the proper channels, you shall be paid promptly."

Jackson hesitated briefly before leaving Margaret's office. "If I might make a suggestion," he said, choosing his words with care. "I'd be very careful in any dealings you may have with McCutcheon. I like what I've seen of him, but don't misunderstand me. I'm guessing anyone who's underestimated him in matters of importance has paid dearly."

"I seldom underestimate individuals with whom I

wish to do business," Margaret replied thinly, her tone of voice conveying her irritation that Jackson had had the temerity to offer unsolicited advice. "Neither you nor"—Margaret smiled coldly—"Mr. McCutcheon need have any concern along those lines."

Albany, California
Friday, March 11, 1994

Claude was not asleep when the telephone rang but then neither was he fully awake. He was in bed, on his futon, the down comforter drawn up to his chest. His first reaction was to check the time, a little after nine in the morning, and then, while deciding whether or not to answer, to wonder idly who it might be. After the fifth ring, for no particular reason, he picked up the receiver. "Hello?"

"Mr. McCutcheon? Mr. Claude McCutcheon?"

A woman's voice. An attractive woman by the sound of it, but not one he knew. He nodded absently but did not answer. After a long second the caller continued.

"Please excuse me for calling you at home but you're a difficult man to reach at your office."

"And who might you be?" He didn't really want to know but felt he had to ask.

"My name is Margaret Stewart Tikkanen and I'm calling from New London, California."

"Indeed."

"I hope I didn't wake you."

"Not quite, but close. What can I do for you?"

"I was calling with regard to a possible representation. You *are* an attorney in private practice, are you not?"

Claude smiled at the irritation evident in his caller's voice. "I am, but unfortunately I'm not taking on any new clients at the present time."

"I assume that you would at least be interested in knowing the nature of the matter at issue?"

"And who exactly *are* you that you would assume such a thing?" Claude yawned again and stretched to his full length on the futon. He reached down and cupped his testicles in his right hand, rolling them lazily around in their scrotal sack. The image of Humphrey Bogart as Captain Queeg came suddenly to mind.

"I am the president and chief operating officer of the Northwestern Lumber Company."

"And?"

"The company is the largest private landowner in Humboldt County, if not in all of Northern California, and our mills process, on average, in excess of two hundred million board feet of lumber annually. We are the county's largest employer, with well over a thousand men and women on our payroll, and we are a hundred percent family owned."

"Whose family?"

"Mine."

"Well, now, Miss Margaret Stewart Tikkanen, what in the world could such an important person as you possibly need with a small-time sole practitioner such as myself? I would imagine that you've got tens if not hundreds of lawyers at your beck and call, none of whom, I'll wager, are still in bed at nine o'clock in the A.M."

"I'm sure you can appreciate our need for new counsel from time to time, Mr. McCutcheon."

"No, actually I can't." He could hear the anger creeping into his caller's voice and he suspected that she was a woman who had little tolerance for fools. *Fuck her if she can't take a joke,* he thought. *Time to wrap this up and let me get a pot of coffee brewing.* "Miss Tikkanen—"

"Won't you at least meet with me so I can tell you more about the company?" Margaret interrupted before Claude could finish his sentence. "I would be more than happy to pay whatever fee you consider appropriate for such a meeting, whether or not you ultimately decide to represent us."

He was suddenly curious about what she looked like and why she was so determined to see him. "I doubt seriously that there's anything I could do for you that's not already being done, but I suppose it would be considered rude not to meet with you since you've asked so nicely. And by the way, I never charge for first meetings so you needn't bring your checkbook. When are you planning to be in the Bay Area?"

"Actually, I was hoping I could entice you into coming up to Humboldt County. The company owns a Learjet, which could pick you up at the Oakland airport at your convenience and return you after our meeting. I could show you our operations in New London firsthand that way."

Claude shook his head as if Margaret could see him. "No, to tell you the truth, I'm not that interested. Why don't you call me when next you're down this way and we'll set up a meeting at my office."

"Would Monday morning be convenient?" Margaret asked.

"That'll be fine," Claude said, noting once again the irritation evident in her voice. "How does eleven o'clock sound?"

"I'll see you at eleven at your office."

Claude hung up and considered for a second the vagaries of life. He sighed and dialed his office. "Hello, Emma? What's going on down there this morning?"

"Good morning, Claude. Nothing much. Bobby Norton called and wondered why you hadn't called him back."

"Did he leave a number?"

"Yes. Do you want it?"

"No. Call him back and and tell him to call me here at home. Tell him to wait ten or fifteen minutes before he calls, though, because I'm getting ready to take a bath. Anything else?"

"Not a thing."

"I just got a call here from a woman by the name of Margaret Stewart Tikkanen. You didn't happen to give her my home telephone number, did you?"

"You know I never give anyone your home number. What did she want?"

"Beats me. I agreed to see her Monday morning at eleven o'clock."

"Are you coming in today?"

"I don't know yet. Depending on what that nitwit Bobby Norton wants, probably not until after lunch. I don't think I have anything on the calendar, do I?"

"Nothing. Unless you need me for something, I was thinking of taking the afternoon off."

"No problem. I'll see you in the morning."

Claude got up and filled the tub, luxuriating for long minutes in the hot water. He shaved, using an ivory-handled straight razor his father and grandfather before him had used. The steel blade had been honed and stropped so many times that it was worn almost completely away. Claude used it only once or twice a month, whenever the mood struck him. As with many old things he owned, just the sight of it pleased him, as did, for instance, his grandfather's shaving mug. When he had finished in the bathroom he padded softly into the kitchen, the paver tiles cool beneath his bare feet. Thurman, hearing Claude moving around the kitchen, bounded through the open kitchen window and nuzzled Claude's hand.

"What have you been up to this morning?" Claude asked, bending over to buss the cat lightly on the head. "Out looking for crippled old mice to slaughter?"

Before Thurman could answer the phone rang. Claude picked up the extension in the kitchen. "Hello?"

"I thought you said you were going to call me last night."

It was Bobby Norton.

Claude shook his head for Thurman's benefit. "If you'll recall I told you not to wait breathlessly by the telephone. As it turned out I was unavoidably distracted by other business. What can I do for you?"

"Man, like I tol' you yesterday, we need to talk, and quick."

"We are talking," Claude pointed out.

"I mean in person. When are you going to be in your office? Man, I never knew anybody wasn't around the office as much as you are."

The frightening thing, Claude thought, *is that I can actually understand what he's trying to say.* He looked at his watch. "It's ten-thirty now," he said. "I'll meet you at my office at noon."

"Great, we can get some lunch, too."

"Are you buying?"

"Man, the lawyer's supposed to buy the client lunch."

"Think again. My advice is to eat before you get there."

Claude hung up and set about making himself a café latte. Thurman, who hated the hissing and gurgling of the espresso machine, leapt from the counter and stalked into the sleeping area, the lure of the down comforter on the futon irresistible. While waiting for steam Claude peeled two oranges and a banana. When the espresso machine was ready he ground enough beans for a double latte and steamed a cup of milk. His breakfast prepared, he sat at the plank trestle table and quietly ate, following the fruit with a large piece of baguette topped with a generous portion of a double-cream brie. He sipped the latte slowly, savoring the rich flavor of the espresso nestled between folds of the steamed milk. At eleven-fifteen he rose and rinsed off the plate and glass he had used for his breakfast. He opened a fresh can of cat food for Thurman and placed it on the counter next to the window. For the day Claude chose to wear his usual: faded Levi's, a casual linen shirt, and butter-soft horsehide cowboy boots. The shirt was made by two seamstresses for whom he had helped obtain a minority-preferred small business start-up loan. Although as a matter of principle they generally refused to make or mend men's clothing, they agreed to make him, in lieu of a fee, half a dozen hand-tailored shirts.

"I've got something here that's going to make us both rich," Bobby said. He and Claude were seated opposite each other in Claude's office—Bobby on one of the leather side chairs, Claude on the love seat. Emma had already left before Claude got there, leaving the two men in complete privacy. Bobby nodded toward the imitation leather briefcase he held protectively in his lap. "You know what I'm saying?"

"Let me guess: You found something in Myron Hirsch's office after he was murdered. Something you think someone, perhaps Hirsch's murderer, might be interested in buying from you. Am I getting warm?"

"That's why you're my lawyer," Bobby said, beaming. "You know everything."

"I'm not your lawyer and believe me, a simpleton could have figured it out. And the answer is no."

"Aw, man, wait'll you hear what it is before you make up your mind."

Claude raised both hands. "Stop. Don't say another word. I don't want to know what it is, or what your plan is." He pointed a finger at Bobby. "Listen for a minute, will you? What you're planning to do is illegal. Worse, it's stupid. Whoever killed Hirsch would, I expect, be tickled plumb to death to kill you for the same reason. Also, by withholding evidence in a capital crime you're committing a felony, not to mention making yourself an accessory to murder. So when the police solve the crime, and you can rest assured that the odds heavily favor the police in crimes of this nature, they'll reel you in like a fat, dumb flounder." Claude cut his eyes toward Bobby's briefcase. "Whether or not you've managed to sell your little package. If, and it's a big if, you're still alive."

"Man, the police don't know shit."

Claude nodded, his face set in a sardonic smile. "The California penal system is chock-full of assholes who thought the police didn't know shit. It won't take a genius to solve Hirsch's murder, just a little patience, believe me. So what you better do is march your tight little ass down to the Berkeley PD and come clean while you still can. I told you the other day that Jim Malone is looking for you, which tells me he already suspects that something's queer with your three monkey bullshit. And the fact that you're avoiding him, staying out of sight, just confirms it. Take my word for it: Keep fucking around and you're going to get your dick slammed in the door, big-time."

"Fuck that motherfucker Malone," Bobby blustered. "Hey, man, listen." His tone softened considerably. "I'm just trying to make a score here, you know what I'm saying?"

"I know what you're saying and I'm telling you to forget it. You're in over your head already."

"Listen, if you don't want to help me, at least let me leave this"—he nodded again at the briefcase he was still holding—"with you for a while, you know what I'm saying?"

Claude shook his head. "No fucking way," he said with finality, although not unkindly. "Listen, Bobby, I'm telling you, man, you're making a big mistake. Let me call Malone for you. I think I can work things out with the DA so you won't take any heat about not telling the police the whole story in the first place."

"No can do, man." Bobby stood up, suddenly nervous. "Hey, Claude, you won't rat me out to Malone, will you?"

"You know me better than that. But you're on your own." There was no mistaking Claude's tone of voice. "Don't call me again unless you want me to go downtown with you."

"Later, man." Bobby turned and left.

Yeah, later, Claude thought. *Mucho fucking later.* He shook his head, a gesture of resignation and release. *At least I'm out of it,* he thought. *It's someone else's heartache, not mine.* The telephone rang.

"Claude McCutcheon here."

"Claude, it's Bernie Beck."

Claude smiled. "Bernie, how're you doing?" Beck was a lieutenant with the Albany Police Department and an old friend of Claude's. "I assume you've called to tell me you've shaken down an ex-felon for two tickets to a Warriors game."

"You wish. No, it's been a while since we spoke so I thought I'd call and see what's up."

"You know me, Bernie, same old shit."

"Heard anything from Rita Johnson, the FBI lady?"

"Lord, no, not in the longest time. Not since the postcard from London, and that must have been, what, damned near a year or more ago. Why do you ask?"

"Just curious. I always sort of thought you two made a nice couple."

"Yeah, right. Why'd you *really* call?"

Bernie cleared his throat. "Well, now that you mention it, I did have one thing I was going to tell you."

"Yeah? What's that?"

"A private dick has been asking around about you. A guy by the name of Rod Jackson."

Claude leaned back in his chair and closed his eyes. *Now what the fuck?* "Rod Jackson? I never heard of him. Local guy?"

"Yeah, office over in the City. After he called I checked up on him. Nothing special, ex-FBI, keeps his nose clean and does all the usual stuff—skip tracing, asset location, shit like that."

"Why's he asking about me?"

"I thought maybe you could tell me."

"I haven't the faintest. What'd he want to know?"

"The usual. Whether or not the Albany PD knew you or had a file on you. Whether or not you're involved in any questionable activities. Your reputation in the community."

"What'd you tell him?"

"I told him the only questionable activity that I personally knew you to be involved in was the practice of law." Bernie laughed. "No, seriously, I didn't tell him a damned thing. When I asked him who he was working for and the nature of his investigation he clammed up, so I told him to take a hike."

"Sounds to me like you were too harsh with him," Claude said dryly. "Hell, private dicks gots to eat too, you know."

"What's going on over there, Claude? Does this have something to do with Myron Hirsch's murder?"

"Beats me. That nitwit Bobby Norton's been going around telling everyone that I'm his lawyer so God knows who might be snooping around. Maybe Hirsch's insurance company."

"You're not representing Norton, are you? In fact, if he told the Berkeley PD the truth I don't see why he even needs a lawyer."

"No, I'm not his lawyer, and as to the truth, well, where Bobby Norton is concerned the truth is a rare and wondrous commodity."

"Do you think he was involved in Hirsch's murder?"

"I don't *think* anything," Claude said pointedly. "I *know* that I don't represent Bobby and anything he does or does not know about Hirsch's murder is between him and Jim Malone over at the Berkeley PD."

"Somebody must think otherwise or they wouldn't have hired a private dick to check you out."

Claude shrugged. "What can I tell you? Whoever it is is wasting their money and their time."

"I hear what you're saying, but I've been a cop long enough to know that nobody wastes money and time just for the hell of it. Somebody thinks you know more than you do and until you figure out who it is I suggest that you keep your eyes and ears open."

CHAPTER 4

Albany, California
Monday, March 14, 1994

MAY I GET YOU A CUP OF COFFEE?"

Margaret could see that the woman, obviously Claude McCutcheon's secretary, was impressed. *Watch a person's eyes,* Joseph had taught her, *they'll tell you everything you need to know.* Emma's eyes had widened almost imperceptibly when Margaret had come into the office, and her pupils had dilated ever so slightly as she looked with open admiration at the clothes Margaret wore. Dressing that morning in New London she had chosen a conservatively cut tan-and-navy suit, the skirt falling to midcalf, the fabric an extraordinary linen and silk blend.

"I love your suit," Emma added.

"Thank you. And no, no coffee." Margaret looked at her watch, a little annoyed. "Is Mr. McCutcheon always late for his appointments?"

Emma smiled. "Not generally, although to be honest . . ." She paused, listening. "There he is now." Claude's footsteps coming up the stairs could be clearly heard.

"Morning, Emma." Claude tossed her a small package, redolent with the rich smell of freshly ground coffee. "Here. Jamaica Blue Mountain. Why don't you throw that swill"—he gestured toward the coffeepot behind his secretary—"out and make us a fresh cup of coffee." He extended his hand to the woman seated across from Emma's desk. "Hello, I'm Claude McCutcheon. Margaret Stewart Tikkanen, I presume?" Before she could answer Claude spoke again. "You have extraordinarily beautiful eyes."

"How do you do?" Margaret reached out and took Claude's proffered hand, felt the strength in his fingers as he carefully grasped hers. *He's tall,* she thought, noting both the blue jeans and boots and the fact that on him they looked like anything but an affectation. *And there's a presence about him, something Rod Jackson's briefing should have prepared me for but didn't.* Oddly enough, she felt almost as if this were a social introduction, not the usual businesslike, formal meeting between the chief executive officer of the Northwestern Lumber Company and an eager vendor of legal services. She could not remember when last she met a man strictly as a man. Her annoyance at his slightly late arrival seemed suddenly trivial.

"Sorry I'm a few minutes late." Claude looked back toward Emma. "Thurman seems to have gotten himself under the weather and I thought I better take him over to Doc Warner's for a look-see."

"Oh, my," Emma said, concerned. "I hope it's nothing serious."

Claude shrugged. "Who knows? Warner wanted to keep him today, do a few tests, run up the bill, that sort of thing." He winked at Margaret. "I told him that if it was going to cost more than twenty-five dollars to shoot the sonofabitch."

"That's terrible," Emma clucked. "If anything happened to Thurman they'd have to shoot you, and you know it."

"Thurman is your son?" Margaret asked, disconcerted that the conversation seemed to have taken off without her. Rod Jackson hadn't said anything about children.

"No, no, my cat. Or, more truthfully, *a* cat. Thurman doesn't belong to anybody, he just decided to live with me about six or seven years ago." He gestured toward his office. "Won't you come into my office? Emma'll bring our coffee in when it's ready."

"How do you take your coffee?" Emma asked.

"Black."

"Wait'll you taste this Blue Mountain coffee," Claude said as he escorted Margaret into his office. "A small, family-owned coffee-importing business over in Alameda gets a limited amount in for me every year. God Herself drinks it. Or would if She could get it. Have a seat." Claude indicated that Margaret should make herself comfortable on the love seat and he settled onto one of the facing side chairs.

"What is this flooring?" Margaret asked, looking closely at the dark, red hardwood beneath her chair. "I don't believe I've seen anything like it before."

"It's beautiful, isn't it?" Claude bent down and ran his fingers across several of the boards. "It's a Brazilian hardwood from the Amazon basin that hasn't been imported into this country for ten or twelve years."

"How did you get it?"

Claude shrugged. "I did some work for a friend who went broke in the exotic lumber business. He had just enough of this particular wood stockpiled in his warehouse to do this office. He milled it for me and the two of us installed it one weekend before his Chapter 11 creditors' committee found out about it."

"It would be a shame if you lost your lease and had to leave something irreplaceable like this behind,"

Margaret noted. *Could something as small as that be a point of leverage?* she wondered, making a mental note to have the ownership of the building researched.

"I doubt there's much likelihood of that happening," Claude said dryly, "but there's risk in everything, isn't there? In any event, why don't we get down to business. You, Margaret Stewart Tikkanen, were born in the bucolic little village of New London in Humboldt County on the eighth day of October, 1951. Graduated with honors in economics from Stanford in 1972, followed by a master's degree in business administration from Harvard in 1974. Only child of Joseph Tikkanen and heir apparent to the lumber business started by F. M. Stewart." Claude paused while Emma served the coffee. After she had withdrawn, closing the door behind her, Claude smiled at Margaret. "Does Rod Jackson work for you? By the way, I like your suit."

"Thank you." Margaret had chosen it with care that morning and was, despite herself, pleased that it had been noticed by both Claude and his secretary. On the other hand, she was somewhat uncomfortable with Claude's directness. It seemed to assume a casual familiarity that was inappropriate. *Or is it?* she wondered. *Why am I allowing this man to assume control of this meeting?* She was also annoyed with herself that she hadn't anticipated questions about Rod Jackson and was unsure how to answer. She looked at Claude's faded blue jeans and cowboy boots and decided to take the offensive. "I must say that you dress somewhat differently than other attorneys with whom I've done business."

"I expect that that's because your attorneys, being primarily concerned with the prompt payment of their fees, dress in a manner calculated to satisfy your sense of business propriety, while I dress to please only myself."

"You're not concerned with the payment of your fees?"

Claude shook his head. "Not in the least."

"You mean you don't care whether or not you're paid for your services?"

"I didn't say that. I said I wasn't concerned about such payment. There's a difference. In any event you were about to tell me about Rod Jackson."

"Mr. Jackson on occasion does work for the Northwestern Lumber Company. In this instance, I asked him to provide me with background information, nothing more, nothing less."

"To what end?"

Margaret raised her eyebrows a fraction of an inch. "I would never consider hiring or doing business with someone I knew nothing about, a trait you obviously share. I trust you are not offended by my use of Mr. Jackson?"

"Indeed not. Were you comforted by what Mr. Jackson was able to find out about me?"

"Quite. Perhaps we could now get on to the matter which brought me here. Unfortunately, I have little time to spare this morning."

"Do you like the coffee? The Blue Mountain?"

Margaret took a sip. "Frankly, coffee to me is just something I normally drink to start the morning. As far as I'm concerned, one is as good as, or at least no worse than, another."

Claude smiled politely. "I expect you're right. Why exactly did you wish to retain my legal expertise, such as it is?"

Margaret unconsciously sat up straighter. *Finally,* she thought, *down to business.* Once again, she felt oddly discomfited by Claude, in a way she could not easily put her finger on. *Keep in mind,* she cautioned herself, *that this man is almost certainly the key to recovering the documents his client took from that bastard Myron Hirsch's office.* Thinking of Myron Hirsch, dead, almost caused her to smile.

"The Northwestern Lumber Company is thinking about buying a large tract of commercial property here in the East Bay," Margaret lied. "Recent events have led me to suspect that one or more attorneys at the firm we usually retain have used inside information for personal profit. We have taken steps to uncover any such activity, but in the meantime, of course, I'm reluctant to use the firm for matters in which confidentiality is of the utmost importance. Therefore I am proposing to retain you, in confidence, for the purpose of having you available to represent the company in the event we decide to proceed with the acquisition." Margaret paused and withdrew a check from her briefcase. "I have here the company's check for twenty-five thousand dollars to be used as a retainer against your hourly rate. By the way, what exactly is your hourly rate?"

Claude laughed. "I've got more different hourly rates than Carter's got pills. How exactly did you select me out of the seemingly hundreds of thousands of attorneys in the Bay Area?"

"You were highly recommended by an individual whose name I am not at liberty to divulge."

Claude checked his watch. "I don't know about you, but I'm hungry. I know it's a little early, but if you would be so kind as to join me for lunch we could continue our discussion at leisure." He stood up.

"I didn't realize we were having a 'discussion,'" Margaret said in a businesslike tone. She, too, rose. "I was offering you an opportunity to represent the Northwestern Lumber Company. Will you or will you not accept the retainer?"

"Your question is premature. You know nothing about me, Mr. Rod Jackson notwithstanding, and I know even less about you. Maybe I'll represent you and maybe I won't. After we've dined and chatted and spent the better part of the afternoon together I may be in a position to make such a determination. On the other hand, I may not. We'll just have to see."

"To be perfectly frank, Mr. McCutcheon, I had counted on a more professional response."

Claude smiled. "I assume that by 'professional' you mean you thought I'd almost break your arm snatching that twenty-five-thousand-dollar check out of your hand."

The barest hint of a smile creased Margaret's lips. *I almost hope you* don't *know anything about the documents,* she thought.

"If it's 'professional' you want," Claude continued, "the Bay Area is literally crawling with lawyers that fit that description and I suspect that here in the East Bay alone you could even find four or five that would undertake not to cheat you too badly. My advice, for which I have no intention of charging you, is to lighten up and have lunch with me. Odds are that once you get to know me you won't want to hire me anyway."

Margaret looked at Claude for a long second. "May I use your telephone?"

"It's not long-distance, is it?" Claude quickly held up both hands and smiled. "Just joking." He pointed toward his desk. "Help yourself. I'll wait outside for you."

"What does she want?" Emma asked after Claude had closed his office door.

"I don't know. Something about wanting to buy commercial property and not trusting the firm they usually use." He shook his head. "Didn't make a lot of sense."

"What did you say?"

"Nothing. I invited her to lunch."

Emma, exasperated, waved a pudgy finger at her boss. "You better be careful. I don't trust her."

"Neither do I." He smiled at Emma. "But how about those threads?"

"I'll tell you something, darling." Bette Beal leaned over the table to refill their coffee cups. "This hound"—her thumb jerked in Claude's direction—"has brought some fancy women into my place, but for *my* money"—the thumb jerked toward herself—"you go right to the top of the list." She shook her head admiringly. "And where'd you *ever* get that suit?"

Bette Beal was the owner and proprietress of Kate's, a café on Fifth Street in Berkeley. She wore her jet black hair short and dressed with plenty of Brylcreme.

"Bette Beal, I'd like you to meet Margaret Stewart Tikkanen," Claude interjected. "Margaret is a woman of independent means," he added cryptically, "with an interest in a family business up north."

"Well, that certainly covers a multitude of sins," Bette said sarcastically. She winked at Margaret. "You're welcome to come back anytime you'd like, particularly without him." She again jerked a thumb in Claude's direction.

"Thank you," Margaret said to Bette. "A woman in Phoenix made this for me." Margaret smoothed an imaginary wrinkle out of the skirt. "She owns a fashion design studio."

"She's in the right business," Bette responded. "She knows how to make a woman look like a woman and I ought to know." She winked at Claude. "I've been looking at women since I was fifteen." She laid the check for their lunch on the table. "Give me a yell if either of you wants any more coffee."

"I'll take that," Margaret said, picking up the check before Claude could. She glanced at it and placed it back on the table, covering it with a fifty-dollar bill she took from her purse.

Claude didn't object. "Thank you for lunch," he said. "It was most enjoyable."

It had been difficult getting Margaret to talk about herself, but Claude had finally succeeded, to a small degree, by asking her about her grandfather. Although the old man had been killed when she was a baby, she spoke of him reverentially, recounting, with obvious pride, the manner of his death.

"Sounds like he was rough as a cob," Claude said politely. *And about as stupid as one,* he thought. *What is it that makes some people think someone is rough and tough just because he's a particularly obnoxious asshole to work for?* "I can see why you and your father would want to carry on the traditions he started." He looked at her contemplatively. *I wonder if she's got some jitney Paul Bunyan servicing her up in the north woods.*

"My father came to this country from Finland in 1948 and went to work for my grandfather in one of his mills. Within four months he was able to demonstrate how the entire layout of the mill could be changed to increase production with fewer employees per shift. Within a year he was supervising three of my grandfather's mills. In 1950 he married my mother, my grandfather's only child. By 1952 he was acting as the chief operating officer of the company."

"And when your grandfather died your father took over."

Margaret nodded. "And I in turn have taken over from him, although my father remains active in the business."

Bette Beal stopped at their table with a fresh pot of coffee. "By the way," she said with a smirk, filling Claude's cup, "I saw in the *Trib* that you're now a fancy criminal defense lawyer."

"That's right," Margaret said as Bette moved to the next table. "I saw the same article. It said you're involved with the gentleman accused of killing that radical lawyer, Marvin Hirsch."

"You managed to get three things wrong in just one sentence," Claude said. "In the first place, the decedent's first name was *Myron,* not Marvin, and secondly, Bobby Norton, the man with whom you inaccurately describe me as being 'involved,' has never, to my knowledge, been even a suspect in the killing, much less charged with or accused of the crime." Claude smiled. "And lastly, Mr. Norton is no gentleman."

Margaret laughed. "In any event I'd say that you may have just had your fifteen minutes of fame."

"Fifteen more than I had any interest in whatever, I can assure you."

Later, out at the general aviation facility adjacent to Oakland's International Airport, they shook hands in a businesslike fashion.

"Thank you for driving me out here," Margaret told him. She nodded toward the '55 Chevy pickup. I'm not sure when I was last in a truck of that vintage."

"It was my pleasure," Claude said. "As for the truck, well, half the people that see it think I'm crazy and the other half try to buy it from me." He smiled, clearly pleased that she seemed to like it. "Again, thank you for lunch."

"You're welcome," Margaret replied. "Will you consider representing the company?"

"No." Claude shook his head.

Margaret nodded, her face frozen in an expressionless mask. "I see." She tapped her foot on the tarmac, suddenly unsure of herself. She looked at Claude, wondering if perhaps he had been toying with her throughout lunch, waiting to see whether she might put her cards on the table and make a preemptive offer for the return of the journals. "May I ask why not?"

"I doubt that I'm the right person for the job." Claude paused for a moment, looking at the sleek Learjet into which Margaret was about to embark. "Quite a contrast," he said.

"I beg your pardon?"

Claude nodded first at the jet and then back toward his truck. "You're about to go from the ridiculous to the sublime, or," he smiled, "vice versa." He took his sunglasses off so she could see his eyes. "I would like to see you again, though. In a nonprofessional capacity. If you feel the same why don't you give me a call in the next day or two."

She watched him walk away and then turned and boarded her aircraft. Inside, she passed through the main cabin and into the cockpit. The pilot, a thin, middle-aged, bespectacled man who had shot down three MiGs over North Vietnam while flying F-4s with the 435th Tactical Fighter Squadron out of Udorn, Thailand, in early 1968, looked up from his preflight routine.

"I'll handle the takeoff," Margaret told him, sliding into the copilot's position.

Later, after they had passed out of the FAA's Bay Area Flight Control Zone, Margaret rocketed the jet a hundred miles offshore and up to forty thousand feet, where she threw them through a series of Immelmann turns, barrel rolls, and high-speed yo-yos. Her enjoyment was quelled somewhat when she noticed that her pilot was sitting, obviously unimpressed, with his arms folded across his chest. *What is it about men,* she wondered, *that won't allow them to acknowledge a job well done by a woman?* She decided to fire him as soon as they were on the ground. In the meantime she turned the controls back over to him for the flight north and tried to concentrate on the task of retrieving the documents taken from Myron Hirsch's office. Her thoughts, however, kept returning to Claude. And his tight behind as he had walked away from her in Oakland.

"How did lunch go?" Emma asked.

Claude shrugged. "I don't think she liked my lizard boots." He looked down and shook his head. "Maybe I should have worn the horsehides."

"I can't imagine why anyone would hire a lawyer who dresses like you do," Emma groused.

"I don't think she wants to hire a lawyer."

Emma looked puzzled. "That's not what I understood."

"I don't know what she wants but it's not to hire me as her lawyer." He smiled slyly. "Maybe she heard about me on the grapevine and had to see for herself."

"Give me a break. What do you think she's after?"

"Your guess is as good as mine. The only thing I can think of is that we've done some work for somebody that interests her and this was a backhanded way of trying to get information."

"Who could it have been?"

Claude shrugged. "Could have been anybody, I suppose, even something years ago."

"What did you tell her after lunch?"

"I told her I wasn't interested in representing her but that she could buy me lunch anytime." He yawned and stretched. "Anything going on this afternoon?"

"You wanted me to remind you to finish up the correspondence on the Parker estate. How much are we going to charge for the probate?"

Claude thought for a moment. Attorney's fees for probate matters were fixed by law and consisted of a sliding percentage of the value of the estate entered into probate. "Let's take half the statutory amount. Old man Parker didn't leave a hell of a lot and you did most of the work anyway. We'll cover our overhead and write the rest off to good karma. Anything else?"

"Are you going to represent the Klein couple?"

Claude shook his head. The Kleins, Ruth and Joshua, had asked Claude to represent them in a dispute with a building contractor who had done some remodeling work for them. "They struck me as an unhappy and fractious couple. Most likely after we got done suing their contractor they'd turn around and sue me. Why don't you prepare a letter telling them that after due consideration I've decided I would be unable to give the matter the attention it so richly deserves."

"Do you want me to charge them for the consultation?"

"That would only give them the satisfaction of not paying. Best just to kiss them off, period."

Claude worked until four o'clock, tidying up matters on several of his active cases. At four he walked out of his office and placed a dictation tape on Emma's desk.

"There's a couple of letters on there together with the schedule for the Parker probate." He looked at his watch. "I'm going to go on over to the vet's and check out Thurman."

"Do you want this stuff to go out today?"

"Yeah, you can sign the letters for me and get them into the mail. Do the probate schedule in rough-draft form and I'll look it over tomorrow."

Emma nodded. "I hope Thurman's going to be okay."

"I'm sure he will. I expect he got hold of a bad mouse and it's given him a stomach ache."

Emma wrinkled her nose. "That's disgusting."

"I'm sorry, Claude, there's nothing I can do."

"And you're sure of the diagnosis?" Claude's face was impassive. He and Ben Warner were standing in a small examining room in Ben's small-animal clinic in Albany.

Ben nodded. "I did two separate blood tests. Both came in positive for feline leukemia. And the symptoms confirm it."

The two men looked down at the cat sitting on the examining table before them.

"He got sick awfully fast," Claude said, speaking more to himself than to the veterinarian. "I mean, just three or four days ago he was fine, then, day before yesterday he starts moping around." He looked up at Ben. "I won't have it done here," Claude continued. His words seemed to be coming from a distance. "Not here."

"I'll come by your house later this afternoon if you'd like. Say about, what, six o'clock?"

"That'll be fine." Claude gathered Thurman up in his arms and left the clinic. He drove home slowly, the heavy cat content to rest in his lap, uninterested in what was going on around him.

"What's wrong with Thurman?" Wayne Fryar, a neighborhood youngster, bored with his schoolwork, was bouncing a basketball on the sidewalk in front of Claude's house. "Is he sick?"

Claude nodded. "Powerful sick, Wayne."

The boy cradled the basketball in his arms, unconsciously mimicking the way Claude was holding Thurman. He frowned. "Is he going to die?"

"I'm afraid so."

Claude fumbled with his front door key for a second. He could see that the boy had several hundred more questions he wanted to ask, for death mystified children as much as it frightened them, but for the life of him he didn't want to enter into a prolonged discussion about the mortality of cats and men at that moment in time. He went into the house and closed the door behind him, leaving the boy to straggle home alone. In the house, Claude laid the cat gently on the futon, fluffing up the comforter around him. He offered both water and food, but his old friend evinced interest in neither. Claude sat on the futon next to the cat and gently stroked its fur. *Your spirit's already left, hasn't it?* he thought. *You sonofabitch, you wander in here eight years ago and take over my life and now you've gone and died on me. And worse, left me with the task of hurrying your body along.*

It was already full dusk when Ben Warner knocked on the door, a sound Claude had been dreading. He answered it and with a nod of his head indicated that Thurman was back in the sleeping area on the futon. The two men walked back and Claude sat once again on the futon. He took Thurman into his arms. Ben quickly took a hypodermic syringe out of his jacket pocket and knelt down beside Claude. He slipped the plastic guard off the needle and, without a word, injected the syringe's contents into the cat. Thurman trembled once and died.

Ben replaced the the protective cover over the syringe's needle and stood up. "Claude, I . . ."

Claude, still holding Thurman, shook his head silently, indicating that the vet should leave without saying anything, while he, Claude, could still control his grief. As soon as Claude was alone he began to cry, tears streaming over his cheeks and onto the still body he continued to hold in his arms. As sadness and despair settled over him, time itself seemed to warp and shift.

He found himself back in Vietnam, reliving a moment he thought he had left behind. Phu Bai, 1968. He'd been with the 82nd only three weeks when his company was assigned to put out platoon-sized ambushes for three nights in a row. Claude's platoon drew the first night.

Three slicks had lifted the understrength platoon from the base camp to the ambush site. Claude remembered deploying the Claymore mines and settling into his position, with the detonators for the Claymores in easy reach.

For the first several hours he'd remained intensely alert, his entire nervous system fueled by a high level of adrenaline. The night brought sounds both familiar and strange and he felt completely alone in the universe. Unseen, a helicopter quartered high above, well out of range of hostile small arms, come and gone in seconds. Shortly before midnight, from a great distance, the rattle of automatic weapons fire, three long bursts and then silence. An odd, unidentifiable masticating sound to his left and rear startled him, bringing to mind the specter of unknown and presumably unfriendly mammals and, even worse, large, poisonous snakes.

Midnight came and went, marked only by the passage of the faintly luminous hands on Claude's watch. Mind and body began to relax as time passed and hormonal levels slowly dropped. Claude caught himself dozing several times, snapping angrily awake, appalled that he could be so careless as to let his eyes shut under such circumstances. An hour before dawn, confident that his first ambush would be a fruitless one, his thoughts wandered home.

A sound. Claude froze. A sound had come, he was certain, from up the trail. Again. Unmistakable now, someone was walking down the trail. His heart pounding, he shifted to bring his M-16 fully into his arms, simultaneously reaching in the darkness for the Claymore detonators. Three human shapes came into his field of vision, walking slowly but confidently down the trail toward the ambush. It was too dark to see their faces but they wore the ubiquitous black pajamas of the Vietnamese peasant. One was carrying what appeared to be a weapon and, without conscious thought, Claude's hand tightened on the detonator.

The explosion, after an entire night of silence, was stunning. A roar filled his ears as the men of the platoon, half of whom had probably been sound asleep when the Claymore mine went off, opened up.

Everyone was firing on full automatic, and tracer rounds filled the kill zone, lighting the trail with flickering reds and oranges.

Dawn came quickly on the heels of the ambush and first Claude and then, in ones and twos, the platoon sheepishly eased out to see what they had wrought. The three Vietnamese were badly shot up and, of course, quite dead. The one Claymore Claude had fired had swept the trail obliquely at about knee height, raking the flesh from the legs of the three men with astonishing efficiency. Since each of Claude's men had fired at least one full magazine through their M-16s and the two machine gunners had cranked off at least fifty to seventy-five rounds each before ceasing fire, Claude quickly estimated that somewhere in the neighborhood of five hundred bullets had passed through the kill zone shortly after he had detonated the Claymore. From the looks of the bodies it was unlikely that the three men had had time to even be surprised.

For the longest time Claude had worried about the three anonymous men caught in his ambush. They had, of course, just left the bodies sprawled on the trail where they had been killed. *Were they ever found by their comrades, and properly buried? Or did they just disappear, nobody even knowing how, or where, or even if they'd died?*

Albany, California
Friday, March 13, 1994

Dawn was a promise unfulfilled, a grudging progression from darkness to the mere absence of darkness. A viscous, heavy fog had rolled in through the Golden Gate overnight and brought the new day's sunlight and warmth to a shuddering halt just east of the Carquinez Straits. Nobody in Claude's neighborhood was yet awake when he stepped out into his backyard, a small, indistinct bundle under one arm and a long-handled shovel under the other. He dug earnestly, the soft earth yielding up dirt almost effortlessly. A clandestine observer, had there been one, would have been puzzled by the size of the hole as it steadily grew far beyond that needed for Thurman's earthly remains. Two feet down it extended, then three, as its perimeter expanded accordingly. When he finally stopped digging Claude stood in a grave almost four feet deep and three feet long. He laid the cat's body, wrapped in a beautiful woolen Chief Joseph Pendleton blanket, at the bottom of the grave. "You were a good friend," he said quietly, wanting to cry but having no tears left. "I know you won't mind sharing . . ." He paused and looked up, his eye caught by a light coming on in one of his neighbors' houses. He looked back down at the grave he had dug. Big enough for a man, let alone a cat. Or three men.

CHAPTER 5

Albany, California
Friday, March 13, 1994

LAW OFFICES OF CLAUDE MCCUTCHEON."

"Emma, it's me, Claude."

"Aren't you coming in this morning? I've got a rough draft of the Parker probate schedule ready for your review."

"Thurman died last night."

"Oh, Claude, I'm so sorry."

"Thanks, Emma. Listen, call Jack Anderson for me and see if he can take over the Parker probate. Tell him I agreed to do it for half the statutory fee."

"You're not going to do it yourself?"

"No, I've decided to take a little time off and the Parker thing is the only active matter that needs tending to. Don't worry about Jack not wanting to take it for half the fee. He owes me a couple of favors and this will give him a chance to square things."

"How long are you going to take off?"

"I don't know. A few days, a few weeks, whatever. Just mind the store, and I'll see you when I see you."

"Well, Claude, can I do anything for you? I mean, I'm worried about you, taking off like this."

"Don't be. I just need a little time off. If anyone calls tell them I'm unavailable."

"Where do you think you might go?"

Claude shrugged as if Emma could see the gesture over the telephone. "I'm thinking I might drift up north a ways, up towards the Mendocino coast." He shrugged again. "Hard to say where I might end up."

"What if that Margaret Tikkanen calls?"

"I doubt she will."

"What if she does?"

"Tell her I'll be in touch."

Claude took his time, driving slowly and enjoying the unseasonably warm early-spring weather. He headed north on Highway 101, paralleling the Russian River past Healdsburg and Cloverdale, Hopland and Ukiah. At Calpella he turned east, driving through the Potter Valley into the Mendocino National Forest. He stopped at the Forest Service Ranger Station, introduced himself, and had a cup of very bad coffee with the ranger.

"Where were you planning on camping?" the ranger asked. Her name tag identified her as Mary Beth Wilson and she had the shiniest brown ponytail Claude thought he had ever seen. She wore glasses, which made telling her age somewhat difficult, but he guessed she couldn't have been more than twenty-three or twenty-four.

Claude went to the large-scale topographical map that adorned one wall of the ranger's cabin. He studied it for several seconds and then stabbed at a point with his index finger.

"Right about here. Well north and a little east of Lake Pillsbury. There's a little place just across one of the tributaries that feed the lake that I found a number of years ago. Very private."

The ranger nodded. "There are very few campers in the park this early in the season, and none that I know of in that area." She studied her coffee cup carefully before speaking again. "For how long were you planning to camp?"

Claude smiled. "Probably not more than two, maybe three days. I've always found this to be a nice time of year to get out into the woods. Not enough people or flies yet to annoy you." He stood up and stretched. "Thanks for the coffee. Tell you what. If you want, stop by my campsite. You shouldn't have any trouble finding it. Just look for my old truck." He nodded out toward where the Chevy was parked. "I'll make you a cup of the best coffee you've ever had."

It took Claude the better part of an hour to negotiate the progressively worse dirt road north of Lake Pillsbury. The campsite itself, a spot he believed only he had ever camped in, was down a steep bank from the road and across a large, boulder-strewn floodplain. From the floodplain one had to wade some twenty feet across an unnamed tributary that ultimately fed into Lake Pillsbury. Fortunately the stream was relatively shallow, no more than three feet at its deepest. Across the stream lay a fringe of undergrowth that opened into a clearing surrounded on three sides by steep limestone escarpments and on the fourth by a chuckling brook that emptied into the wider tributary. Claude ferried his gear from the truck to the bank of the tributary in two trips and then, after taking off his pants and changing into an old pair of tennis shoes, made two crossings to the campsite. The tributary, fed mostly by snowmelt from the northern Sierras and the Trinity Alps, was icy cold. When he had everything across he quickly dried himself and set about making camp. That night he saw an uncommonly large meteor streaking across the sky from east to west.

"Good-bye, old friend," he murmured, lifting his coffee cup in a salute to his departed feline companion. "I hope there's a fat, old mouse waiting to show you around wherever you've gone, just to prove there's no hard feelings." He took a drink of the Irish whiskey in his cup. "I hope to Christ there's no hard feelings," he repeated quietly, more to himself than to Thurman's spirit.

"You didn't tell me you had to ford a river to get to your campsite."

Claude stood on his side of the tributary and smiled broadly. "It's hardly a river," he called out. He had watched the ranger leave her Forest Service Carryall on the road behind his pickup and make her way confidently down the embankment and across the boulder field. "And, you didn't ask. Come on over and I'll put a fresh pot of coffee on the fire." He saw her hesitate. "Wait a minute." He ran to the campsite and took his tennis shoes from the rock on which they had been drying since his own crossing. Back at the tributary he threw them, one at a time, across to the young woman. "Put the tennis shoes on and hold your shoes and socks over your head. I've got a clean, dry pair of pants you can change into on this side."

"It better be damned good coffee," Mary Beth said, shivering from the cold water as Claude helped her up the bank. "I can't believe I'm doing this."

Claude led her through the underbrush that concealed the campsite and quickly dug a pair of cotton trousers out of his knapsack. "Here," he said, handing them to her, "you can use the tent to change." Before she could respond he thought of something else. "Wait a minute." He dug back into his knapsack and pulled out a pair of clean, white Jockey briefs. "You can wear these too, if you'd like."

Mary Beth took the proffered articles of clothing

and disappeared into the tent. Claude busied himself at the fire, inserting several slices of fatwood kindling amongst the red-hot embers. Next came the coffeepot, an old-fashioned percolator, which he filled with water from the brook.

"I thought this was all in a day's work for any of America's forest rangers," he called over his shoulder.

"What is?" Mary Beth yelled back from inside the tent.

"Fording ice-clogged rivers, fighting off hungry bears, stuff like that."

"Think again." Mary Beth emerged from the tent tucking her Forest Service–issue khaki blouse into Claude's trousers. She held her wet clothes in her right hand.

"Here," Claude said, "spread those wet things on these rocks next to the fire. He smiled. "So if rangers don't spend their time doing the things I thought they did, what exactly *do* they do?"

Mary Beth sat down on a large rock to the leeward side of the fire. "Ticket speeders, break up domestic disputes at the campsites, and deal with complaints about loud boom boxes and drunken campers."

"No bears?"

Mary Beth shook her head and rubbed her hands near the fire. "All the bears around here were shot generations ago."

"The job doesn't sound like what you must have had in mind when you majored in animal husbandry, or wildlife biology, or whatever it was that got you here."

"And what exactly do *you* do for a living?" Mary Beth asked, a hint of irritation in her voice.

Claude laughed. "Damned little, to tell you the truth."

"Nice work if you can get it."

"Maybe." He poured a cup of rich, black coffee and

handed it to the young ranger. "Maybe not. Where are you from?"

"Nevada. I live here in the park, but I guess I'll always think of Nevada as home."

"Where in Nevada?"

"North of Winnemucca, just south of the Oregon border. Place called McDermitt." She took the cup of coffee that Claude handed her and shook her head. "My mother and I were what might now be described as rural poor. Food stamps and a little welfare kept us from starving but not by much."

They sat quietly for several minutes, each sipping their coffee and staring into the fire. Suddenly, Mary Beth laughed, a sound strangely devoid of humor.

"A couple of years ago, when I was still in college, a professor in one of the classes I was taking made the statement that the Gobi Desert was generally thought to be the most desolate place on the face of the earth. I raised my hand and asked him if he'd ever been north of Winnemucca, up around the Fort McDermitt Indian Reservation." She held out her cup for a refill. "Nobody knows desolation that hasn't spent a winter where I grew up."

"Does your mother still live there?"

"She died the year I finished high school. The constant wind blowing across the high prairies drove her mad as a hatter and as soon as she felt she could she just gave up and died. After the county buried her an Indian boy I'd gone to school with drove me down to Reno. I got a job dealing twenty-one at Harrah's and started taking classes at the University of Nevada. The rest, as they say, is history." She looked up and smiled at Claude. "How about you?"

"I grew up in rural North Carolina, just my dad and I. Left as soon as I could." He smiled, thinking of how he'd returned from Vietnam to the small town in the middle of the night, the cab from the airport dropping him off in front of the drugstore. He'd planned on just sleeping there on a bench until he could get a ride out to the old man's house in the morning. He had just lit a cigarette and was watching the bats fly in and out of the cones of light thrown by the streetlamps when he heard the police car turn onto Main Street and drive in his direction. It stopped in front of him and a powerful flashlight beam centered on his face.

"What's your business out here this time of night?"

Shielding his eyes with the flat of his hand, Claude smiled, pleased that he recognized the voice. It was Otis Ferguson, oldest of the three Ferguson boys. Claude had gone to school with the youngest one, Tom.

"It's me, Otis, Claude McCutcheon. Turn that light out, you're fixin' to blind me."

"No shit, is that you, Claude? What in the world are you doing back here? You home on leave?"

The patrolman got out of his car and walked gingerly up to Claude, still unsure if he could believe his eyes and ears.

"Yeah, it's me, Otis. No, I'm not on leave. I've been discharged, finished my hitch. I'm just back from Vietnam."

"Well, goddamn, Claude. What in the hell are you doing out here in the middle of the night?"

"I just flew in and figured I'd wait here until morning and then get someone to give me a ride out to the house. I don't know if anyone's been looking after it since the old man passed. It was already so late I didn't think it made a lot of sense to get a hotel room in Raleigh. Say, if you don't mind, maybe you could run me out to the house now."

Otis shifted his feet and looked away for a minute. "Jesus, Claude, we were all sorry about your daddy dying, especially what with you being overseas and all." Otis paused and cleared his throat. "I'm afraid

there's a slight problem about you going out to the
house right away."

"What do you mean, problem?"

"Well, because you were away, old Judge Grover
had to appoint what you call an executor to look after
your daddy's affairs until you could get home. And,
since no one knew for sure when that might be, the
judge allowed the executor to rent the house out so it
could generate some income to pay the bills."

"What bills?"

"Well, damn, Claude, you know. It costs money to
get buried properly, and legal fees for the estate,
things like that. Hell, can't nobody die for free in
Johnston County anymore." Otis shifted his feet
again, plainly embarrassed. "Look here. You can
come on down to the jail and sleep there if you'd like.
Then tomorrow you can get yourself situated."

"Thanks, Otis, but if it's all the same to you I think
I'd just as soon stay here. I'm thinking in the morning
I'll catch the bus to Raleigh and get me a room or
something. Say, how about the old man's Ford? Is it
still around?"

"No, Claude, I'm sorry. The judge ordered it sold.
In fact they pretty much sold off everything except
some personal things the lawyer has stored in Raleigh."

"How about the old man's dogs?"

"I'm afraid they're gone too."

"I'll be damned," Claude had said.

"Does he?" Mary Beth asked.

"I'm sorry." Claude looked up from the fire, chagrined. "What did you ask?"

"I asked if your father still lived back in North
Carolina."

"No," Claude said quietly, shaking his head, "he
died some years ago." *In fact, we both died at just
about the same time,* Claude thought bitterly but did

not add. *Him a lot and me not as much.* He held up the percolator. "Would you like some more coffee?"

They chatted quietly in front of the fire for the better part of an hour. The superficial warmth the early-spring sun brought to the small campsite quickly dissipated as evening approached. Mary Beth shivered as a sudden zephyr, chilled by the snow on the western slopes of the Trinity Alps, swirled through the clearing.

"Would you like to stay for dinner?" Claude asked.

"Thanks, but I've got several things that have to be done before it gets too dark." She rather awkwardly handed Claude one of her Forest Service business cards with her address and telephone number without saying anything.

Claude took it and, like Mary Beth, said nothing further. He watched carefully as she negotiated the swiftly flowing tributary. On the other side she shook the water from her hair and yelled something that was lost in the sound of the rushing water.

"What's that?" Claude called out, cupping his hands around the words.

"I said, you make good coffee."

Claude continued to watch as she turned and crossed the boulder field, climbing quickly back up the steep embankment to the Forest Service Carryall. She waved once and drove away immediately.

Richmond, California
Thursday, March 17, 1994

Bobby Norton was more than a little pleased with himself. In one week's time he had managed to turn Myron Hirsch's untimely demise into something of a personal and professional windfall. The late Myron's brother, his only heir, had just the day before agreed to sell to Bobby, at a price a disinterested third party would have considered more than fair, the building in which his, Bobby's, after-hours nightclub was located. In anticipation of the close of escrow Bobby peremptorily closed the club and engaged his brother-in-law, a licensed contractor, to undertake a complete remodeling of the facility. Additionally, and potentially far more profitably, he had been able to identify a number of individuals whose likely interest in the document he had taken from the unfortunate Mr. Hirsch's office could be tested in a private auction. Although it was not yet noon he indulged himself with a small glass of Napoleon brandy in the deserted club. As he sipped the brandy, he surveyed the large main room, imagining how it was going to look after the construction was completed. He planned to take full advantage of the improvements to the physical plant by upgrading his clientele as well, and that very morning had become a member of the Richmond Chamber of Commerce. He looked forward to the monthly luncheons the Chamber's executive secretary had told him about, and he realized that he needed to start involving himself in Richmond's political affairs. He finished his brandy and with a flourish picked up the telephone on the bar in front of him to place the first of several important business calls.

Feather Rainforest, born Ruth Rosenblum, grew up in a colorless political world of black and white. Radical in the extreme, both her mother and father believed that American society could be improved only by violent revolution, and viewed the social upheaval of the 1960s as irrefutable proof that such a revolution was under way. Unwilling to sit in class while others stormed the ramparts, Feather (then still known to her revolutionary comrades-in-arms as Ruth Rosenblum) dropped out of college in 1971 to join an active cell of the Weather Underground. She demonstrated a flair for the design and assembly of delayed-action explosive devices, and her products were soon in demand in urban areas and on college campuses from New York to Wisconsin. Her budding talent soon came to the attention of the FBI, and she quickly topped the charts as the single most wanted *soi-disant* student radical in the country. Ruth's world collapsed in the spring of 1972 when one of her devices exploded prematurely, wiping out most of the leadership of a black Maoist revolutionary group that had been transporting it in a stolen 1968 Sedan de Ville to the world headquarters of the Chase Manhattan Bank. Delighted, the FBI decided to take advantage of the opportunity by spreading disinformation to the effect that, as a result of bitter dissension within the revolutionary movement, Ruth had deliberately timed the device to kill the leaders of the rival group.

Revolutionaries being what they are, the disinformation was accepted at face value and three rather clumsy attempts on Ruth's life were made in quick succession. Although a college dropout Ruth was by no means a fool, and she realized that mere honest denial was useless in the ultraparanoid world of radical politics. Within hours of the third attempt she left New York in the company of a Lakota Sioux construction worker who was wanted in connection with a liquor store holdup on Staten Island. Long before they reached the Black Hills of South Dakota she was pregnant and bearing a new faux-Indian identity: Feather Walks Far.

Abandoned by her Indian friend in Rapid City, Feather pushed on to the West Coast, following an inner yearning that was more instinctive than conscious. In San Francisco she settled into the Haight-Ashbury district to await the birth of her child. She lived on welfare and food stamps and, while obviously pregnant, enjoyed some modest success as a panhandler in Golden Gate Park. Her son, Wolf Walks Far, was born in the happy confines of the Haight-Ashbury Free Medical Clinic in a bed next to a nineteen-year-old girl from Fresno who was suffering from early-stage dementia brought about by a particularly virulent strain of syphilis.

The birth of her son was a turning point in Feather's life. Social issues, until then the dominant focus of her existence, began to recede in the face of overwhelming evidence that the ecology, and the preservation of Mother Earth, were primary. Her blood ran cold as anecdotal tales of the assault on the last of the world's old-growth redwood trees by soulless lumber companies began to filter down to San Francisco and she summarily changed her name from Feather Walks Far to Feather Rainforest. With the newborn Wolf riding on her hip, Feather hitchhiked north, determined to save the redwoods. She settled first in Eureka, immediately filing applications with the county for welfare, a monthly rent subsidy payment, and Aid to Families with Dependent Children. The county's social-services caseworker, a young man who had recently graduated from Humboldt State College with a degree in sociology and a confused sense of his own sexual identity, was awed by Feather's philosophy of feminine self-empowerment and introduced her to Eureka's disenchanted and disorganized leftist intellectual elite.

Three months were enough to convince Feather that Eureka was a poor situs from which to launch an all-out assault on the harvesting of old-growth redwood. The region's economy (not to mention Feather's welfare payments) depended, in one way or another, almost exclusively on the lumber industry, and few individuals were willing, at least publicly, to attack that industry. Casting about for more fertile ground from which to build her power base, Feather settled upon the tiny community of Redway, a motley collection of cabins along the Eel River housing an unattractive mixture of burnt-out, brain-dead hippies and hard-core unemployed rednecks.

After several years of intense effort had failed to produce any decline whatever in the harvesting of timber in the county, Feather decided that a change in tactics was called for. By the late 1980s she was forced to conclude that she would never be able to reduce timber-harvesting activities in any meaningful way by lawful means.

But, she knew, there were other ways.

"Yes, this is Feather Rainforest. Who is this?"

The voice at the end of the line chuckled. "Don't you be worrying about who this is. All you need to know is that I got the documents. The ones that whoever killed Myron Hirsch was trying to get his hands on, you know what I'm saying?"

Feather's breath caught in her throat. "What do you intend to do with them?"

The caller laughed at the foolishness of the question. "What the fuck do you think I intend to do with them, bitch?"

Feather bit back a curse. "You're thinking about trying to sell them."

"Shit. Not *thinking about* selling them, *going* to sell them. I'm just calling now to let you know that I've got them. I'll get back to you in a few days with the important details like where, when, and how much. In the meantime, if you want in the game, you need to be liquidating assets, you know what I'm saying?"

"Do you have any idea how valuable those documents are? In the right hands they could effect a powerful change for good, for environmental . . ." Before she could finish her appeal to the caller's sense of eco-responsibility he hung up with a laugh. "Goddamn it." Feather's voice surged with anger as she slammed down the telephone, outraged that so important a document, by all rights *her* document, had entered what could probably now best be described as commercial channels.

Wolf Walks Far looked up from the knife blade he was honing to a razor-sharp edge. "How much does he want for it?" A large-boned, heavyset young man, he had inherited his absentee father's classic Native American facial features but none of his openhanded good nature and charm. His face bore a perpetual scowl and that, together with his size, intimidated and frightened most people who encountered him. As a fifteen-year-old he had spent one year incarcerated with the California Youth Authority for savagely beating a convenience-store clerk in the course of stealing a twenty-five-cent candy bar.

Feather looked at her son and shrugged. She felt an overpowering urge to wrap her meaty hands around someone's neck, and Myron Hirsch, had he still been alive, would have done just fine. "He didn't say. I'm to wait for his call, when we'll discuss terms and arrangements."

"It hardly matters what he asks, we don't have any money anyway," Wolf grumbled.

Feather said nothing, unwilling to discuss their lack of funds and furious anew that that weasel, George Hough, had welched on his original agreement to give her the documents with which she planned to destroy the Northwestern Lumber Company.

"Why do you suppose," George, Feather's mole in the company, had asked Feather during a furtive meeting over a year ago at her cabin in Redway, "the company has been able to operate essentially without meaningful oversight by any public agency, including even the state Department of Forestry? And why do you further suppose that the major environmental organizations, such as the Sierra Club and Greenpeace, have never taken the company to task for its massive annual harvests of old-growth redwood and Douglas fir?"

Feather had silently shaken her head, having learned over the past five years that George liked to answer his own questions. He was an environmentalist's dream—a disaffected clerical worker with access to confidential company documents. Unfortunately, most of what he passed on to Feather was of little more than nuisance value, and she had recently begun to lose patience with his overly dramatic mannerisms.

"The so-called philosophy of sustained-yield harvesting." George smiled. "Joseph Tikkanen is a very smart man. In the 1950s, well before anyone began to think about conservation and question the right of a lumber company to do pretty much as it pleased in the matter of timber harvesting, he began to develop the public relations concept that the company used the so-called sustained-yield method of timber harvesting. They claimed they only cut down in a given year the approximate board footage that was calculated to have grown in the year before. It was a stroke of genius."

"Wait a minute." The thought that the company's widely vaunted philosophy of sustained-yield harvesting was fraudulent rocked her. "Are you saying that the company does not harvest its redwood and Douglas fir using a sustained-yield method?" She looked skeptically at the diminutive file clerk.

"They do not. And they never have. They've gotten away with it because the company's holdings are so vast, and their financial and other documents so private, that no one outside the company could possibly calculate how much timber grows each year relative to the actual annual harvest. It's all been a public relations scam, a way to lull the environmental movement into a false sense of security."

Feather had been stunned by George's revelation. *My God, could this really be true?* "How, exactly, did you come by this information?"

"Believe it or not, the Tikkanens, father and daughter, apparently keep a confidential company journal, a sort of corporate diary, where they record all significant events and decisions. I overheard them talking about it in the old man's office. It sounded as if the diary contains all of the confidential cruise information gathered by the company's foresters over the years, providing detailed records of just how much old-growth forest is left and how fast it's being depleted."

Feather's palms had gone suddenly damp. "You, we, have got to get our hands on that journal."

It took George the better part of the following year to accomplish his mission but, in the dogged manner of clerks the world over, accomplish it he did. In three months he had discovered the location of the personal safe Joseph and Margaret used. It was set flush into the hardwood floor of Joseph's office, behind the leather sofa that ran along the west wall opposite the old man's massive desk. Obtaining the combination itself was rather more difficult. After months of fruitless cogitation on how to gain access to the safe's contents short of resorting to dynamite, the solution presented itself to George on a silver platter, as it were. Joseph suffered from rheumatoid arthritis, and occasional flare-ups of the disease made it difficult for him to manipulate the safe's combination mechanism. So some years back he had given the combination to his longtime secretary, demanding that she memorize it and under no circumstances divulge it to anyone else. The elderly woman, having no head for figures, knew she could never keep the combination in her head and so, contrary to Joseph's instructions, wrote it down on a small piece of paper she kept in her desk. Months of surreptitious observation paid off when George noticed her consulting the paper in her desk's top drawer before going into Joseph's office.

Somewhat to George's surprise, the safe contained not one but two journals, both expensive, leather-bound ring binders. The first, as he had expected, contained details of the yearly annual harvest, broken down by species, and provided comparisons of actual board feet harvested versus timber cruise estimates. The figures showed that the company was harvesting its timber, including the last massive stands of old-growth redwood in all the world, at a much faster pace, particularly in recent years, than reforestation and stump regeneration could possibly keep pace with. The second journal, however, when he examined it by flashlight on the floor of Joseph's office, truly rocked him. Page after page, it memorialized the company's clandestine relationship with elected officials, including, to the penny, amounts paid for services rendered with regard to key support for, or opposition to, specific legislation. It showed that regular cash payments were being made to local, state, and federal officials, both elected and appointed. Names of the payees and places of payment were detailed, and, in a number of cases, descriptions of phony fronts such as nonprofit voter registration organizations used to funnel illegal payments to elected officials.

Feather knew instinctively that George had somehow chanced upon far more than the two of them had anticipated when he informed her by telephone that he had changed his mind and was now planning on doing business with Myron Hirsch in the Bay Area. *Whatever it was, I can only hope the sonofabitch is rotting in hell this very minute,* she thought grimly, *together with his erstwhile partner Myron Hirsch.* No one had seen or heard from George Hough for several weeks and she wondered when that bastard Joseph Tikkanen and his whore daughter Margaret had discovered the loss. *I doubt it took them long to sweat the truth out of the little putz once they got their meat hooks on him. But not soon enough.* She looked at her son, determination anew on her face. *And with a little luck I'll still beat them to the prize.*

"Don't worry about the money," she told her son, her voice full of contempt at the very notion of actually *paying* for something she desired. "We'll get what we want the same way we always have. By taking it."

CHAPTER 6

New London, California
Friday, March 18, 1994

DO YOU HAVE AN APPOINTMENT WITH MISS TIKKANEN?"

The plainly dressed, middle-aged woman eyed Claude, particularly his three-day beard and rough, outdoors clothing, with open skepticism.

"She's quite busy, and seldom sees anyone without an appointment."

Claude smiled. He was in the foyer of the administration building of the Northwestern Lumber Company in New London, California. It was a tidily maintained two-story frame building painted, as were all the buildings in the company town, white with forest green trim. A large sign attached to the front door warned in bold letters: NO CAULKS ALLOWED. *What's a caulk?* Claude wondered, vaguely amused.

"I understand," he said politely. "Just tell her that Claude McCutcheon's come to call and would like to buy her lunch if she's otherwise unencumbered."

The woman's eyes widened in shock. Claude didn't doubt that in all her many years with the company this was the first time a gentleman had paid a social call on Miss Margaret Stewart Tikkanen. "Please wait here," she managed to croak in an oddly formal way as she rose from her desk. "I'll inform Miss Tikkanen you're here."

Claude waited for a moment and then walked outside to stand on the small front porch that framed the building's entrance. Built on a promontory overlooking most of the company town and its three large mills, the office building was clearly both the physical as well as the psychological focus of the small community. A loud steam whistle sounded the noon hour and, as Claude watched, hundreds of workmen streamed from the mills and hurried the short distances to their company-owned houses. He was struck by the similarity of what he was seeing with the images in his mind of what life in the late-nineteenth- and early-twentieth-century industrial towns and cities must have been like, particularly the company towns of such industrial giants as Krupp and Vickers and Carnegie. Here they were milling lumber but it could just as easily have been steel and iron fabrication.

"Mr. McCutcheon."

His reverie interrupted, Claude turned. "Ms. Tikkanen, as I live and breathe." *Whoa,* he thought. She was wearing a long gray wool skirt, black, low-heeled shoes, and a matching gray cashmere sweater. The gray of the skirt and sweater perfectly complemented the red tones of her auburn hair and the striking blue of her eyes. *I don't believe I'd get much work done around this woman.* "You look . . . um . . ." Embarrassed, he foundered, wanting to compliment her on her appearance but not wanting to offend or sound banal.

Margaret let him sweat for a moment before suggesting an adjective. "Businesslike?"

Claude smiled, knowing that she knew exactly what he was thinking. "Just the word I was looking for."

Before she could respond he pointed down from where they stood to the scene below. "Tell me, why is everyone in such a hurry?"

Margaret looked at Claude. "They have only half an hour for lunch."

He smiled. "And you, Ms. Tikkanen, do you also have only half an hour for lunch?"

Ignoring his question she gestured with her arm to the small parking lot adjoining the building. "Shall I drive?"

"Why do I have the feeling that hundreds of eyes are focused on us even now?" Claude asked as they walked to her car.

"Little out of the ordinary is permitted in this community, and you, Mr. McCutcheon, are most definitely out of the ordinary."

They got into a company-owned four-wheel-drive Dodge pickup with an extended cab. Claude noted with silent approval the expert way Margaret worked her way through the gears as they left the busy company town and, heading north, merged with the light traffic on Highway 101.

"To what do I owe the pleasure of this visit? Have you decided to represent the company after all?"

Claude shook his head. "No, I'm afraid not. I was just in the area and thought you might enjoy having lunch with me."

Margaret looked at Claude, skepticism evident in her glance. "Just in the area? In New London? Three hundred miles north of the Bay Area?"

"That's it. I decided to take a few days off and do a little camping down in the Mendocino National Forest." He smiled. "I will admit that I came a little further north than I otherwise might have done had I not wanted to see you again."

"You're not in any particular hurry, are you?" she asked, taken with Claude's honest reply. She glanced at him out of the corner of her eye. He needed a shave and probably a shower too, but she was pleased, quite pleased, to see him. Such a romantic gesture deserved a bold and spontaneous response.

"It's been my experience that hurrying, in any situation, invariably leads to dissatisfaction and stress."

"Good." Margaret picked up the cellular telephone that rested on the console and pressed the speed-dial button for her office. "Hello, Miriam? Yes, that's right. Call Carl up at Arcata and tell him to roll the Lear out and prepare a quick flight plan for Portland. Then call Carlucci's in Portland and tell them that I want a table for two. Be sure and speak with Gianni." She cradled the telephone receiver between her shoulder and her ear while she looked at her wristwatch. "Tell him I'll be up there sometime before two o'clock and that he's to prepare something special. Wait a minute." She looked over at Claude. "Sorry, this will just take another minute."

"Take your time."

"Miriam? After you've spoken with Gianni I want you to call Roscoe Emerson at Georgia Pacific and cancel my two o'clock meeting with him. Tell him I'll call tomorrow and reschedule it. Oh, and call Ben Lomond at Mill Two and cancel this afternoon's productivity meeting. Have you got all that? Good." She hung up and looked innocently at Claude. "Have you eaten at Carlucci's?"

"The one in Portland?" Claude shook his head. "Actually, no, although I've been meaning to for the longest time. You don't suppose we'll have any trouble getting a table at this late hour, do you?"

"I don't think so," Margaret replied. "I own it."

Claude finished the last of his peach-and-blueberry cobbler and put his spoon down with a sigh.

"If I ate like this every day I'd be as fat as a pig in no time," he said, nodding as Margaret ordered two cappuccinos from the attentive waiter. They were the last two diners in the restaurant and were seated at a window table with a view of a snow-capped Mount Hood.

"I have some trouble picturing you fat as a pig," Margaret said, pouring the last of the second bottle of chardonnay they had ordered.

Claude held his wineglass up to the light, admiring the pellucid character of the crisp fruity vintage. He nodded his head toward the empty bottle. "Despite the fact that damned little Latin was taught at Johnston County High School, I suspect that that label, *Semper Virens Vineyards,* is more than a coincidence."

Margaret laughed. "Subtle it isn't. We, my father and I, have owned a good deal of land in the Anderson Valley east of Ukiah for years, and we've sold our grape production to several wineries. I finally decided to get into the winemaking business myself."

"Are you making any money?"

"Not yet. What you're drinking is one of our first wines to hit the market. I suspect we're at least five to ten years away from seeing a return on our investment."

"It's an extraordinary chardonnay."

Margaret nodded. "It is, isn't it? I was extremely lucky in acquiring a woman I consider to be the finest young winemaker in the state. She's an oenology graduate from UC Davis who was going nowhere with a small, undercapitalized operation in the Napa Valley. I made her the boss of *Semper Virens* and gave her all the resources she needs to eventually produce what I expect to be one of the most sought-after wines in the world."

Margaret paused as their waiter brought two cappuccinos to the table.

"That will be all for now," she told him when he asked if he could bring them anything else. She looked at Claude when they were once again alone. "It's my practice to find the best person available for any given job, pay them well, and get out of their way. I provide strategic planning and establish timelines for goals and objectives. If they succeed, we both profit."

"And if they fail?"

Margaret smiled. "Only a fool tolerates failure. If someone I employ fails to reach agreed-upon objectives within the time frame I establish I get rid of them." She took a sip of her cappuccino. "Fortunately, by selecting only the very best I limit the number of disappointments. Take this restaurant, for example. I frequently travel to Portland from New London on business and saw an opportunity when this place became available. Since I know next to nothing about the restaurant business I employed a consultant to help me select an executive chef/manager. The person we found, John Carlucci, was a graduate of the California Culinary Institute. He was young, a veteran of both the Santa Fe and Berkeley gourmet ghettos, but he was a bud waiting to blossom. All he needed was the impetus of total responsibility. I brought him up here, gave him a small but, contingent upon success, steadily increasing share of ownership, and turned him loose." She finished her cappuccino. "And I told him to change his first name from John to Gianni."

"He knows how to cook," Claude allowed.

"More importantly, he knows how to make money. By this time next year we'll have two more restaurants open, one in Seattle and one in Vancouver."

"Watch out, McDonald's."

"Indeed." Margaret looked coyly at Claude. "Knowing what you know now, aren't you at least a little bit sorry that you decided against working with me?"

Claude shook his head. "To tell you the truth, I don't care anything about how you do business or how much business you do. In fact, sitting here now, with you, I don't even care what your *real* interest in me is." When Margaret started to speak he held up his hand, cutting her off. "What I *do* care about is you and the fact that I find myself strongly attracted to you." Claude finished his cappuccino and leaned across the table toward Margaret. "Neither one of us are kids anymore so I'm going to be honest with you. I want to get you into bed, find out what makes you tick as a woman, and let you see me as a man, not some two-bit lawyer you're trying to buy or some low-rent bozo you think you can impress with how much money you make or how many businesses you own." He leaned back and lit a Camel. "Now, if going to bed with me is not on your agenda my suggestion is that we ease that Learjet of yours on down to California so you can get back to making money and I can continue my little vacation."

"And if it is on my agenda?"

Claude nodded toward the telephone on the maître d's table. "Call home and tell them you're going to be in Portland for a while."

The insides of Margaret's thighs were raw from the roughness of Claude's beard. For three days and two nights they had not left the four-room Lumber Baron Suite on the top floor of Portland's majestic downtown Benson Hotel, a fact that greatly impressed most of the hotel's staff. Whenever they got hungry she called Gianni Carlucci and had him prepare and deliver full-course meals complete with chilled aperitifs and wines. *My God,* she thought, reclining nude on the king-sized bed's pillows and watching Claude shave through the bathroom's open door, *who would have guessed such a thing?* She smiled. *And he had needed a shower, just like I guessed when he first showed up at New London.* However, far from offensive, the musk of his body odor as he covered her the first time had intoxicated her as no brandy ever could have. And his body. She couldn't keep her eyes off him, even though he was just shaving. A tidy waist, not too small, a man's waist, from which his back spread alarmingly wide to meet his shoulders. Dropping her eyes downward, she lingered on his tight, hard butt, joined from below by impressively muscular thighs. *And a scrotum to die for,* she thought.

After Claude finished shaving, he walked back into the bedroom, his penis swinging lazily from side to side.

"I'm thinking I should probably give Emma a call and let her know I haven't fallen off the earth," he said.

"Who's Emma?"

Claude sat on the edge of the bed next to Margaret and picked up the telephone receiver. "Emma, my secretary and person Friday. You met her when you first came to my office." He dialed his office number and winked at Margaret. "Emma? Hello, darling, it's me, Claude. What's that? No, I haven't been kidnapped. Who the hell would pay a ransom for an old fool like me?" He listened a moment. "Portland. Yes, that's right, Portland, Oregon. None of your business. No, I'm leaving today."

Margaret slid her torso around Claude's thighs and took his flaccid penis into her mouth. It was at once somewhat odd and yet strangely compelling, its very limpness exciting her as she remembered how its erect counterpart had recently so completely possessed her. Claude laid a hand on the back of her neck and continued his conversation with Emma.

"Who called? Did she say what she wanted?" As Claude listened to Emma's reply he felt a familiar tingle in his scrotum as blood pulsed into his cock and the head began to swell and the shaft lengthened in Margaret's mouth. "Call her back for me and tell her that I'll be back in Berkeley . . ." He consulted the

Rolex lying on the nightstand next to the telephone and did a quick calculation. "Late this afternoon and I'll call her then, okay? I'll see you in the morning." He hung up and shifted his body on the bed, leaning against the headboard as Margaret moved to lie between his legs, both taking care that their movements not dislodge the object of their attention from her mouth. He closed his eyes and smiled, silently thanking whatever gods might exist that he'd been born a man.

After the Lear had climbed to altitude, Margaret left the copilot's seat in the cockpit and joined Claude in the small main cabin.

"Can he manage up there without you?"

"I think so," Margaret answered. "He had many thousands of hours flying jet fighters for the air force before I hired him."

She sat beside him on the leather sofa that ran along one of the cabin's bulkheads and placed an affectionate hand on his thigh. "I'm sorry you have to return to the Bay Area right away."

Claude smiled. "I can scarcely imagine the impact that my staying would have on the simple folk of New London."

"You may rest assured that every person in New London over the age of five as well as probably one out of every three people in all of Humboldt County already know that we've spent the past three days passionately coupling in Portland."

"That's as may be."

Margaret reached down and stroked one of Claude's boots. "Why is it that every time I see you you're wearing blue jeans and cowboy boots?"

"You've only seen me twice, to be exact, hardly a sufficient number of times to assume that you've spotted a trend. In this case, though, you have indeed noted a peculiarity in my character. I love cowboy boots beyond all reasoning. I've got eight pairs, all with different hides and colors." He nodded down at the pair he was wearing. They were a soft, buttery-looking tan. "These happen to be current favorites of mine. Horsehide, and so soft they're like slipping on a condom."

Margaret laughed. "Have you always been so inclined?"

"No, only the past fifteen years or so. It came on me one day out of the blue. 'Claude,' I told myself, 'you're never too old to be a cowboy.'"

"When you spoke to your secretary you mentioned calling a woman when you got back. Is that why you have to leave right away?"

He shook his head. "No, I'm not leaving right away just because of the phone, although the woman in question, Claire Williams, is an old friend. Nothing for you to be concerned about." He paused and chose his words with some care. "In fact, I think we need to have a little time apart to think about the past three days. I don't think either one of us believes that it was just a quick fling. On the other hand, I don't think either one of us knows yet exactly what it was."

Both fell silent and remained that way until the Lear was on the ground and taxiing to its private hangar. They spoke but little on the drive back to New London, inconsequential things of the sort said by people who would rather be silent. In New London, Margaret handed Claude a slip of paper.

"It's my telephone number. At home."

Claude nodded. "I'll call you." He smiled. "Soon."

Claude's first reaction when he walked into his house was to look around for Thurman. Almost immediately he realized what he was doing and he knew that he would be a long time forgetting his old companion. *How could something so small, relatively speaking, take up so much room in one's house and one's heart?* he wondered as he stowed his camping gear and undressed. He was tired after the long, five-hour drive south from New London and, although he knew he had promised to return Claire Williams's telephone call, he sank down onto the futon and immediately fell asleep.

CHAPTER 7

"**G**ODDAMN."

Claude looked again at the Rolex, unwilling to believe that he been asleep for almost sixteen hours. But the hands on the face of the watch obdurately refused to change their positions, Claude's dismay notwithstanding. It was nine A.M. *I must be getting old,* he thought, as he rose and walked into the bathroom. He smiled as he took his penis in his right hand, noting with pleasure the fact that the shaft was still somewhat irritated from the friction of three days' hard use at the Benson Hotel in Portland. He placed his left hand against the wall behind the toilet and leaned forward, pleased with the force of his stream into the toilet bowl. After brushing his teeth he stepped into the tub, sighing with pleasure as the hot water closed over his body.

Revitalized, he quickly dried himself and pulled on a fresh pair of jeans. In the kitchen he took a container of coffee beans out of his freezer and emptied a portion into his hand-powered coffee mill. Without looking he gestured with his right arm, indicating that his next-door neighbor, Sally Pinter, whom he assumed was watching his activities through the kitchen window, should join him for a cup of coffee.

"Where've you been?" Sally asked before she was completely through the screen door leading to Claude's kitchen.

"Away," Claude said noncommittally. "You want a cup of coffee?"

"Lord, yes. How do you like my hair?"

Claude smiled. He enjoyed her shameless vamping for him and wondered idly what she would do if he ever indicated an interest. He handed her a cup of strong, black Sulawesi coffee.

"Your hair always looks nice," he assured her.

"Mmm, good," she murmured, sipping the coffee. Unlike most women he knew, Sally enjoyed her coffee as strongly brewed as Claude did his, and unadulterated with either sugar or milk. "Thelma"—her hairdresser—"says it makes me look just like Debra Winger."

"Who's Debra Winger?" Claude asked.

Sally ignored Claude's question. "Were you off with a woman these past few days?"

"Debra Winger wouldn't have to ask."

The telephone rang. Before Claude could move to answer it, Sally rose and started to leave.

"I expect that's your new girlfriend," she said archly as she walked out the screen door. "You'd better be careful or you're going to end up like the governor of Idaho or Nebraska or wherever."

Claude took a sip of his coffee and watched Sally cross over to her own backyard before picking up the telephone. "Claude McCutcheon here."

"Hello, Claude. It's Emma."

"If it can wait I was going to start for the office in a couple of minutes."

"I wasn't sure when you might come in so I thought I'd better call and let you know that Claire Williams called again this morning. She sounds upset."

"Damn," Claude muttered, annoyed with himself that he hadn't called her the night before as he had said he would. "I'll call her from here and then come down to the office. Everything else okay?"

"Fine. I'll see you soon."

Claude dialed Claire's number at work and then, patiently, worked his way through two layers of clerk-secretaries to her actual desk.

"No wonder taxes are so high," he said when she came on the line. "The first person I talked to didn't know who you were or for which justice you worked, and the second, although claiming to know you, wasn't sure how to put my call through to you. It's the grace of God that we're actually talking to each other."

Claire laughed. "We were going to get a new telephone system this year, one where all the staff would have their own direct-dial numbers, but the legislature cut the court's budget."

"Well, at least those morons in Sacramento are doing something right. I just wish they'd cut even more of your budget as well as the budget of every other taxpayer-supported entity in the state. What can I do for you?"

"Meet me for lunch?"

"How about some other day? I just got back into town and haven't been to the office yet. I'm calling from home. How about tomorrow?"

"I'll come over there. I could take BART and you could pick me up at the North Berkeley station. I have to talk to you. It's about—"

"Don't say it," Claude interrupted, "not over the telephone." He sighed, knowing what Claire wanted to talk about. "Call me at the office when you're ready to leave. We can have lunch at Kate's."

"Mornin', Emma."

"Well, if it's not the traveling Mr. McCutcheon." Emma fixed a gimlet eye on her boss. "You've been up to no good the past few days and there's no use denying it."

"Why, Emma, how could you even think such a thing?"

"And I know with whom you've been cavorting."

"Oh, yeah? With whom?"

"That Margaret Tikkanen from up north. You and she have been up in Portland together and don't say you haven't."

"Who told you that?" Claude asked with mock severity.

"I don't need anybody to tell me what's as plain as the nose on your face." She wagged a finger at Claude. "That woman's going to be nothing but trouble for you, mark my words." Emma handed Claude a telephone message slip with a flourish, satisfaction evident on her shining oval face. "She called a few minutes ago. Informed me that you would know what she was calling about." Emma sniffed with disdain. "As if I wouldn't."

Claude took the message and put it into his shirt pocket. "I'm having lunch today with Claire Williams."

"She's the one you should be taking to Portland or wherever. What kind of trouble has she gotten herself into?"

"I haven't the faintest," Claude lied. "What else happened while I was gone? Did you hear anything more from or about Bobby Norton?"

Emma shook her head. "Not directly, although both Sergeant Malone of the Berkeley PD and Bernie Beck called."

"What did they want?"

"Wouldn't say. Malone sounded annoyed so I assume he hasn't had much success in identifying Myron Hirsch's killer. I told him I expected you back in a few days and he said he'd call again. Same with Bernie Beck, though he didn't sound annoyed about anything. More like he was just calling to see if everything was okay."

Claude looked at his watch and picked up the telephone on Emma's desk and began punching in the number for the Albany Police Department. "I'll speak to Bernie now, if he's in. To hell with Malone. I've already told him that I've got nothing to do with Norton." He held up a finger, indicating that the call had been answered. "Yeah, is Lieutenant Beck available, please?" He looked at the message slip Emma had written out regarding Margaret's call and smiled. "Bernie? Claude. I understand you were trying to get in touch with me. What's up?"

"Nothing in particular, Claude, I was just following up on our conversation about Rod Jackson. You hear anything more?"

"Yeah, as it turns out the Jackson thing has nothing to do with the Hirsch murder. A prospective client was just doing a background check."

"Prospective client? I never heard of prospective clients hiring private detectives to investigate lawyers they were thinking about hiring. Who are you representing these days?"

Claude shrugged. "I guess it is a little odd, but what can I tell you?" *That she's an extraordinary woman that now I can't get out of my mind?*

"You can tell me who the client is."

"It doesn't matter since I decided not to represent them. Look, Bernie, I'd like to chat but I've got a lunch meeting coming up. You got anything else?"

"Jim Malone's pissed off at you. Big-time. He thinks you know more than you've told him and—"

"Fuck Jim Malone," Claude interrupted, suddenly angry, and then, just as suddenly, over it. *Jesus Christ, I'm starting to sound like Bobby Norton,* he thought, chagrined. *Plus, Malone's right.* "Hey, I'm sorry, Bernie, I didn't mean to say that. It's just that I've already told Malone several times that I don't represent Bobby and that I can't help him out." He looked at his watch again. "Listen, I've got to go. I'll talk to you later, okay?" He hung up the phone and shook his head. "To hell with those guys," he told Emma, a smile once again teasing his lips.

"Where are you taking Miss Williams to lunch?" Emma asked, suddenly suspicious.

"Kate's, why?"

Emma shook her head. "I might have known. Why do you have to take her to that nasty place?"

"You're just jealous because none of the ladies there pay you any mind." He ducked to avoid the eraser she threw at him and ran down the stairs. "I'll be back," he called over his shoulder.

"I always feel like I'm on display when we come to Kate's."

Claude and Claire sat at the rearmost table, the one affording the most privacy in the raucous café atmosphere of the lesbian eatery. He couldn't help but notice that the suit Claire wore, though well tailored and quite appropriate for an attorney on the staff of the California Supreme Court, conveyed none of the effortless elegance of the outfit that Margaret had worn when he brought her here a week ago. By comparison Claire's suit seemed rather dowdy and middle-aged. He thought it somewhat odd he had never noticed such a thing before.

Claude smiled. "You are. On the other hand, Bette Beal doesn't allow any cruising so all the ladies can do is look and admire." He signaled to their waitress, a beefy young woman with a pronounced Texas twang and a small but highly detailed black-and-brown steer's head tattooed on her left wrist. Her name tag identified her as "Ropin' Roslyn."

"What'll it be, pardner?" she asked Claire.

"Just a spinach salad, no dressing, with several lemon wedges on the side, please. And a Perrier."

"Dieting?" Claude asked, thinking of three days of sybaritic dining in Portland with Margaret. He looked at the waitress. "I'll have a slice of the meat loaf," he said, "and tell Bette I'd like one of her sherry-cream sauces with it." After Ropin' Roslyn left the table with their orders he turned his attention back to Claire. "I presume that Nina"—Claire's daughter—"is continuing to see Ralph Martini."

Claire nodded and ran a hand through her hair, a gesture of despair and defeat. "I'm afraid she's becoming addicted to crack cocaine. I found some in her dresser last week and she's come home high several times in the past two weeks. I know she's getting it from Martini because I've followed her there after school."

"Have you talked to her about it?"

Claire shrugged. "I've tried, but she refuses to even respond. Nothing works anymore, not threats, not tears, not pleading. She's even told me that if I keep hassling her she'll run away, and I believe her. Martini has taken complete control of her. Plus, I have no doubt that he's abusing her sexually when he gets her high. Three nights ago she came home and passed out on her bed fully clothed. When I started to undress her I found that she had no panties on and that the insides of both her thighs were heavily bruised, as if she'd been struck repeatedly."

Claire paused as their food was served. She picked at her salad for several minutes, eating very little, and then pushed the plate away from her.

"I never thought something like this could ever happen to me. I always assumed that Roger's running away with his secretary shortly after Nina was born would be the worst thing in my life." She tried to smile at Claude. "I was wrong." She began to cry, silent tears that ran down her cheeks and onto the table. "And the police still won't help. They say that without Nina's cooperation there's no evidence that Martini sold or gave her the crack, or whatever. There's always a reason why they can't do anything." She slammed a fist down on the table, a startling gesture born of fear, anger, and frustration. "Damnit, he should not get away with ruining my daughter's life." She looked at Claude, defeat in her eyes. "There should be a special hell for people like him, people who sell drugs to children."

Claude reached across the table and took her hand. "Go home. Take the rest of the day off. Get a good night's sleep. Forget that we had lunch together today and that you told me anything about this matter." He held her eyes with his own, not allowing her to look away. "Can you do that? No matter what happens, can you forget ever discussing Mr. Martini with me or anyone else?"

Claire nodded, recognizing the full implication of what Claude was saying. "I can," she whispered. She squeezed Claude's hand as hard as she could and looked down at the table. "I never thought I was capable of even thinking, much less saying such a thing, but I want him hurt." She looked up at Claude. "Badly."

"Amigo, it is good to see you." Rocky Martinez smiled and the late-afternoon sunlight danced warmly off the gold in his front teeth. He spread his arms. "Welcome to my home."

Claude took his hand in a firm grip. "The pleasure is mine." He smiled at Rocky's wife, Carmelita. "I hope you don't mind an unexpected guest for dinner."

Carmelita brushed Claude's comment away as if she were shooing flies from her kitchen. "Since when is Claude McCutcheon a guest?" Her face took on a mock severity. "But I am angry with you for not coming more often." She called out to her eldest daughter. "Gloria. Set another place at the table, *por favor.*"

They spoke quietly of ordinary things at dinner, the weather, Rocky's job, how the children were doing in school. After dinner, Carmelita bustled the children out of the small dining room, leaving Claude and Rocky to relax with cigarettes and strong, black Mexican coffee. Neither man spoke, both content to sit quietly and study the smoke rising from their cigarettes, to savor the complex bitterness of the darkly roasted coffee. Finally, Rocky spoke.

"What can I do for you, my friend?"

Claude nodded, pleased that Rocky had made it unnecessary for him to ask. He nodded toward the rear of the house, where they could hear Carmelita putting the children to bed.

"How old is Gloria getting to be?"

"Fifteen this year."

"She's a good girl, isn't she? All your children are good, but particularly Gloria, no?"

Rocky nodded. *"Si."* Gloria was his first-born, the anchor of his soul. "Gloria will go to college, perhaps to be a doctor." He shrugged. "Whatever she wants to be. Such a thing would never be possible in Mexico, not for the child of Rocky Martinez." He looked closely at Claude. "Were it not for you, amigo, Gloria would have no chance." He held up a hand when Claude started to protest. "It is true. You fought the INS for me, you lent me money to bring Carmelita north from Oaxaca. You charged nothing for your services. Now I see that something is troubling you and perhaps I can, in some small way, begin to repay a debt that can never be truly repaid."

Carmelita came into the room to refill their cups and she did not linger. Both men lit fresh cigarettes and again sat quietly for a time.

"I have a friend," Claude said, finally breaking the comfortable silence, "a woman, with a daughter, a child the same age as Gloria." He paused and smiled. "One of the wonderful things about children is how trusting they are. They find it difficult to believe that someone, an adult they admire perhaps, would do anything to harm them." The smile left his face. "This child, this girl of Gloria's age, the daughter of my friend, has come under the influence of a man who is doing her great harm. He is giving her drugs and has begun to take advantage of her sexually."

Rocky remained silent but his face hardened.

"My friend, the woman, has no man, no husband, to protect her child in this matter, and of course the police are of no assistance."

"How may I help?" Rocky asked.

Claude smiled. His friend, as he had known he would not, had not let him down. He reached over and put a hand on Rocky's shoulder, a startlingly intimate gesture between the two men.

"I don't need any help," he said, "at least not directly. I will deal with this man, tonight, on my own. It is possible, however, that I may need to be able to tell the authorities, the police, that I spent the evening here in Oakland, with friends. You and Carmelita. I don't anticipate needing to, but," Claude shrugged, "you never know."

"Are you going to kill him?"

Claude shook his head. *The question sounds so unremarkable,* he thought, *the words so innocuous.* "No. Certainly not. I do plan to hurt him though. He must be convinced never to attempt such a thing, at least with this child, again."

"Tonight?"

Claude nodded but said nothing.

"Bueno." Rocky nodded as if the matter were closed. "I will go with you." He quickly put up a hand, stifling Claude's protest. "I will not interfere, but I will not let you go alone. As you said, one never knows. We will take my car, which nobody knows or will connect with this man." He paused and thought for a moment. "In fact, my cousin Hector, who you have met once, lives in the City, in the Mission District. If necessary, he will say that we, you and I, came to the City and spent the evening with him and his wife."

Ralph Martini lived in a rundown stuccoed apartment building on 28th Street off Valencia in the City. Claude had Rocky circle the block twice while he scanned the neighborhood, familiarizing himself with the street and observing the few people out and about.

Once a bastion of blue-collar respectability, drugs and rootlessness had turned much of San Francisco's Mission District into typically urban mean streets. The gang culture, both Hispanic and black, had turned brutally violent, no more than a sidelong glance often sufficient provocation for murder. Martini's neighborhood was typical, rundown apartment buildings cheek-by-jowl, darkened streetlights, and a pungent aroma of failure in the stagnant air.

When he felt comfortable Claude had Rocky park. Before getting out of the car he reached inside his jacket and withdrew the Colt .45 automatic he was carrying in a concealed shoulder holster. Rocky watched silently as Claude chambered a round and returned the weapon to its holster. The building's foyer was empty when they entered and Claude quickly found Martini's name on the mail slots.

"Apartment 201," he said to Rocky, noting that there were fifteen units on three floors.

They took the stairs two at a time and encountered only trash on the stairs. A dimly lit hallway reeking of stale urine and industrial disinfectant led from the stairwell to the five apartments on the second floor. From upstairs, somewhere on the third floor, a stereo blared out a muffled rap, the insistent bass line traveling down the walls and across the floor joists. Martini's apartment was next to the stairwell. He nodded to Rocky, who knocked quietly but firmly on the door.

"Yeah, who is it?"

As he and Claude had agreed upon, Rocky responded in a flood of rapid Spanish, a language Claude was reasonably certain Martini would not be able to understand. The idea was to get him to open the door so Claude, with the element of surprise, could then swiftly force his way inside. It worked.

"What the fuck—"

Martini threw the deadbolt and yanked the door open, aggressively thrusting his head forward to see who was bothering him. Before he could react Claude thrust a shoulder savagely against the partially opened door, propelling both men into the apartment. Rocky quickly followed and shut and bolted the door behind them.

"Check the apartment," Claude said over his shoulder to Rocky. He turned his attention back to Martini. "I told you, you sonofabitch," he cursed through clenched jaws, his eyes locked on the terrified man in his grasp. "I told you to leave that girl alone."

"We are alone, Claude," Rocky called from the rear of the apartment.

Claude looked to his right, momentarily distracted by the unexpected sound of Rocky's voice. In that instant Martini dug his right hand into his pants pocket and withrew a knife, which he immediately plunged into Claude's left side. The blade tore into Claude's thick latissimus dorsi muscle and raked downward, flaying the muscle and skin in a deep incision seven or eight inches in length. Claude's reaction to the fiery pain in his side was unthinking and instantaneous. "Fuck," he gasped as he instinctively reached for the Colt inside his jacket, thumbing the hammer back as he freed the weapon from the holster. He thrust the heavy automatic into Martini's midsection and pulled the trigger. Even though Martini's body absorbed much of the sound of the gunshot, the report nonetheless filled the squalid, three-room apartment. The round took Martini squarely in the solar plexus, driving the breath from his lungs with an audible grunt and pinning him for several seconds against the wall. He looked at Claude with a look of utter surprise before sliding to the floor.

"Claude! *Amigo!*"

Claude gradually became aware that Rocky was talking to him. He remained crouched over the body of Ralph Martini like a bird of prey protecting a kill from scavengers, the Colt still clutched in his right hand.

"Amigo." Rocky's voice was taut with tension. "It is over. You have killed him."

Claude looked down and saw that his friend was right. Ralph Martini was slumped on the floor, his knees drawn up toward his chest, his eyes staring blindly toward the ceiling. A copious amount of blood had already pooled next to the body. Claude noticed with a certain hysterical clarity that in death Martini's jaw muscles had relaxed and his tongue was protruding from his mouth.

"We must get out of here," Rocky hissed, "and quickly." He gestured toward Claude's left side. "You have been cut."

Claude straightened up and returned the Colt to its holster. He felt a heavy, pulsing wetness down his back and side and knew instinctively that it was his own blood.

"Christ," he mumbled, unconsciously echoing what Rocky had just said, "we better get the fuck out of here."

Rocky grabbed Claude's arm and pulled him from the apartment, slamming the door behind them. He half carried him down the stairs, praying that no one would look out their door and see them. A wonderful darkness enveloped them as they left the building and stumbled out onto the sidewalk. At the car Claude paused for a second, trying to clear his head before getting in.

"Sorry about the blood," Claude mumbled as Rocky helped him into the car. He knew that he was getting blood all over Rocky's front seat.

Rocky ignored Claude's apology as he started the car and pulled away from the curb. "Hector lives very close," he assured Claude. "We will go there and decide what to do."

"Madre de Dios!"

Claude could see that Hector was stunned at the sight of so much blood. He smiled giddily, suddenly remembering Bobby Norton's description of all of the blood in Myron Hirsch's office. *Hold on,* he told himself. *Now's not the time to be going into shock.* He heard Rocky and his cousin Hector discuss the situation in rapid Spanish as the two of them led him into the kitchen of Hector's small apartment overlooking Mission Dolores Park.

"His wife is at work," Rocky finally told Claude. He helped him into a straight-backed wooden chair.

"She is working a night shift at the airport," Hector added. "It is a very good job."

Rocky silenced him with a glance. He helped Claude remove his shirt and winced when he saw the extent of the wound.

"You are badly cut, my friend," he said, gesturing for Hector to bring him a clean cloth soaked with warm water. He gently cleaned around the wound, which was still bleeding, although not as copiously, and looked at his friend with concerned eyes. "It is too deep a wound to heal without stitching, and you will need medicine." He paused momentarily, searching for the proper word in English. "For the infection, no?"

Claude shook his head. "Give me a cigarette. I can't see a doctor like this." He paused as Hector held a match to his cigarette. "Any fool can see it's a knife wound and would report it to the police." He shook his head again.

"Is it painful?" Hector asked, both repelled and fascinated by the large wound.

"Not yet," Claude answered, "but it sure as hell will be soon." The wound's throbbing had increased in intensity in just the past few minutes, and he knew that when the shock and adrenaline rush of the violent encounter wore off the pain would be considerable. He fell silent, thinking while Rocky continued to wipe blood from his side. "Listen," he finally said, "I've thought of someone who can help me." He looked at Hector. "Have you got any strong tape? Duct tape or something like that?"

"Si."

"Good. Get the tape and four or five of your wife's sanitary napkins."

Under Claude's direction Rocky and Hector layered four sanitary napkins over the wound and then bound them down with long strips of gray duct tape.

"Tighter," Claude insisted as they pulled the tape across the bulky pads. He grunted with pain as the two men complied. "The pressure will help keep the wound closed until I can get it stitched."

When they were done Rocky wadded Claude's bloodied shirt and placed it into a grocery bag. "I will burn this at home," he assured Claude. He and his cousin then helped Claude into one of Hector's clean

T-shirts. As they were leaving Rocky asked his cousin to say nothing of the evening's visit to his wife.

"Don't worry about the seat covers," Rocky assured Claude as they were driving back to the East Bay. "I'll take the car tomorrow to Jesus and have them replaced."

Claude nodded, knowing that Rocky was referring to a cousin-in-law, Jesus Vilar, who owned and operated a small auto repair shop out on the San Pablo Dam Road in Contra Costa County.

"Tell Jesus to send the bill to me," Claude grunted, his attention focused on the growing pain in his side.

"There will be no bill," Rocky assured him, smiling at the very thought. "I just wish I knew a doctor we could trust."

"Don't worry, old friend, I know a woman who will help me." He spoke with perhaps a touch more confidence than he felt. *No need to worry about it*, he thought, *she'll either help me or she won't.*

"Let me take you there now."

Claude shook his head. "You've done more than enough already."

They pulled into the yard in front of Rocky's house and sat for a moment in Rocky's car.

"What of the police?" Rocky asked. "What should I say if they question me?"

"Nothing. We've got nothing to fear from the police," Claude responded, not wanting to talk because of the now-unremitting pain in his side but knowing his friend needed reassurance. "Martini was a paroled felon, convicted of selling drugs to children. The police will think he was killed in the course of a drug transaction and will not spend much time or money searching for the killer. Nobody, the police least of all, will care about the death of a man like Ralph Martini." He paused for a second as a wave of nausea rolled over him. He put his hand on Rocky's shoulder. "I'm glad you were there." *Glad wasn't nearly enough,* he thought, *but how to say more?*

"Come into the house. Carmelita will be able to put a better bandage on you."

Claude got out of the car, wincing with pain, and got into the cab of his pickup truck. He rolled down the window and leaned his head out.

"No, you've done more than enough already. Don't worry, I'll be fine. I'll call you in a couple of days."

He started the truck and backed carefully out of Rocky's yard. He was unable to lift his left arm sufficiently to use it for steering and had to shift gears while steadying the steering wheel with his right knee. A quick look at the Rolex once he reached the highway told him that it was almost 1:00 A.M.

Later, when he looked back on it, he could remember nothing of the drive north, nothing of the six and a half hours it took to drive from the Bay Area up to Humboldt County and the little company town on the Eel River. Somewhere along the way a fever got started, and by the time he pulled into the gravel parking lot behind the administration building of the Northwestern Lumber Company his cheeks were flushed and his eyes were shining luminously. His entire left side felt as if it were on fire, and the pain rolled through his body in rhythmic waves. It was seven-thirty when he turned his engine off. The company's administrative employees had already been at work for thirty minutes. He knew from the wetness down his side and back and into his pants that the wound had been seeping blood continuously and he frankly doubted that he could walk. After sitting quietly for several seconds he saw a young boy walking by on the way to school. He signaled with his right arm and the boy stopped and looked at him curiously.

"Son, I want you to do me a favor," Claude called out. "Go into the office there and tell Miss Margaret

Tikkanen that Claude McCutcheon is here and would like to see her. Can you remember that? Claude McCutcheon."

The youngster stood looking wide-eyed at Claude for a second and then walked quickly into the office building. Several seconds passed, during which time Claude thought that the rich, coppery smell of blood in the pickup's cab was going to make him ill. Finally, he saw Margaret come out onto the building's small front porch and peer in his direction. He waved with his right hand and she started his way, a smile lighting her face.

"What in the world are you up to, Claude McCutcheon," she said as she neared the truck, clearly pleased to see him. "Why didn't you—" She gasped and put her hand to her mouth in shock when she looked through the truck's open window and saw the bright red blood soaking Claude's entire left side.

Claude tried to smile and didn't quite make it. "It's damned good to see you, Maggie," he said, using the nickname he had given her in Portland. He was breathing in short gasps, and now that he had reached his destination, for better or worse, he felt weakness flow through his body in concert with the pain. "I've gotten myself into a bit of a jam, don't you know?"

A look of puzzlement flickered across his face as he lost consciousness and slumped to his right on the seat.

CHAPTER 8

MARGARET'S EXECUTIVE INSTINCTS AUTOMATICALLY kicked in the instant Claude passed out. Out of the corner of her eye she saw her father Joseph come into the parking lot and beckoned him to Claude's truck. "It's Claude McCutcheon," she said almost absent-mindedly, her mind busy with how best to deal with the situation. "We've got to get him over to the dispensary."

"I'll call the fire station," Joseph said, referring to the paramedics stationed with the firemen. When he saw Claude slumped over the seat, covered in blood, his eyebrows rose a fraction. "Our documents?"

"I don't know," Margaret said firmly. "I do know that this"—she indicated Claude with a gesture— "has to be taken care of quietly so I suggest we take him directly to the dispensary ourselves. The less people involved, the better."

At the dispensary, the company doctor, Morley Rose, was startled to see Joseph and Margaret bringing in what appeared to be a badly injured employee.

As soon as they got the man up on an examining table Joseph left. Dr. Rose cut away the blood-soaked shirt and peeled the duct tape from Claude's skin. The soaked sanitary napkins fell with a wet plop to the floor, and he nudged them under the table with the toe of his shoe.

"Louise"—his nurse, an elderly widow who had been employed by the company for over fifty years—"called in sick this morning," he said nervously.

"I'll assist you," Margaret said brusquely.

Margaret took several sterile sponges and, using a disinfectant and cleansing agent, began to clean the wound while Dr. Rose prepared to start a blood plasma transfusion using a cutdown procedure at Claude's left ankle.

"I'll be damned."

"What is it?" Margaret asked.

Dr. Rose pointed to the inside of Claude's ankle. "Look here. Somebody's already done a cutdown on this man, years ago."

"What's a cutdown?"

"A procedure we use to quickly get to a vein to give a transfusion. It's usually done when the patient is unconscious or badly wounded. You see it done in the military quite a lot, with combat injuries and wounds."

After starting the plasma Dr. Rose turned his attention to the wound itself. Margaret had cleaned the entire area of old blood. Some eight inches long and in places up to two and a half inches deep, the lips of the wound remained pulled apart, clearly revealing the striated muscle underneath. The bleeding slowed to a steady seep. Dr. Rose drew a deep breath and began sewing.

"This is a knife wound," he mumbled as he worked. "I'm required by law to report such a wound to the police."

"You'll do no such thing," Margaret said, her voice

steely with authority. "This man is my responsibility. Under no circumstances will word of this matter be communicated to *anyone* without my approval." She paused and held Dr. Rose's eyes with her own. "Do I make myself clear?"

"Of course, I didn't mean to suggest that I would notify anyone without your approval," Rose stammered. Beads of perspiration appeared on his forehead. "Clearly, in a case such as this, there will be no need to involve the outside authorities." He paused for a second and nervously cleared his throat. "I'm not sure what they'll say in Eureka, however."

"What are you talking about?"

"Well, um, of course, we'll have to transport him to the county hospital in Eureka as soon as possible. A wound like this—I mean, with the likelihood of infection, he should be in the hospital for at least several days so they can monitor his condition and give him the right medication." He noted Claude's flushed face and rapid, shallow breathing. "He's already running a fever."

"No." Margaret shook her head. "We'll move him to my house here in New London. You start him on antibiotics and I'll have Dr. Jenkens follow up."

At the mention of Dr. Jenkens's name, Morley Rose breathed a sigh of relief. If the man died, a not wholly unlikely possibility depending on what type or types of infection took hold, he, Dr. Rose, would not necessarily be the attending physician, burdened with the need to complete and sign the death certificate for the coroner's office. On the other hand, he remembered, the county coroner owed his undergraduate education to the company, and would be unlikely to delve too deeply into a matter so obviously important to Margaret. As soon as she had gone Morley Rose took a big drink from a bottle of vodka he kept in his filing cabinet.

* * *

Bob Jenkens had grown up with a big-time crush on Margaret Tikkanen. She filled his adolescent dreams throughout junior high and high school, and it was not until he was well into his medical school education at Stanford that he could smile at his infatuation. Since he was the son of an employee, the company had underwritten his education at UC Berkeley, and later, after Joseph learned of his intention to attend medical school, the company paid all of his tuition and expenses at Stanford on the condition that he agree, after completing his residency, to practice medicine in Humboldt County for at least ten years. Although his schedule as chief of surgery at the county medical center together with a thriving private practice was such that he seldom had time to even think of Margaret, he retained an interest in her life. They occasionally met at county charity functions, especially since the Northwestern Lumber Company was a large contributor to the hospital's budget and Margaret chaired the hospital's board of directors. He never forgot that he owed his education, his very life as he lived it from day to day, entirely to the company, not once doubting that were it not for the company's largess he would never have become a physician, and, by Humboldt County standards at least, a wealthy man with no educational debt. He did not allow criticism of the company to be voiced in his presence, and he had absolutely no doubt that the good the company did for the entire county far outweighed any alleged evil.

"What sort of wound?"

Although busy with a patient when Margaret's call came in to his office, Dr. Jenkens's staff knew enough to interrupt him whenever a Tikkanen called.

"A cut," Margaret answered. "A deep cut approximately eight inches long."

"What sort of a cut? Why don't you just have the man transported by ambulance to the hospital here in

Eureka." Jenkens, puzzled, thought for a moment. "Dr. Ross is on duty right now in the emergency room and is quite competent."

"Dr. Jenkens, this is important to me, otherwise I wouldn't be calling you personally." Margaret's voice, though quiet, bore an undertone of demand. "I don't want to transport this man to your hospital. I want him cared for here in New London. The wound is severe, and I don't feel that Dr. Rose is competent enough to care for the patient without supervision. I would like you to come here, to New London, immediately if possible, and prescribe a course of treatment. If you can't, please tell me so that I can get help elsewhere."

Bob Jenkens did not hesitate. "I'll leave at once."

"What's his blood pressure?"

Dr. Rose, startled, began to stammer. He had not thought to take Claude's blood pressure.

Dr. Jenkens, not surprised, grimaced. He ordered Rose to hook up a blood pressure cuff and did a quick visual inspection of Claude's body. He noted the plasma IV and the ankle cutdown and shook his head, doubting that such a procedure had actually been necessary.

"How many units of plasma have you given him?"

"This is the second," Dr. Rose answered, clearly nervous that he had done something else wrong.

"Why haven't you started him on whole blood? Have you typed him yet?"

"Yes, I've just finished that. He's A positive."

"Have you ordered the blood from the bank?"

Dr. Rose shook his head.

"Well, why not?" Dr. Jenkens asked, exasperated.

"*She* told me not to." Rose looked toward Margaret, who was standing with them in the examining room.

"May I ask why?" Jenkens's voice softened considerably as he addressed Margaret.

"I have A positive blood," she replied. "I told Dr. Rose that I would donate whatever is necessary."

"That's not exactly practical," Jenkens explained patiently, "nor entirely safe. I doubt Dr. Rose has all the equipment he needs to transfuse your blood to this patient. These days, only hospitals and blood banks are prepared to do that." He turned to Dr. Rose. "Call the blood bank immediately and tell them I want three units of A positive."

Margaret held up a hand. "I'm concerned about confidentiality in this matter."

"And I'm concerned about saving this man's life," Dr. Jenkens responded somewhat testily. "Listen to me. This man is seriously ill. He's lost a great deal of blood, far more than you realize, and a serious infection is already under way. We can argue about record keeping later."

Margaret nodded at Dr. Rose. "Order the blood."

Dr. Jenkens removed the dressing and examined the wound. "These stitches are going to have to come out. A wound this deep needs subcutaneous sutures and then closure with staples." He looked up Margaret. "This is, you know, a knife wound."

"I am aware of that."

Jenkens smiled, pleased to have, for the first time in his life, something that Margaret Tikkanen desperately wanted. The smile disappeared and he was once again the physician.

"Dr. Rose will assist me. This'll take some time so you might as well return to the office." Margaret began to protest, but Jenkens firmly shook his head. "I don't want you here. There is nothing you can do to help and having you looking over my shoulder will only complicate matters." He resisted the urge to take

one of her hands in his. "I'll call you when I finish."
He saw her unspoken question. "And no one else."

"How is he?"

Margaret stood before her father's desk. She
shrugged in answer to his question. "Dr. Jenkens is
working on him now."

"We probably should have called Jenkens first,"
Joseph said contemplatively. "One day soon we're
going to have to retire Dr. Rose." He took a sip of his
coffee and looked closely at Margaret. "Tell me about
this Claude McCutcheon. You seem to have developed an, um, affection for him."

"I'm not sure how I feel about him."

Joseph grunted. He loved his daughter beyond all
measure and he knew enough about men and women
not to take her response at face value. *She's fallen in
love with him,* he thought. *Whether or not she knows it
yet herself it is certainly a fact.* "In light of today's
events, what do you think now about his involvement
with Norton and the recently deceased Myron
Hirsch?"

"He may or may not be involved." She ran a hand
through her hair.

"That's hardly a response." Joseph allowed some of
his annoyance to show in his tone of voice. "You were
reasonably certain he was involved not too long ago.
You assumed him to be a typically opportunistic
lawyer trying to . . . let me remember, how did you
put it, 'trying to get his finger into the pie.'" The
sudden flush of anger on his daughter's face told
Joseph he had struck a responsive nerve. *This will
have to be handled delicately,* he thought. *I need to use
her anger to get her to see the danger here.*

"What I did or did not—"

"Let me finish," he interrupted. "My only concern
here, as it has always been, is the company. You are

now the majority shareholder and chief executive and as such you must ask yourself whether or not you're allowing your personal feelings for this man, whatever they may be, to interfere with your judgment as to what's best for the company."

As quickly as it had come Margaret's anger left. "I understand what you're saying," she assured her father. "I don't think that now is a particularly good time for this discussion, but your point is well taken."

"Good. There'll be plenty of time to look into the affairs of your Mr. McCutcheon when, and if"—both Joseph and Margaret unconsciously turned their heads and looked through the window of Joseph's office to the dispensary—"he recovers."

"My life would be a great deal easier if you'd let me transfer him to the hospital in Eureka."

Bob Jenkens had helped Dr. Rose and Margaret move Claude from the dispensary to her home. They had loaded him into the company's ambulance for the two-block ride to the lovely two-story Victorian home Margaret had had built overlooking the Eel River. Rather than carry him up the stairs to one of the bedrooms on the second floor, they put him in the dining room, on a twin bed Drs. Jenkens and Rose brought down and set up. Margaret dismissed Rose as soon as Claude had been shifted from the ambulance gurney to the bed. Jenkens set up the stand that held the second unit of whole blood now being transfused into Claude. When they changed from plasma to whole blood at the dispensary, he had put a stitch in the cutdown performed by Dr. Rose and started the new IV inside Claude's right elbow.

"When the blood has been transfused just remove the needle and put on a Band-Aid," he told her. "I'm pretty sure that two units will be enough, together with the plasma Morley already gave him." He was momentarily distracted by the expression on Margaret's face as she looked down at Claude. *My God,* he thought, *whoever this man is, she's in love with him.* "I've got him loaded up with antibiotics and I'll run the blood I took before we began the transfusion through the hospital lab to see if I can get a better handle on the infection."

"How long will he be unconscious?"

"Hard to say. The shock of the wound itself, the effects of the infection and fever, the loss of a great deal of blood—all these things add up to one sick puppy. Fortunately, the antibiotics we have today are quite powerful. I am concerned about the fever, though, so you'll need to monitor it carefully. Call me at once, at home, if it spikes and stays up. If that happens he could get delirious." Jenkens smiled. "Another reason he should be in the hospital for a few days," he chided gently.

"Don't think I don't appreciate what you're doing," Margaret said. "I will remember your courtesy."

Jenkens put his hand up. "I'm so far behind in favors owed your father and this company that I'm just happy I can help. But I warn you—if his condition materially worsens, I *will* remove him from here and take him to the hospital."

"Fair enough, but I think he's going to be just fine."

"Frankly, my doctor's intuition tells me the same thing. My sense is that he's quite a tough character. Plus, he's obviously used to being treated this way."

"What do you mean?"

Jenkens put his index finger next to a scar on Claude's lower rib cage, on the right side. "My guess is that this is a bullet entry wound. You can feel, here, where it shattered the rib. I presume this scar"—he pointed to an obvious surgical scar five inches in length—"was the result. And on the back of his left thigh is another scar that reminds me of photos of shrapnel wounds I saw in medical school. Do you know if he was in the military?"

Margaret nodded. "Vietnam."

"That probably explains it. Well, like I said, he's obviously a tough man to have survived all of that. My guess is he'll survive this, too." Jenkens paused, framing his next words with care. "This wound was no accident. Somebody obviously meant to kill this man, which is why the authorities, reasonably enough, like to be notified when doctors treat gunshot and knife wounds. Are you quite certain that neither you nor he are in any, shall we say, present physical danger from the person who inflicted this wound?"

"Quite certain. Though I don't yet have all the facts I've been assured that the matter's been settled." *Not entirely a lie*, she thought. *I am certain that Claude would not have come here had his doing so meant I would be in danger.* "And remember, New London is a very small town." There was little likelihood that a stranger looking to harm someone in the confines of the company town would get very far unnoticed.

"Good. I'll be back tomorrow morning around seven. For the time being I'll plan to look in on him twice a day, morning and evening."

"What about pain medication?"

Jenkens shook his head. "I'll decide tomorrow. He's too weak right now to risk narcotics outside a hospital environment. I don't think he's going to wake up before morning anyway. If he should wake up you can give him aspirin with small amounts of water only." He smiled at Margaret and for an irrational instant wished he was the man lying unconscious before them. "I'll see you in the morning."

Margaret did not understand and could not fully explain her feelings as she prepared a light supper for herself. She constantly found herself looking from the kitchen to the dining room, unable to keep her eyes off Claude for more than a few minutes at a time. She became attuned to his breathing, to the rise and fall of his chest, the flutter of his pulse through the carotid artery at the base of his throat. She wanted to touch him, to feel the texture of his skin on her fingertips, and yet she could not. Her usual evening routine consisted of two or three hours of paperwork, typically grinding through daily mill productivity reports, inventory assessments, or timber cruise analyses. With Claude in her dining room, however, she found herself completely unable to concentrate. Finally, after realizing that she had been reading the same sentence for the past ten minutes, she rose from her sofa and walked into the dining room. Pulling up a chair, she sat next to Claude's cot.

"I've been so lonely," she said quietly, and she began, for the first time since she was a child, to cry.

CHAPTER 9

DAWN EASED INTO THE FOG-SHROUDED EEL RIVER VAL-
ley above New London like a sleepy cat. It dawdled,
stretched, groomed itself, and finally, grudgingly,
made a commitment. At five-thirty, objects in Margaret's dining room—an antique table and chairs, an
étagère imported from France—began to take shape,
forming slowly out of nothingness as the earth turned
eastward. Men and women throughout New London
stirred uneasily in their beds, sleepily unknowing
participants in a circadian dance that had begun tens
of thousands of years before they were born.

Margaret was dreaming when she woke up. She was
in an old-growth redwood grove, alone, standing over
a newly dug grave as dense, wet fog, hurried down
from the Gulf of Alaska by a dip in the jet stream,
swirled about her. It was a dream she had had many
times before. There was a feeling of incalculable loss,
grief, and longing as she stood silently in the grove,
not knowing whose grave she was attending. Waking
up in a chair she had dragged in from the living room

left her momentarily disoriented and she started up, looking anxiously about. Of an instant she saw Claude lying in front of her, awake and looking at her, and she fell to her knees next to him, weeping inconsolably. Puzzled, he reached out and carefully put his right hand on her head, trying to comfort her. She looked up at him.

"I love you," she whispered, feeling as though her heart were breaking. "I love you and I never thought I'd say that to anyone, ever."

The words struck Claude like a hammer blow. *I love you too,* he wanted to say, intended to say, but did not, could not. He looked carefully around the room. "Where am I?" he whispered.

"In my home," Margaret said, rising and wiping her cheeks with both hands. "I wouldn't let them take you to the hospital in Eureka." She saw that his face was flushed and his breathing rapid. "I'll get you some water."

"Good." Claude's whisper was barely audible. "I think I have a fever."

"Would you like an aspirin?" Margaret called from the kitchen where she was filling a glass at the sink. When she returned to the dining room she saw that Claude had closed his eyes. "Claude? I have your water."

When he did not respond she grew frightened and felt his face, at once shocked at how hot it felt to her touch. She immediately telephoned Dr. Jenkens at his home in Eureka.

"No, no, that's all right, I was already awake." Jenkens looked at his watch. It was not quite 6:00 A.M. "I'll be there as quickly as I can, but I've got to stop by the hospital pharmacy to pick up more antibiotics for him. In the meantime, you could give him a sponge bath using cold water to help bring down his temperature. That's right. Has he been awake at all?" Jenkens listened and nodded his head, hearing the tension and fear in Margaret's voice. "Try not to worry too much. Cool him down and I'll be along directly."

"Nice body."

Even unconscious, Claude's heavy musculature was impressive. Dr. Jenkens had just finished inserting an IV needle. He noted that his comment had caused Margaret, who was still holding the washcloth she had been using as a sponge, to blush. She immediately pulled the sheet up over his privates.

"Most people would be shocked," he said in a conversational tone while he worked on Claude, "at the humorous comments doctors and nurses make about their patients while they're anesthetized." He smiled at Margaret. "Actually, I think it's a perfectly natural way of dealing with the constant tension in operating and emergency rooms." He could see that Margaret was unimpressed with his banter and wished that he had the courage to tell her to lighten up. "The IV I just started is a saline solution with an antibiotic," he said. "I want to hit that infection hard, and a constant infusion like this is the best way. Meanwhile"—he looked sideways at her—"I want you to sponge him down with cold water every hour until that fever comes down."

Before Margaret could answer Claude opened his eyes.

"Well, well," Dr. Jenkens said, using his dulcet bedside voice, "look who's joined the party. How are you feeling?"

Claude nodded and licked his dry lips. "To tell you the truth, I could use a touch of water."

Margaret looked at Dr. Jenkens, who indicated his approval, and quickly brought Claude a glass from the kitchen. She knelt down and, when Claude lifted his head, tilted the glass to his lips. Unfortunately, in her haste to help him she tilted the glass too steeply. More water ran into his mouth than he was ready for and he choked and coughed as he aspirated a small amount. The coughing obviously irritated his wound, for he gasped with pain and grimaced.

"Goddamn, darlin'," he managed to say after several seconds, "let's take it a little slower next time."

Margaret, horrified that she had caused Claude additional pain, looked to Dr. Jenkens for help. He couldn't help smiling.

"Maybe a straw would be a little easier," he suggested. When she went into the kitchen to search for one he bent down next to Claude. "That's a pretty good scratch you've got there," he said quietly. "Would you mind my asking how you got it?"

Claude shook his head. "Not at all," he responded, his voice somewhat stronger. "I cut myself shaving."

Before Jenkens could say anything Margaret returned with a straw and helped Claude take several small sips.

"That's much better," he said, winking at Margaret. He looked at Jenkens. "I don't believe we've been introduced."

"Excuse me, I'm Dr. Jenkens. Miss Tikkanen asked me to consult on your case after your initial treatment by Dr. Rose."

Claude lifted his right hand. "Pleased to meet you, I'm sure. I feel like I've got a fever."

"That's what's sapping your energy right now. You've got a pretty good infection going from the wound, but my guess is that it'll respond quickly to the medication I've started." He nodded at the IV running into Claude's arm.

"How long do you think I'll be laid up?"

Jenkens shook his head. "Hard to say. The good news is that you're obviously blessed with what used to be called rude good health. The bad news is that you're not a kid anymore. If I may be so bold, how old are you?"

Claude smiled at Margaret. "Forty-five." He looked back at Jenkens. "How old are you?"

"I'm thirty-nine and you look better than I do. You must be living right." He laughed. "At least most of the time," he amended. "In any event, my guess is that you'll probably be able to move around on your own in a couple of days, but you're going to be pretty sore for some time."

"How many stitches did I take?"

"Actually, I stapled you, after putting in some forty subcutaneous stitches. No need to worry about the stitches, they'll dissolve as you heal. We'll take the staples out in ten days or so if everything goes well. Meantime, for today and tonight, I prescribe sleep, and plenty of it." He handed a small bottle of pills to Margaret. "These are codeine pills. You can give him two every four hours if he needs them. I'll be back this evening, say around seven or so, and we'll see how things are going then. Oh, and don't forget the sponge baths until the fever comes down. Every hour."

Margaret saw Dr. Jenkens to the door and stood for several minutes chatting with him about hospital matters. When she returned to the living room, she discovered Claude sitting at her desk in the living room. He had just hung up the telephone.

"I needed to make a couple of calls," he explained. "I hope you don't mind me using your phone without asking."

"Don't be ridiculous. Of course I don't mind. I just wish you had waited until I could have helped you. You might have fallen."

Claude stood, an involuntary grimace evidence that movement, even slow, careful movement, was painful. "I had this"—he nodded at the wheeled IV stand—"to use as support." He shuffled from the living room back to the bed in the dining room. "If you don't mind, I think I'll lie back down for a while." He smiled wanly. "I'm afraid I'm not going to be a very scintillating house guest for another day or two."

"Can I get you anything? Some water?"

"Believe it or not, I'm hungry. Some soup would be great. And a glass of milk."

Margaret went into the kitchen and found a can of condensed tomato soup. "Did you call your secretary?" she asked as she began heating the soup. "Is everything all right?"

"Marvelous," Claude answered noncommittally.

Margaret walked into the dining room with the milk. "Does your secretary know about your, um, accident?"

"No." Claude took the glass and struggled to sit up so he could drink. "I told her I was going to be incommunicado for several days. She will assume that means I am with a woman and she will further assume that that woman is you."

"I'm flattered." Margaret took the glass from Claude and hesitated before returning to the kitchen. She decided to be direct and blunt. "Are the police looking for you?"

"No, they're not. At least," he amended, "I doubt very seriously that they are." He looked carefully at Margaret. "I was cut doing a favor for an old friend."

"Must have been some friend."

Claude smiled. "She *is* a good friend, and the favor badly needed doing. Her daughter, a child of only fifteen, was being abused by a drug dealer, a man who was giving her drugs and sexually molesting her."

"The child's mother came to you instead of going to the police?"

"No, she came to me after the police told her, essentially, that it was her problem. I think I smell the soup burning."

Margaret jumped up and ran to the kitchen, emerging several minutes later with a bowl and a large spoon.

"I better help you with this," she said. "It's quite hot."

She placed an additional pillow under Claude's upper body and began to feed him, blowing carefully on each spoonful before placing it carefully between his lips. After a time he held up his hand, indicating that a short pause would be in order.

"You know," he said, choosing his words with care, "I think that it must be difficult for most people living in a closely knit, rural community like New London to appreciate how bad things have gotten in our major urban areas."

"We do get newspapers and television up here," Margaret pointed out. "And we do have our share of drug problems, even, surprisingly enough, in the tiny communities up and down the Eel River."

Claude shook his head. "Drugs and violence are merely symptoms of what I'm talking about—the breakdown of the basic social fabric, the unspoken contract that used to exist between the members of a community."

"Did you kill him?"

"You are direct, aren't you?" Claude nodded, pleased that now he did not have to worry about dancing around the issue. "I had not intended to, but, yes, I killed him. During the confrontation I got stupidly careless and he managed to pull a knife and cut me. I reacted without thinking."

"Are you at all concerned about the police?"

"Not really. I was careful to leave no evidence and my experience tells me that the police are notoriously poor in solving crimes, if you want to call what I did a crime, wherein the solution is not striking them in the face. They'll assume the instant case was one of a dispute arising out of a drug deal and after no more than a perfunctory investigation will be only too happy to leave it for more profitable matters. As far as they'll be concerned, he's just one more cockroach someone stepped on." He looked up at Margaret. "Thanks for the soup."

"Even if it wasn't quite up to the standards of Gianni Carlucci?"

"I trust you haven't forgotten what happened the last time we ate his food?"

Margaret leaned down and lightly brushed her lips across his. "I've thought of little else since then," she whispered.

Shadows moved slowly across the room and Margaret sat quietly by Claude's side until he fell asleep again.

A casual observer would readily have concluded that Joseph loved his office at the Northwestern Lumber Company as few other men or women ever loved anything, and yet as a matter of fact the office itself, as a physical *place,* meant little to him. His massive, handcrafted oak desk was impressive, as was the obviously expensive leather furniture, and yet in the old man's absence nothing about the room itself made it stand apart from countless other executive offices one might encounter. It was when Joseph *occupied* the room, as he had on a daily basis for almost fifty years, that it came alive. Oddly enough, only when Joseph sat at his desk did one really notice the double row of framed, 8½-by-11 black-and-white photographs on one wall. All were of various politicians posing with Joseph, some in New London, others in Sacramento and Washington, D.C. Strikingly, in all of the photographs the politicians, including several governors and a liberal sprinkling of assorted representatives and senators, were smiling into the camera lens, while Joseph's expression, if it could not be said to convey actual distaste, displayed no more than conscious neutrality. Disturbingly, upon reflection, the photographs, in each and every instance, clearly portrayed not equals, nor even expedient political allies, but rather master and man.

Since turning day-to-day operation of the company over to Margaret, Joseph had become increasingly contemplative, content to spend a good deal of his time in the office looking back on a life he considered more than well spent. The theft of the company documents and the later appearance of Claude Mc-Cutcheon represented both a unique threat and, he was coming to believe, a unique opportunity for both the company and his daughter. He was examining the matter in his head as one might examine a newly discovered piece of unexploded military ordnance when his telephone rang. He listened to the obviously muffled voice for several seconds, a cold smile beginning to play across his face.

"Mr. Norton, I presume?"

Bobby Norton laughed and took the handkerchief he thought would disguise his voice off the telephone. "You're a clever old man, I'll give you that, but I've got the documents."

"I suspected as much," Joseph said dryly, leaning back in his chair. He shifted his telephone from one hand to the other. "Although, to be honest, I would like to hear you read a passage or two now, to convince me." He listened and nodded his head as Bobby read from one of the entries. "I presume you are willing to return them for, what shall we call it, a finder's fee?"

"Not exactly. What I had in mind would be more like an auction."

"An auction presupposes not only more than one interested party, but also more than one interested party who can afford to bid."

"You can presuppose anything you want. I'll set everything up and call you back in a few days with the rules of the game. Oh, and one other thing."

"Yes?"

"The documents have been given to a third party for safekeeping."

"A third party?"

"That's right. Someone who's been told to make them public in the event anything happens to me before the auction is completed." Bobby chuckled. "I don't believe a man can be too careful after what happened to Myron Hirsch, you know what I'm saying?"

"I believe I do."

After Bobby broke the connection, Joseph sat quietly for several minutes before calling Margaret at her home.

"When did you get the call?"

Margaret reached across her father's desk and took a cigarette from the open pack sitting on his leather-bordered blotter pad.

"Just now," Joseph answered. "I called you immediately."

"And he called it an *auction?*" Margaret couldn't keep the amusement out of her voice.

"I fail to see the humor in it." Joseph looked as if he had smelled a bad odor. "Perhaps your involvement with Mr. McCutcheon has, is, affecting your judgment in this matter."

"My involvement, as you call it, with Claude McCutcheon is none of your affair." Margaret matched her father's steely-eyed glare unwaveringly. "I'm quite aware of the threat to the company that the documents pose, and want them back as much as you do. Keep in mind that at the moment neither one of us knows what, if any, involvement Mr. McCutcheon has in the matter. But if he's a threat to our interests I'll respond accordingly. In the meantime I suggest we concentrate on the one who claims to have the documents."

Joseph spread his hands placatingly. "Agreed," he said. "Now, as I indicated, Norton told me that he would be conducting an auction between ourselves and other parties with an interest in the documents."

"And he won't say who."

"That's correct. He said the purpose of this first call was merely to alert us to the fact that he had the documents and was fully aware of their significance. To prove he had them he read several passages. He said he would be getting back to me soon with the bidding rules."

"Sounds like he's thought the thing through."

Joseph nodded. "He finished our conversation by warning me that he had entrusted actual physical possession of the documents to a third party, with instructions to make them public should anything happen to him before a deal could be consummated."

"A third party?" Margaret unconsciously looked past Joseph's desk, through his office window, to her home. "What are your thoughts?" Margaret's voice was businesslike, her eyes once again on her father.

Joseph shrugged. "As regards Norton, for the present I have none. I am willing to believe that he has the documents and that he's given them to a third party. We have no choice but to wait for his next move. As to the unnamed third party, well, good fortune may have turned her face on us. Clearly Mr. McCutcheon is involved with Norton to one degree or another, as evidenced both by his actions in representing the man before the Berkeley police and in Mr. Norton's own words."

"Although he has denied to the media and others, including the police, that he represents Norton."

Joseph smiled. "Let's see what Mr. McCutcheon has to say. Recent events seem to me to be more than mere coincidence. One thing is certain. Mr. McCutcheon is clearly now greatly in our debt. Who knows? We may discover that he is a man with whom we can profitably do business. Has he told you yet how he came to be wounded?"

"Just now." Margaret relayed Claude's story.

"Do you believe him?"

Margaret shrugged. "Such a story coming from almost anybody else I could imagine, I'd say no, I wouldn't believe it. But coming from this man . . ." She paused and shrugged again. "There's something about him that tells me he isn't lying." *I don't believe, after Portland, that he would lie to me about something like this.*

Joseph pondered the desk in front of him. "You may not be entirely, shall we say, objective in the matter."

Objective? she wanted to shout. *How can I be objective about a man I've fallen in love with?* "I recognize that, and that's why I'm trying to keep an open mind. But there's no question he's an extraordinarily strong man, with values not unlike our own, so I can't dismiss his explanation out of hand."

"If he is telling the truth, such a man would . . ." Joseph paused again and looked closely at his daughter. "Such a man would fit in well here in New London."

He steepled his fingers in front of him. Outside a cold rain was falling and he could see, in the near distance beyond the corner of Mill 1, a lone worker with a long pike jumping from log to log across the huge mill pond. A single blast from the town's steam whistle sounded, and both Joseph and Margaret unconsciously checked their watches. Margaret made a mental note to postpone that afternoon's production meetings with the mill superintendents to early evening.

"Perhaps we've taken the wrong tack with Mr. McCutcheon," Joseph continued. "Perhaps such a man would respond more positively to some form of the truth."

"What are you talking about?" Margaret wasn't at all certain she liked what she was hearing.

"I would guess that Mr. McCutcheon's decision, admittedly under extreme duress, to seek aid from you would indicate that he has developed an, um, affection for you. Certainly a trust. Let's assume for the moment that Mr. McCutcheon *doesn't* have the documents, *isn't* in league with his erstwhile client. Regardless, he clearly does have some sort of influence with the elusive Mr. Norton and presumably could, if he so chose, intercede in some fashion on our behalf. It could be that if I were to meet with him now, alone, and be somewhat more forthcoming about our particular interest in him, perhaps letting him know that his cooperation would be appreciated and rewarded, he would be disposed to help us."

Also letting him know that I've been lying to him from the beginning, Margaret thought. *He'd never trust me again, not after Portland.* Outside, the rain intensified and the sky darkened enough for the town's automatic streetlights to begin coming on.

"No," she said, shaking her head. "We'll continue for the time being exactly as we began. I think it would be a mistake to change course until we know more precisely what threat, if any, he poses to the company." She took a deep breath and stood up. "I need to get some work done."

New London, California
Monday, March 28, 1994

"I can't say I'm surprised at how rapidly you've thrown off the infection, but I must say I'm pleased."

Dr. Jenkens stood beside the bed looking down at Claude. Margaret stood next to him.

"I owe it all to Nurse Tikkanen," Claude said.

"I think we can safely dispense with this now," he said, wrapping up the IV gear. He handed Margaret a bottle of pills. "I do want him to continue on antibiotics for another seven days, though, as a precaution. See that he takes one of these three times a day, at least as long as you're caring for him."

Margaret knew that the doctor was obliquely inquiring into how long Claude would be sharing her house. "Thank you," she said, taking the bottle, declining to provide the information he sought.

"And I think we can dispense with the sponge baths at this point as well," Jenkens added dryly. He had Claude sit up so he could remove the dressing to check the wound. "Everything looks fine," he said.

Margaret noted Claude's involuntary wince as Jenkins touched the skin adjacent to the wound and couldn't help reflecting upon and admiring how stoic Claude had been throughout the entire experience.

"Sorry," Jenkens added as he continued probing about the wound, "I'm afraid that this area will be quite tender for some time to come."

"When do you think I should be able to become more, um, active?"

"That depends entirely on your capacity to put up with discomfort. I don't want you doing much of anything for at least two or three more days; otherwise you run the risk of pulling the wound open, despite the staples. After that, I'd say several more days of very limited activity. You may move around cautiously on your own, but with a definitely limited range of motion. Then we'll take the staples out and you can gradually resume normal activites, although I'd advise against any strenuous athletic activity for probably three months." He smiled in an attempt to soften the impact of his words. "I know that seems like quite a while, but keep in mind that deep muscular trauma such as you've undergone takes a great deal of time for the body to repair. A great deal of time," he reiterated, emphasizing the point. "Even a body in such good shape as yours. In fact, athletic men and women often take longer to heal than their less fit counterparts because they push themselves too far too soon."

The doctor quickly re-dressed the wound. He listened to Claude's heart and lungs, took his blood pressure, temperature, and pulse readings, and recorded everything in the medical file he had begun after his first visit.

"I must warn you," he said jokingly to Claude, "that having your physician, as opposed to a practical nurse on staff, doing these rather mundane but essential tasks is expensive."

"Which reminds me," Claude interrupted, "I wanted to tell you that I would be taking care of your fee directly. That is, I see no need to get my insurance carrier involved in a private matter like this. If you would like, I'll have my secretary cut and mail a check immediately."

Margaret cleared her throat to speak, but before she could do so Jenkens raised his hand to interrupt her. "Actually," the doctor said, speaking directly to Margaret, "there will be no fee for my professional services." He turned to look at Claude. "You see, Mr. McCutcheon, you are a guest of the Northwestern Lumber Company." He turned back to Margaret. "Nothing more need be said on the matter of fees. Well, I'll drop in again in the morning. Assuming there are no complications like the infection coming back, after tomorrow morning I'll plan to visit just once a day. You can reach me, of course, at any time."

"I'm impressed," Claude told Margaret after Jenkens had left. "'A guest of the Northwestern Lumber Company,'" he repeated.

"Actually," Margaret corrected, "you're *my* guest,

not the company's, although there's no need to correct Dr. Jenkens."

"He already knows."

"What do you mean?"

"I mean," Claude said, "that Dr. Jenkens knows that you and I are lovers and he is, at least in a small way, quite jealous. I expect he's been carrying a torch for you for some time."

"Don't be ridiculous. How in the world could you possibly know such a thing?"

Claude reached out and put his hand on Margaret's left calf, and began stroking the back of her leg. "Because I'm a man, as is the good doctor. And you, Maggie dearest, well . . ." He paused, looking up into Margaret's eyes. "You know, I've been sleeping in your house for almost three days and you haven't yet kissed me." Margaret started to protest but Claude shook his head. "That wasn't a kiss, that was a peck. Kneel down here next to the bed and kiss me."

Redway, California
Monday, March 28, 1994

"It's me again."

Feather Rainforest's heart rate jumped as she recognized Bobby Norton's voice on the phone. "Yes?" was all she could think to reply.

"Are you getting your shit together like I told you? For the documents you want so bad?"

"Yes, but—"

"Listen, bitch," Bobby interrupted, "you either get some cash put together or you're fixin' to be on the outside looking in, you know what I'm saying?"

"How much do you want?" Feather was desperate to keep him talking while she tried to figure an angle.

"It ain't gonna work that way. You and the other

interested parties are going to bid. I'll tell you what everyone else is bidding and give you a chance to come up with more. Like an auction. I'm going to give you just a little more time to liquidate your assets, refinance your house, whatever. And look here— don't be thinking about trying anything stupid because I don't have the documents myself, you know what I'm saying? They're with a third party, safe and secure." He hung up the phone with a laugh.

Livid, environmental curses burst from Feather's throat as she slammed down the receiver. "He's going to hold an auction," she snarled to her son Wolf. "Norton's going to sell the documents to the highest bidder."

Wolf looked as shocked as his mother. "An auction?"

"That's right," Feather snarled. "A goddamned auction." She felt mad enought to spit.

Wolf thought for a moment. "What do we care what he plans to do?" He slammed a huge fist down onto the table in front of him. "We'll just have get to him first, before he has a chance to hold his auction."

Feather shook her head. "He's still one step ahead of us. He said that he doesn't have the documents personally, he's given them to someone else for safekeeping."

"The lawyer."

"McCutcheon. That's what I think." Feather nodded grimly. "God curse all lawyers to hell. They're worse than the worst possible criminals." She went to the rough, homemade dresser that stood against the wall and took out two pistols. Wolf's eyes lit up when she handed one to him. "Start packing. You and I are going south, to Berkeley, and we're going to get our hands on lawyer McCutcheon before anyone else does. We can stay with Jean-Luc."

Jean-Luc Dugre, an assistant professor of sociology at UC Berkeley, was a clandestine financial supporter of Feather and her small band. A veteran of Quebec's violent separatist movement, Jean-Luc had fled French Canada in the late 1960s in the wake of a terrorist bombing in Ottawa that he feared could be traced to him. Finding Berkeley and the university amenable to his intellectual theories of violent social change, he quickly became a popular lecturer on campus, so much so that his application for a tenure-track position in the sociology department was approved in record time. In addition to occasional financial contributions, Jean-Luc passed along any field intelligence he became privy to that might be of interest to Feather.

Wolf smiled. "Don't worry. If McCutcheon has the documents or knows where Norton is it won't take me long to beat it out of him."

Feather looked at her son, unable to resist the thought that none of this would be happening if only she and Wolf had gotten their hands on Myron Hirsch before he had managed to get himself murdered. "It better not," she muttered in response. "And what do you mean 'don't worry'? Do you think this is just a game?" Her voice rose with anger at Wolf's nonchalance. "If Joseph Tikkanen and that bitch of a daughter of his get those documents before we do, things around here will turn ugly in a hurry."

"Huh?"

Feather sighed. *He really is stupid,* she thought. *Just like his father.*

CHAPTER 10

Albany, California
Wednesday, March 30, 1994

THE HOUSE LOOKED GOOD TO HIM, DAMNED GOOD, although he was in quite a bit of discomfort by the time he got back to the Bay Area. The five-hour drive in the old Chevy pickup had taxed his limited physical reserves, but once inside, in his own house, amidst his own possessions, the pain began to ease. He automatically looked around for Thurman, even called his name once, before remembering.

"You dumb bastard," he said to himself, the words strangely comforting in the empty house.

In effect, those were the words Margaret had used when he told her that morning that he was returning to his home in Albany.

"You can't possibly be thinking about leaving," she had said. "The staples won't be removed for another four or five days at least."

"Don't worry," he had reassured her, "I'll come back when it's time for Jenkens to take them out. And anyway," he teased, "wouldn't it be nice if you came down and spent a little time at *my* house for a change?"

Though midafternoon, the house was cold after many days with no heat and he set about laying a fire, being careful to favor his left side as he bent and stooped with the firewood. As he was putting match to kindling a familiar feminine voice rang through the kitchen.

"Claude McCutcheon, where in the world have you been these last I-don't-know-how-many days? We've been worried sick about you."

"We?" Claude smiled at Sally Pinter, his next-door neighbor. "I doubt seriously that Bud was too terribly worried about me."

"Where have you been? And what's wrong with you?" She had seen the awkward way Claude stood up from the fireplace. She shifted her pelvis to the right and put her hands on her hips. "Everybody tells me I look exactly like Geena Davis when I stand like this."

"None of your business and I pulled a muscle. And who the hell is Geena Davis?" He winked at Sally. "Do you want a beer or what?"

"You don't think it's too early for a beer, do you?"

"Not for a couple of kids like us," Claude teased. "But you'd better remember to chew some gum or something before Bud comes home, otherwise he'll think you've been out running around." He got two Anchor Steams from the refrigerator and joined Sally at the kitchen table. "So, what have you and Bud been up to?"

"Not much." She made a face after sipping the dark, rich-tasting beer. "I don't know how you can drink this stuff. I like Coors Lite. Oh"—she waved her hand in sudden excitement—"I remember what I wanted to tell you." She put her beer bottle down and leaned toward Claude. "I think there's been somebody looking for you the last day or two."

"What are you talking about?"

"Course, Bud thinks I'm crazy, but I could swear that they've been watching this house, looking for you."

"Who has?" Claude thought immediately of the private detective, Rod Jackson, who had been working for Margaret. *But he shouldn't still be snooping around,* Claude thought, *unless Maggie hasn't told me something.*

"A man and a woman, driving a beat-up Ford van."

"What did they look like?"

"Like hippies." Sally saw the look of disbelief on Claude's face and she giggled. "Really," she continued, "they looked like hippies. The woman was heavyset and fortyish and the man was younger, much younger, in his early twenties I'd say. And they both had long, dark, greasy-looking hair."

"Anything else?" Claude could not help feeling skeptical.

"The man looked like an Indian."

"An Indian? From India?"

"No, an American Indian. At least he had his hair braided on both sides of his head like an old-time Indian. The woman looked like a regular, well, white woman." Sally wrinkled her nose as if certain they smelled bad as well. "But they both looked like hippies."

"How many times have you seen them?"

Sally held up two fingers. "Just twice. That's why Bud thought I was imagining things when I told him about it. But I'm sure they were looking at your house both times."

"Were they parked on the street when you saw them?"

"No, both times they were driving by, but real slow, like they were looking to see if anyone was home."

"I can't imagine who or what it might be," Claude mused. "The only thing I can think of is someone noticed that I was away and was casing the house for a possible break-in."

"That's what I thought so . . ." Sally produced a small slip of paper from her pocket. ". . . so I wrote the license number down."

"Hello, Bernie? Claude here. Not bad, how about you? Say listen, Bernie, do me a favor, will you? Yeah, right. I need an ID on a license plate. California. Got a pencil? It's HLM 421. I don't know. One of my neighbors spotted it cruising the street, looking at houses. Couple of times. A Ford van, old and beat-up. Man and a woman, greasy-looking, long hair. The woman's white, heavy, the man possibly Indian or Chicano. That's it. Yeah, probably nothing, but these are parlous times we live in. Call me when you get something. Yeah. Thanks, Bernie."

Claude broke the connection and dialed again. "It's me, Claude," he said when Margaret answered.

"I was worried," she said. "Did you get home all right?"

"Just fine. I've got to tell you, this old house looked mighty good when I got here."

"I can't believe I let you go. Even Dr. Jenkens thinks you should have stayed another day or two."

"Doctors get paid to think that way. Besides, if I'd stayed any longer your daddy would have come after me with a shotgun."

Margaret laughed. "Seriously, how are you? I was afraid that bouncing around in that old pickup of yours would reopen the wound."

"I'm fine. A little sore, maybe, but basically fine. I've got a nice fire going in the fireplace and I'm about to pour myself a little Irish whiskey. After that I'm going to take a hot sponge bath and go to bed and hopefully sleep for about twelve hours."

"Sounds nice."

"I'll be happy to repeat the entire procedure anytime you'd care to join me."

"I was thinking I might fly down day after tomorrow. Friday afternoon. Would that work out for you?"

"How long were you planning on staying?"

"Just the weekend. I need to be back by early Monday morning."

"Sounds great. Call me just before you take off and I'll pick you up at the airport."

There was a pause during which neither of them spoke.

"I miss you," Margaret finally murmured.

"I'll see you Friday," Claude said.

The telephone woke him. It had been a long night, full of dreams and visitations that left him disoriented and troubled. Once during the night he woke to find himself standing beside the futon, his Colt .45 automatic in his right hand, unsure where he was or, for a bad second or two, who he was. He rolled to his left on the futon to pick up the telephone receiver and cursed when the weight of his body came to bear on his wound. He gasped and blinked his eyes, waiting for the pain to subside, ignoring the insistent ringing of the phone. He sat up and reached carefully across his body with his right hand.

"Yeah?" he said, his voice heavy with sleep.

There was silence at the other end of the line, as if the caller were trying to figure out whether or not they had reached a wrong number.

"Mr. McCutcheon? Mr. Claude McCutcheon?" A woman's voice.

"That's correct. Who is this?"

"My name is Julia Morton, Mr. McCutcheon, although the name won't mean anything to you because we've never met."

"Well, Ms. Morton, what exactly can I do for you?"

"I was calling to make an appointment to meet with you, soon. I apologize for calling at home but your secretary was unsure exactly when you would be returning to your office." She paused for a second. "I hope I haven't called you at a bad time."

"No, I was about to get up in any event." Claude fumbled for the Rolex sitting on the small tonsu next to the futon. It was just after 9:00 A.M. "Unfortunately, I'm not accepting any new clients at the present time. If you could give me an idea of what sort of legal services you need I'm sure I could refer you to another attorney."

"Actually, I'm not interested in retaining your services as an attorney. Your name has come to our attention in a matter of utmost importance, and, well, I know I'm not being very clear about this—"

"A remarkable understatement," Claude interrupted, suddenly struck with a coincidental thought. *That's vaguely similar to what Margaret said when I asked her how she had gotten my name in the first place.*

". . . yes, thank you, as I was saying, I know I'm not being very articulate but if you would agree to meet with us we would take only a little of your time."

"We?"

"Yes, my companion and I traveled here together from Virginia."

"I thought I recognized the accent," Claude said, stifling a yawn. "Well, since you've come all the way from Virginia I suppose the least I can do is meet with you. Let's meet here, at my house, in an hour. Would that be convenient?"

"Yes, that would be fine."

"By the way, your companion wouldn't happen to be an Indian, would he, or, as they say in these politically correct days, a Native American?"

"Hardly." Julia laughed. "I think it's safe to presume that A. G.'s ethnic background is solidly Anglo-Saxon."

"A. G.?"

"Yes, A. G. Farrell of Hopewell, Virginia."

CHAPTER 11

CLAUDE McCUTCHEON WAS MOST DEFINITELY NOT what he had been expecting. From his many years of experience with lawyers both in Richmond and at the law school in Charlottesville, A. G. expected to meet a well-barbered, well-dressed, and probably overweight barrister. He certainly did not expect blue jeans and cowboy boots.

"Good morning," the man who opened the door said with a deeply resonant voice. "I'm Claude McCutcheon. You are Mr. Farrell, I presume? And Miss Morton?"

"That is correct, sir. I am indeed A. G. Farrell of Hopewell, Virginia." He took Claude's right hand in his own. "Folks just call me A. G."

"What does the A. G. stand for?" Claude asked, still gripping the old man's hand.

"Augustus George. May we come in, sir?"

"You may," Claude said, stepping back from the threshold and inviting them both in with a sweep of his arm. "I trust you're not selling Bibles? Or dispensations?"

A. G. laughed heartily. "Indeed not, sir, although one might say that the journey which led me here has been almost biblical in its breadth."

Claude led them into the kitchen. "I was just about to make some coffee. Have you had breakfast?"

"We have," A. G. assured him, "although a cup of coffee would be nice. I fear we have interfered with your morning routine."

"Not to worry. Have a seat at the table and I'll get the coffee going. Miss Morton . . ."

"Please, call me Julia."

Claude nodded. "And you both may call me Claude. Julia told me that my name had come up in a matter of some importance to you."

"It has," A. G. confirmed. He sat quietly for a moment, watching Claude go about the business of grinding coffee beans and folding a filter. "You have almost no accent but everything about you tells me that you are a gentleman of the South. Am I correct?"

"You are," Claude replied. "Born and raised in North Carolina, although I've lived in California for many years." He put out coffee mugs and broke a baguette into several sections. "You were about to tell me how my name came to your attention."

A. G. smiled. "Indeed I was." He paused while Claude poured the steaming coffee into their mugs. "However, if you would be so kind as to indulge an old man, before we discuss how I learned of your name, I need to tell you a story." He took a sip of his coffee. "An almost unbelievable story, actually, one that began almost fifty years ago in North Africa. The facts, as far as I've been able to piece them together, are these . . ."

Tunisia, North Africa
July 7, 1943

For almost two years the men of the Italian tank division Ariete (Ramshead) had crisscrossed North Africa between Tripoli and Tobruk. Once the pride of the Italian army, its men now traded pistols and ceremonial daggers for chickens and goats with the Bedouin who skulked on the fringes of the great armies massed in the desert. For the past two weeks company-sized tactical units of the division had engaged Montgomery's tank corps in a running retreat toward the coast. The division commander hoped that if he could reach the coast at Cape Bon the remnants of the Italian navy could evacuate his troops under cover of night. The glory years of the Ethiopian campaign and the Spanish Civil War were long since forgotten, and the division's officers and men concerned themselves now with survival, many reckoning that POW status would be far more likely to assure such survival than escaping North Africa merely to fight the Allies again on another, European, battlefield.

Lieutenant Angelo Tavecchio was a tired man. Not a professional soldier, he had been a businessman in Verona before the war. The proprietor of a small, family-owned manufacturing concern, he had been called into service during the Spanish Civil War, and because of his manufacturing and engineering background, he had been assigned to a mechanical maintenance combat support unit after receiving his commission as a lieutenant. Except for a seven-month period from late 1939 through April 1940, he had been out of Italy and separated from his family for five and a half years. Almost three years had been spent in Spain during the civil war, during which time no furloughs or leaves to return to Italy were granted. In fact, the expeditionary force's commanding officer had been told by Mussolini personally that if the Italians failed in their support of Franco they would be left to rot in Spain. Shortly after Germany's invasion of Poland in September 1939 Lieutenant Tavecchio, only seven short months back in Italy, had been reassigned to the Divisione Ariete and once again sent to war. The division went first to France, then the Yugoslavian front, and finally, to Libya in North Africa.

When radio communication with division headquarters was lost, Lieutenant Tavecchio ordered the destruction of all of his unit's equipment save five trucks to be used to transport the men and sufficient small arms to protect themselves from scavenging Bedouin. For two days the unit, 140 enlisted men, five noncommissioned officers, and himself, hid in a deep ravine, carefully camouflaging themselves and their trucks against air attack during the day while awaiting the arrival of British armored units to which they could surrender. On the third day the British came.

Responding to a lookout's cry Tavecchio scrambled up the side of the ravine and at once spotted a line of four tanks abreast moving toward him. He raised his arms and began waving a large white cloth. The tanks approached to within fifty feet before stopping. The tank closest to him bore an odd cargo which Tavecchio, in his somewhat dazed and dehydrated condition, had trouble understanding. Bound with ropes and strapped to the turret next to the main gun was a German officer whose uniform insignia identified him as a member of a Waffen SS division. As Tavecchio puzzled over the meaning of what he saw, a hatch on top of the turret popped open and a British sergeant appeared.

"Do you speak any English?"

"I speak some English," Tavecchio answered, still

clutching the white flag of surrender he had been waving. "I would like to offer the surrender of my men and myself."

"How many men do you have and where are they?" the tanker asked.

"There are one hundred and forty-one of us." Tavecchio waved in the direction of the ravine.

"Will you accept our surrender?"

"Do you have any transportation in the ravine?"

"Yes, we have five trucks."

"With enough fuel to reach Constantine, in Algeria?"

Tavecchio quickly calculated the distance in his head. "I believe so," he said, "but just barely."

"Good." The sergeant took off his leather tanker's helmet and vigorously scratched his head. "I want you to load your men onto their trucks and have them proceed to Constantine. They should be able to reach it in two or three days."

"Do you mean that you are not going to escort us there?" Tavecchio's tone of voice conveyed his surprise.

"That's right," the sergeant answered brusquely. "In case you missed it there's still a bloody war on. I can't spare anybody to shepherd a bunch of POWs back to Constantine. Your men are on their own."

"But what about the American P-38s? Won't they shoot at us if we don't have a British escort?"

"I'm going to radio back to Constantine that your men are on the way. Headquarters will let the Americans know. I suppose if they don't your men will get strafed." The sergeant shrugged. "Tough."

"Why do you keep speaking of my men?" Tavecchio asked. "Am I not to accompany them?"

"No." The sergeant lit a cigarette and shook his head. "See this kraut lieutenant? He's mounted on the front of this tank so that if any of his countrymen should decide to take a shot at us he'll get it first. Also, he speaks English, so if we come across any German units that want to surrender he can translate. You're going to ride on the front of one of the other tanks in the same capacity. If you're lucky, in a few days we'll send you off to Constantine none the worse for wear."

For three days Tavecchio bounced across North Africa, struggling ineffectively to spare his body from the ceaseless pounding it took atop the British Centurion tank as they roared across the desert scrubland of Tunisia. Several times during each day Tavecchio and the SS lieutenant were allowed to dismount and stretch as best they could. They were allowed no opportunity for fraternization, even during rest and refreshment stops. Although they encountered no Italian or German troops during Tavecchio's first two days, they knew that the British forces were closing in on remnants of Rommel's Afrika Korps and knew further that their captors had been advised that the Germans, if not the Italians, were still engaging the Allies in running battles as they retreated toward the North African coast. At midmorning of the fourth day the small unit of four tanks ground to a halt near a large wadi. As the tank crews disembarked to relieve themselves, the two prisoners were untied and allowed to dismount.

"We're going to be engaging a German tank force within the next hour," the British sergeant told them. "Since there's no way either of you would survive I'm going to release you here. You are to proceed, on foot, to Constantine, which is pretty much due west of here, where you will turn yourselves in to the Allied authorities. The entire area is saturated with Allied forces and I'm told that large numbers of POWs are being moved west, so I believe your chances are actually quite good of making it alive."

Before either man could respond, the British sergeant gave each of them a canteen of water. Without saying another word the British tankers remounted their tracked vehicles and roared out of the wadi. Tavecchio turned to the German officer.

"Perhaps we should speak English since my German is quite poor. I remember the British sergeant saying that you spoke it for them."

The SS lieutenant stared at him coldly. "Yes, I speak English."

"Good." Tavecchio smiled to show his comradely intentions. "I think we should start walking. The sooner we reach the road to Constantine the better our chances of being picked up by Allied soldiers and escorted. I am anxious to be reunited with my men."

The two men walked the better part of that day, taking frequent rest breaks due to the oppressive heat. Because the German was so uncommunicative they spoke little, mostly Tavecchio suggesting breaks and his fellow traveler agreeing with a nod of his head. Late that afternoon, during one of their rest breaks, Tavecchio turned to his taciturn companion.

"Based on what the British sergeant told us I believe that we are no more than two or three hours from the road to Constantine. I suggest that we keep walking in an effort to reach it before nightfall."

When the German responded with his perfunctory nod of the head, Tavecchio rose and prepared to resume the march. He had a sense now that he was going to make it, was going to be safely reunited with his men. He was confident that for him the war was over, even as he knew it was over for his nation and their few allies. Placing his hands on the small of his back, he stretched backwards as he heard the SS lieutenant get up behind him. He felt a rock-hard arm thrown across his neck, jerking him backwards as, simultaneously, a knife blade pierced his lower back and right kidney, only to be quickly withdrawn and thrust into his heart. Death was a starburst, a supernova, and Tavecchio was returned to the soil from which his ancestors had sprung.

"That is one hell of a story," Claude said. It was almost lunchtime. A. G. had just finished telling him how the unnamed POW, after taking Tavecchio's identity, had escaped from Camp Lee. "I assume by your very presence here, this morning, that you weren't able to apprehend the escaped POW, whoever he was."

"That is correct," A. G. answered. "We found not another trace of the man, nor, interestingly enough, of the truck he stole in Indianola, Mississippi."

"Perhaps he drove it all the way into Mexico," Claude said with a shrug. He smiled at Julia. "Stranger things have happened."

"In this instance," A. G. said ruefully, *"nothing* can be said to be too strange. In any event, neither the FBI nor countless local law-enforcement agencies were able to turn up a single clue as to the man's whereabouts or activities after Indianola. My own supposition is that he drove nonstop to a Texas border town, probably Laredo, sold or abandoned the truck, and crossed forthwith into Mexico. He was probably already in Mexico, or close to it, by the time the Indianola murder was discovered." A. G. paused and looked at his watch. "Would you be so kind as to allow me to take you to lunch? Old age has left me with a touch of diabetes and I find that controlling it is facilitated by adherence to a regular dining timetable."

"By all means," Claude said. "What sort of lunch did you have in mind? We could have Chinese, Thai, Indian, Lebanese, or American Southwestern, all within just a few blocks of here."

"A hamburger would be fine with me," Julia volunteered.

Claude sighed and winked at A. G. "It's clear to me that a liberal arts education is not what it used to be," he said. "Fortunately, the Lebanese place I was thinking of serves a workmanlike cheeseburger. You and I," he said pointedly to A. G., "will be free to sample more creative dishes."

At the Café Sport Claude introduced A. G. and Julia to Meyer Levine, proprietor of the tiny restaurant.

"Meyer, Mr. Farrell and I desire something light yet memorable. We place ourselves in your hands. Miss Morton"—Claude nodded in Julia's direction—"on the other hand, would like a hamburger."

"Um-hmm." Meyer's response was noncommittal. He had known Claude for too long to risk being drawn into uncharted waters. "What would you like to drink?"

"I'll just have a cup of coffee," A. G. said. "Black. I believe Miss Morton would like a Coca-Cola." He pronounced it "Co-Cola."

"I'll have a latte," Claude said. He smiled at A. G. and Julia as Meyer left their table and walked into the kitchen. "Meyer's family emigrated from Beirut in the late 1960s when he was a teenager. They're dyed-in-the-wool socialists and, in addition to being excellent cooks and bakers, have a demonstrated love for anarchy. In fact, Meyer still believes Nicola Sacco and Bartolomeo Vanzetti were innocent victims of a corrupt capitalist system." Claude paused as Meyer's young daughter Rosa, named after the notorious German socialist agitator Rosa Luxemburg, brought them their coffees.

"Thanks, darling," he said. "Shouldn't you be in school today?"

She tossed her head. "We're striking today in solidarity with our brothers and sisters in South Africa."

"I fail to see the connection between cutting classes at Berkeley High and the fight against apartheid," Claude said sorrowfully, "but I'm sure there must be one."

Like her father, Rosa knew better than to be drawn into dialectical combat with Claude McCutcheon. She smiled at Julia. "I'll bring your Coke in just a second."

"Who were Sacco and Vanzetti?" Julia asked after Rosa left the table.

"Revisionist historians the world over are crying even as we speak," Claude said. "If nobody remembers Sacco and Vanzetti then it doesn't matter who they were, does it?" He turned to A. G. "Tell me more about your friend Spencer Lee. Was his political career everything he wanted it to be?"

"Spencer was killed by a drunk driver in 1952," A. G. said, his voice betraying none of the sadness he still felt after more than forty years. "At the time of his death he was the Richmond, Virginia, district attorney and well on his way to the governor's mansion." A. G. looked carefully at Claude. "It's funny you should ask about him because had he lived I might not be sitting here talking to you."

"Why is that?"

"When Spencer was killed I lost the one source of influence I had. Without Spencer and his political connections few people in Washington were interested in bringing my escapee and murderer to justice."

"So without your friend Spencer backing you they were able to dismiss you as some sort of crank, a small-town southern sheriff chasing a bogeyman."

"Exactly. You must remember, the country wanted to put the war and all of its memories behind it.

Communism was the big threat, and the Korean War confirmed all our worst fears about Soviet intentions to dominate the world. West Germany was now our ally and the former officers of the Wehrmacht, excluding only the war criminals we had imprisoned or executed after the trials at Nuremburg, were essential to the industrial and social rebirth of the country. The State Department in particular was hostile in the extreme to my efforts to uncover the identity of the man who escaped from the POW compound at Camp, now Fort, Lee."

"Lunch is served," Meyer said, wheeling a serving cart to their table. He presented Julia with a hamburger on a toasted French roll. For A. G. and Claude there were salads with feta cheese and ripe Greek olives together with steaming bowls of lentil soup and a plate of pita bread. "Enjoy."

"How long were you sheriff of Prince George County?" Claude asked after they had eaten in silence for several minutes.

"Until 1950. I decided to return to Charlottesville and the University of Virginia for graduate work and stayed for close to forty years."

"A. G. was the head of the philosophy department when he had to take mandatory retirement in 1975," Julia interjected. "He became a professor emeritus the following year and has continued to teach every year."

"And what exactly is your connection to A. G.?" Claude asked pleasantly.

Julia drew herself up in her chair. "We're lovers."

A. G. sighed and laid his spoon down on the table. "I confess I do not share this modern tendency toward complete honesty with regard to relationships between men and women," he said to Claude. "I fear that perhaps more is lost than gained when all is revealed to a salaciously curious world."

"I could not agree more," Claude interjected. *There's obviously some juice left in the old bull,* he thought admiringly.

"Miss Morton and I, as she has indicated, are more than just professor and student, although I hasten to note that our relationship was not consummated until after she graduated from the university." He smiled and took her hand. "I must confess in all honesty, however, that I was mightily tempted." He released her hand and looked back at Claude. "In any event, until Spencer's death I remained quite active in my efforts to identify and bring to justice the murderer."

"How so?"

"Well, for one thing I had a pretty good idea of what our man looked like. The FBI lent me one of their top artists and with the help of the Italian POWs who had accompanied the man to Camp Lee from North Africa we were able to develop an excellent composite drawing—a drawing I was able to take to Italy and demonstrate conclusively that the POW identified as Angelo Tavecchio was in fact someone else." A. G. smiled ruefully. "Unfortunately, that was all I was able to demonstrate."

"Go on," Claude said, eager to hear the rest of the story.

Verona, Italy
May 1946

Getting to postwar Italy had not been as difficult as A. G. had anticipated. As soon as commercial air travel between the United States and Italy resumed in April of 1946 he had, with Spencer's assistance, obtained one of the first tourist visas issued by the new government in Rome.

"What in the world do you expect to accomplish in Italy?" Spencer asked him.

"I intend to confirm that the man who escaped from the POW compound at Camp Lee was not Lieutenant Angelo Tavecchio," A. G. replied patiently. "The first step in identifying any man is determining who he *isn't*. In this case I'm betting that the man we want isn't, or wasn't, Tavecchio."

"Why not let me get someone at the War Department to check it out for you? They could work through the Italian government."

A. G. shook his head. "You know as well as I do that no one in Washington gives a damn about this matter. If they had, we might have captured him back in 1943 while he was still trying to make good his escape. So now, even if you could talk someone in Washington into doing you a favor it'll be done in a half-assed way, which is worse than not doing it at all. No, I want to speak directly with Tavecchio's family myself. That's the only way I'll know that the information I get is both accurate and useful."

The visit with the Tavecchio family in Verona was a wrenching affair for all concerned. Tavecchio's wife, having been informed by the Italian military of her husband's capture in May of 1943, had not heard a word from or about him since his purported escape from the POW compound at Camp Lee. Through an interpreter, a Catholic priest educated in the United States at Notre Dame, A. G. explained that he was trying to determine the true identity of the POW identified by the Allies in North Africa as Angelo Tavecchio. When shown the composite drawing that had been prepared in Virginia Tavecchio's wife became hysterical, and had to be restrained by relatives from injuring herself. Later, after a doctor had sedated the woman, Tavecchio's brother showed A. G. a photograph of Angelo taken in 1939. The two images could hardly have been more dissimilar. Angelo Tavecchio was of classically Mediterranean stock, short and darkly complexioned.

"I believe your brother died in North Africa and that his identity was assumed by this man." A. G. gestured toward the composite drawing he had shown the Tavecchio family. "Why, I do not know. But I am certain that your brother never reached America."

Tavecchio's brother spoke for several minutes with A. G.'s interpreter, Father Antonio.

"He tells me that the sergeant of Lieutenant Tavecchio's unit, a man who was captured at the same time as Tavecchio, has remained in touch with them. He has been, how do you call it, separated from the military and is living in the city of Padua." The priest paused, sensing A. G.'s excitement. "It is only a short drive from here."

Strict postwar gasoline rationing kept the road from Verona to Padua mostly free of automobiles. A. G. let Father Antonio drive the Daimler-Benz he had hired out in Rome, a decision he silently questioned as the priest barreled down the highway like a man with the devil on his heels. In Padua one of the local *carabinieri* directed them to the home of Sergeant Benito Bassino. A. G. stood silently as Father Antonio spoke with the ex-sergeant. In the background, over Bassino's shoulder, A. G. could see a woman nervously watching the goings-on. After what seemed like the longest time Bassino nodded, said *si* three times in rapid succession for emphasis, and invited them into his home. Through Antonio he told A. G. the story of their surrender in North Africa.

"A German?" A. G. was excited by Bassino's revelation that a German officer had been with the British unit to whom the Italians had surrendered "He's sure it was a German?"

Antonio nodded. "He says the uniform was unmistakably of the German Afrika Korps. He thinks it was a Waffen SS unit. The British explained that the German was kept with them to act as a translator should they run into any German units that wished to surrender. He said that they would keep Lieutenant Tavecchio for the same reason and that in three or four days they would be released to the prisoner-of-war authorities in Constantine."

"And he's certain that he never saw Lieutenant Tavecchio again? Not at the Allied POW compound in Constantine?"

Bassino shook his head emphatically. "No, never," he said through the priest. "All of the men were disturbed when the British kept Lieutenant Tavecchio and sent us on to Constantine without him. We were worried that if the British got into a battle Lieutenant Tavecchio might be killed, but of course there was nothing we could do."

Scarcely daring to breathe A. G. handed the composite drawing to Bassino. "Was this the German?"

Bassino examined the drawing carefully and handed it back to A. G. "It is impossible to tell. He was covered with dust and dirt and in any event I was not allowed to get very close to the man." He sensed A. G.'s keen disappointment. "I am sorry."

Albany, California
Thursday, March 31, 1994

"And the trail ended in Italy?"

The three of them had finished eating and Claude signaled Meyer for the check.

"So it might have appeared. And, in fact, *did* appear to all of official Washington."

"But not to you."

A. G. shook his head. "Not to me. Remember, I was pretty sure even before I went to Italy that the escapee was not Angelo Tavecchio nor any other Italian for that matter. A. G., I said to myself when I got back to Hopewell, "think for a moment. How would an officer in the German army have gotten from Mexico or Central or South America back to Europe? Well, sir"—A. G. smiled at Claude—"there were only two possibilities: by air or by sea. Although commercial flights were available throughout the war between a number of South American cities and both Spain and Portugal, my gut feeling was that my man had returned to Germany via submarine. I'll take that." He reached for the bill that Meyer was about to present to Claude. After paying with cash he turned again to Claude. "If the Third Reich was anything, it was organized. I knew that the extraction off the Mexican or South American coast via submarine of an army officer would have certainly been the subject of one or more reports, and would therefore have been memorialized in the permanent records of the German Admiralty. I was certain that if I could get my hands on those records I'd have my man."

Claude smiled admiringly. "You were like a bulldog on this case, weren't you?"

"I can almost understand the first murder—the yard bull. Not forgive it, mind you, not ignore it, but perhaps understand the motivation." A. G.'s face turned somber, and Claude saw more than a hint of the strength that kept the old man vigorous in what was now his ninth decade. "But that farmer in Mississippi"—he shook his head—"that was nothing more than the cold-blooded eradication of an innocent man. And he wasn't the last."

"What do you mean?"

"It took me almost three years but finally, with Spencer's help, I got to Germany. Europe, and Germany in particular, was still digging itself out of the catastrophe that was the world war, and the absolute last thing the U.S. military wanted to do, much less the State Department, was to provide cooperation and assistance in hunting down an unknown Wehrmacht officer who allegedly escaped from a POW camp while disguised as an Italian officer. Keep in mind, by 1949 we were well into the postwar era of strained relations with our ex-friends the Soviets, and our once-bitter enemies, the Germans, were now suddenly our allies. An ally who did not look kindly, you can well imagine, on what was perceived as little more than a witch hunt on my part."

Claude rose from the table. "Why don't we continue this conversation at my office? It's just a couple of blocks from here and we can be more comfortable there."

"If you're sure we're not taking too much of your time," A. G. said.

"Not at all. I want to hear the rest of the story." *Not to mention why you're telling it to me in the first place.*

At the office he introduced A. G. and Julia to Emma.

"What's wrong with your shoulder?" she demanded, sotto voce, after politely greeting his two guests. "Why are you walking funny?"

"It's nothing," Claude demurred. "I just pulled a muscle working out."

Bonn, West Germany
April 1949

"I have found a man who might be able to help us."

A. G., thoroughly chilled, sat outside a *Gasthaus* in the heart of Bonn. Almost exactly three years had passed since the trail had ended in Italy, three years that A. G. had used to badger and harass various officials in Washington to permit him to take the hunt directly to postwar West Germany. Finally, with constant albeit grudging assistance from Spencer Lee and his political contacts, A. G. had made it to Bonn. Across the small table sat Willi Czernic, a displaced Hungarian who, with the help of the International Red Cross, had managed to obtain a West German passport. Willi, a child of twelve when Hitler invaded his country, was a survivor first and foremost. A natural linguist, he spoke five European languages as well as fluent English, a talent that had gotten him a job as a translator with the Red Cross after the war. When A. G. arrived in Germany, a State Department functionary, after happily explaining that no funds were authorized with which to provide him a translator at taxpayer expense, referred him to the Red Cross Displaced Persons office where, with his own money, he might obtain such assistance. That unwitting referral turned out to be a godsend, for it led him to Willi Czernic.

"How can he help us?" A. G. asked.

"He works in the ministry which oversees all of the Admiralty records from the war."

A. G. allowed himself the hint of a smile. Willi Czernic had been a godsend indeed. Recognizing at once that A. G. would receive no official assistance, the young man proved to be, in the old military parlance, a scrounger extraordinaire. Except in this case he scrounged information like a career supply sergeant in almost any army in the world could scrounge otherwise unavailable equipment or materiel. While A. G. continued to push unyielding bureaucrats and department heads, Willi talked to file clerks and bought secretaries drinks after work. He knew better than to waste time talking to supervisors or to *Herr Doktors* or to anyone who might have been an officer in the defunct army of the Third Reich.

"How much does he want?"

"He will ask a great deal but will settle for something reasonable under the circumstances." What

Willi omitted to say but which both he and A. G. understood was: *With me doing the negotiating he will settle for something reasonable.*

"He understands exactly what I want?"

"I have explained in detail, with dates and circumstances as you have provided."

"And he believes he can find the appropriate file or files?"

"He agreed that such an event, the repatriation of an officer from Mexico or South America by a U-boat, a man who had escaped from an American POW camp by masquerading as an Italian national, would almost certainly have been recorded in the files of the Admiralty. Such a one might even have been decorated by the High Command. It is inconceivable that a record of the escape does not exist somewhere."

"Why is your man willing to help me when so many others are not? It can't be just the money."

"The money is important. I would not underestimate its value in these times to such a man. But you are right, it is not the sole motivation. He was an enlisted man, a common soldier during the war. He has no love for the officer class. Soldiers in the German army were shot for things like insubordination. Perhaps now he sees a way to settle a score or two." Willi shrugged. "And make some money doing so."

Two days later Willi reported that the man had the information they sought.

"He will provide us with the actual file documents relating to the man you seek."

"When?" A. G.'s heart was pounding with excitement. *Almost six years, you bastard,* he thought, *but now I've got you.*

"Tonight. I am to meet him, alone, pay him the money we agreed upon, and he will give me the file."

"I'll go with you."

Willi shook his head. "No. He is quite nervous, and said that I must come alone."

"I don't like it," A. G. said. "Why would he mind if I were there? After all, I'm the one paying him for this information."

"He knows you are an American policeman." Willi tried to suppress a smile. "Every official in Bonn knows of you and your 'mission.' For what he is doing, stealing a confidential file, he would at least be fired from his job and probably be criminally prosecuted. Some very powerful people, both German and American, have let it be known that the government has no interest in assisting you, and so he is taking no small risk. He does not want anyone, you included, to know his identity."

"Why does he trust you?"

"He and I are much alike. We both must remain here after you leave to return to America. He knows I cannot reveal his identity without risking my own."

"You'll be careful?"

Willi nodded and took one of A. G.'s cigarettes. "There is nothing to fear from this man." He looked at his watch. It was almost 6:00 P.M. "In less than four hours you will have the identity of the murderer." He inhaled and savored the rich taste of the American bright-leaf tobacco. "I will miss your cigarettes."

"Are you Mr. A. G. Farrell?"

A. G. jerked awake. He had been dozing in the lobby of his hotel, waiting for the return of Willi Czernic. He looked at his watch and then up at the two men who had awakened him. It was almost midnight. "Yes." He nodded, running a hand over his face and standing up. "I'm A. G. Farrell. Is something wrong?"

"Mr. Farrell, my name is Tower Hale. I'm with the American embassy here in Bonn. This gentleman"— a nod in the direction of his companion—"is Herr Bauer. Herr Bauer is with the West German Federal police." Neither man offered to shake hands with A. G. "I'm afraid that Herr Bauer wants to talk to you about a murder, two murders actually, that took place earlier this evening."

Albany, California
March 31, 1994

"I never saw him again." A. G. shook his head, lost for a second in a dark memory. "Alive, that is. Both Willi Czernic and the informant were found dead, murdered."

"And no file," Claude supposed.

"No file. However"—A. G. held up one finger—"the murderer's bullet did not kill Willi instantly. He was able, before he died, to scratch out two words on a piece of paper he had in his hands. 'Not German.'"

"Not German?" Claude repeated. "What does that mean?"

"I believe Willi was trying to tell me that the man I was seeking was not a German national after all. Presumably, before they were shot, Willi learned that the POW, although certainly an officer in the German army, was not himself a German."

"Not much help," Claude observed.

"Indeed not, and certainly not worth two more lives."

"And that was the end of the trail?"

"Pretty much. Oh, I went back in '56 and then again in '65, even hired a German private investigator to do a little snooping, but the trail had gone cold. Any military records had long since been cleaned out by the killer or his friends. I gave up on hoping to find him long ago."

A pause ensued, during which Claude knew that A. G. wanted him to ask the question.

"I'll bite," Claude dutifully responded. "Why are you here, now?"

A. G.'s pale blue eyes never wavered. "Robert Norton."

CHAPTER 12

"ROBERT NORTON?" THE NAME WAS SO UNEXPECTED, SO startling, that it took Claude a second to place it. "You mean Bobby Norton?" He still couldn't believe that A. G. was referring to the man he, Claude, knew as Bobby Norton. "Over in Richmond? California?"

"The same, I believe." A. G. was bemused by Claude's momentary confusion.

"How in the world would you know Bobby Norton?"

"Actually, we don't know him. About two weeks ago I got a telephone call at my home in Charlottesville. The caller was your Mr. Norton."

"He's not *my* Mr. Norton," Claude interjected. "Contrary to popular opinion, I neither represent nor know the present whereabouts of the gentleman."

"I'm sorry to hear that. In any event, as I was saying, Mr. Norton recently got in touch with me to advise me that he was in possession of certain documents in which I would most certainly be interested."

"Myron Hirsch!"

"I beg your pardon?"

"Myron Hirsch," Claude repeated. "Or, more properly, the recently deceased Myron Hirsch. A couple of weeks ago Bobby Norton was a clandestine witness to the murder of a local attorney by the name of Myron Hirsch. Hirsch was a radical environmentalist, almost a lunatic on the subject. In any event, Norton was visiting him at his office on a houseboat at the Berkeley marina when a visitor, still unidentified, shows up. Before the visitor gets to his office, Hirsch sends Norton upstairs to wait until the business with the anonymous visitor is concluded. The business was concluded with Hirsch's murder. A bullet in the heart. With Bobby Norton still hiding upstairs, the murderer was surprised by the harbormaster. After conking the harbormaster on the head the murderer left the scene. Bobby came downstairs, found Hirsch dead and the harbormaster unconscious, and called the police."

"Was he able to provide a description of the killer to the police?" Julia asked, looking at A. G. with wide eyes.

Claude shook his head. "No, he never saw the man. The shooting took him by surprise and the last thing he wanted to do was confront the killer. In any event, the police took him downtown and questioned him, coming up with little of value to their investigation. I've known Bobby for a good many years, which is presumably why he called me from the Berkeley police station. I went down just in time to walk him out the front door. The police believed his story that he was hiding upstairs when the crime was committed."

"How does this tie in to Mr. Norton's call to me?" A. G. asked.

"I suspected almost from the get-go that Bobby hadn't come entirely clean with either the police or me. Oh, I believed him when he said he had no idea who the killer was. It was that something else seemed to be hovering just out of range, if you know what I mean. Anyway, a day or two later he tells me that in fact there was something else. After the killer had fled, and sometime before the police arrived, Bobby found some sort of document in or around Hirsch's desk. Presumably the document the killer was looking for. I advised Bobby to take whatever he had to the police but he wasn't interested in any gratuitous advice. He told me that he thought the document had a certain intrinsic value, not his words, from which he could profit." Claude paused and looked carefully at his two guests. "It doesn't take a degree from Stanford to figure out that, incredible as it may seem, the document Bobby made away with contains both your name"—Claude pointed a finger at A. G.—"and the name of your nemesis, the escaped POW." He shook his head, astounded at the very thought. "Have you got words?"

"I don't," A. G. answered. "In any event, Mr. Norton's instructions to me were to come out here and get in touch with you, his attorney." A. G. held up a hand to forestall Claude's by now oft-repeated denial of representation. "I know, I know, you say you're not his attorney. I am merely echoing Mr. Norton's words." He paused and thought for a moment. "Are the police aware that Mr. Norton is in possession of the document or documents in question?"

Claude shook his head. "I don't believe so. Bobby told me in confidence, and other than you and Miss Morton I have told no one. Again, I advised him as strongly as I could to go to the police but . . ." He shrugged. "Bobby seems determined to profit from Myron Hirsch's bad fortune."

"Have you any idea how the deceased Mr. Hirsch obtained possession of the documents?"

"None whatever. And I'll tell you something else."

Claude leaned forward in his chair for emphasis. "I have no interest in getting involved in this matter. I know that you badly want to nail the man you've been chasing for almost fifty years, but take my word for it, doing business with Bobby Norton, which is to say buying twice-stolen documents, will only lead to heartbreak." Claude sat back in his chair and softened his demeanor. "Bobby's not a bad guy, he's just stupid. If I were you I would presume that he's also contacted everyone else he thinks might have an interest in obtaining the documents."

"If he has contacted the man I am seeking, his life is in grave danger."

"I already told him that whoever killed Hirsch would be only too happy to kill him for the documents."

"Yes, but he has no idea, not really. At the risk of sounding melodramatic, the man I have described to you, despite the fact that he is now an old man, is a battle-hardened soldier, a man to whom life means virtually nothing." A. G. leaned forward and his face hardened as he described the man in almost demonic terms. "If I am correct he has murdered, with his own hands, at least five people, six if he killed the attorney in Berkeley, in order to keep his true identity hidden. Your acquaintance, Mr. Norton, and anyone else"— A. G. looked pointedly at Claude—"who may be involved with him as an accomplice, is in mortal danger, believe me."

A palpable tension had come into the room, which Claude tried instinctively to lessen. "Sort of like Bambi meets Godzilla?" When A. G. failed to smile in response Claude shrugged. "What can I tell you? Bobby's on his own and, if you choose to do business with him, so are you. Out of curiosity, though, nothing more, how much are you prepared to pay him for the documents?"

"Nothing. I have, as you might imagine given my

career in academia, little in the way of liquid assets. I intend to appeal to Mr. Norton's sense of justice."

"Such an appeal is unlikely to have much of an effect on Mr. Norton," Claude observed dryly. "Nonetheless, I wish you"—he smiled at A. G. and Julia—"both of you, well."

"Have you any idea how we might contact Mr. Norton?" A. G. asked as he rose from his seat.

"None whatever. In fact, I discouraged him, as best I could, from getting in touch with me again unless it was to ask me to accompany him to the Berkeley police."

"I see. In the event he does call you would you be so kind as to tell him that I am in town and awaiting word from him?"

"Where are you staying?"

"Miss Morton and I have taken rooms at a small establishment in El Cerrito, the Arlington Arms."

Claude nodded. The Arlington Arms was an old-fashioned residence hotel that catered to a primarily well-to-do elderly trade. Its owner was a friend and occasional client of Claude's. "I know it well. Are your rooms comfortable?"

"Quite. May I assume that you will inform Mr. Norton of our whereabouts?"

"If, and that's a big if, he should get in touch with me, you may so assume." He escorted the old man and the young woman out past Emma's desk. "If you and Miss Morton are free this Saturday evening, I would be pleased to have you over to my house for supper."

A. G. bowed slightly from the waist, a courtly gesture from a bygone era. "We would be most delighted." He took Julia's hand and placed it in the crook of his right arm. "Come, my dear."

"What a delightful gentleman," Emma said after they left. "And such a beautiful granddaughter."

Claude laughed and pumped his right hand and

forearm back and forth in a copulatory motion. "Think again," he said.

Emma's eyes narrowed and she looked at Claude with overt suspicion. "I don't believe it. He seems like a perfect southern gentleman."

"What's that got to do with it? Look at me. *I'm* a perfect southern gentleman myself."

Emma held up a hand. "I don't want to hear it. What you *can* tell me is what they want. Are they going to be clients?"

Claude shook his head. "No, they're not. I'll tell you the whole story sometime when we've got an hour or two to spare, but the short of it is that that nitwit Bobby Norton is trying to sell a document or documents he found in Myron Hirsch's office after the murder. Apparently the information contained in the said documents is of interest to the old man, A. G. Farrell, and Bobby contacted him, telling him to get in touch with me."

Emma's eyebrows rose in surprise. "Do you think Bobby had anything to do with Hirsch's murder?"

"No, I believe his story that he was just in the right place at the wrong time. Or the wrong place at the right time. Whichever. In any event, in true street-rat fashion, that certainly didn't stop him from snooping around Hirsch's office afterwards, before the police got there, in the hope of profiting from Hirsch's misfortune."

"Do the police know about the documents he's trying to sell?"

"I doubt it, though clearly Jim Malone over at the Berkeley PD smells something fishy. He's been trying to run Bobby down so he can talk to him about it."

Claude bent down to pick up a piece of paper that had fallen off Emma's desk and grimaced with pain.

"What's wrong with your left side, and don't tell me nothing because I can see that something's wrong. Have you hurt yourself?"

"No, I just pulled a muscle while I was up north last week."

"And that reminds me, what exactly were you doing last week? First Portland with that woman and then all last week at her home in Humboldt County." Emma paused and examined her boss in a new light. "Are you and she getting serious?"

Claude started to frame a sarcastic reply and then changed his mind. "Maybe. Any messages?"

"Two. Lieutenant Beck called this morning and said you could return the call at your convenience. And Rocky Martinez called. He didn't say what he wanted. You don't suppose he's in any trouble, do you?"

Claude shook his head. "No." He looked at his watch. It was just after three o'clock. "See if you can get Beck on the line for me." He had just settled in behind his desk when Emma buzzed him.

"Lieutenant Beck on line three."

He picked up the receiver. "Bernie, Claude here. Emma said you'd called earlier."

"Yeah, Claude, I got a make on that license plate you gave me yesterday."

"Great, Bernie, I appreciate it. Anything of interest?"

"Possibly. The plate and the van it's attached to belong to a professor out at Cal, a man by the name of Jean-Luc Dugre."

"Dugre," Claude murmured. "The name sounds familiar but I can't quite put my finger on it."

"It should sound familiar. Dugre is one of Berkeley's resident radicals, a sociology professor who still preaches the virtues of violent revolution."

"Bingo." Claude laughed. "I knew I'd heard the name. He's a French Canadian, fled to Cal's welcoming arms after a bombing in Ottawa, if I remember correctly. Jerry Brown, Governor Moonbeam, protected him from extradition at one point or another, didn't he?"

"That's the one," Bernie confirmed. "You'll recall that when Brown was governor damn near any felon on the run could count on refuge in California. All they had to do was hire a radical lawyer and claim political or cultural persecution. The lawyer would hire a press agent and the governor's office would 'study' the matter while fending off extradition by whoever was trying to make the collar. In the case of Dugre the Canadians saw the handwriting on the wall and gave up when UC granted him fast-track tenure." Bernie laughed, a not entirely humorous sound. "I'm thinking they figured that with a governor like Brown California deserved to have a man like Dugre teaching its youth."

"Any idea who the Indian and the white woman driving Dugre's van might be?"

"None. I had a little time on my hands yesterday afternoon, though, so I checked with the State Department of Investigation in Sacramento. I was curious what they might have in their intelligence files on Dugre."

"And?"

"Not much. One thing of interest, though. A year or two ago Dugre got into a public pissing contest with a radical environmental lawyer in Berkeley."

"Let me guess. Myron Hirsch."

"Bingo. SDI's files don't have a lot of information on the matter, but it looks like Hirsch filed a civil suit against Dugre alleging some sort of libel or slander. The suit was eventually dropped and SDI's files show no other relationship between the two. As I said, there's not much there to go on. It could be just a coincidence. Both Dugre and Hirsch are the kind of fringe lunatics that attract each other."

"Except that Hirsch ends up getting murdered and

an unattractive couple driving a van registered to Dugre are seen casing my house. And the only possible connection between these otherwise unrelated events is a local dimwit by the name of Bobby Norton."

"Exactly."

"Do you think Dugre had something to do with Hirsch's murder?" Claude asked.

"Stranger things have happened. The world of radical politics seldom allows for alternative points of view." Bernie paused for a moment. "Have you seen or heard from Bobby Norton lately?" he asked carefully.

"No. The last time I talked to him, well over a week ago, I advised him to stay in touch with Jim Malone over at the Berkeley PD. I haven't heard from him since."

"Speaking of Jim Malone, I've already told him about the couple in Dugre's van casing your house. I hope you don't have a problem with that."

"Not at all. What was his reaction?"

"He was somewhat surprised. Like us he surmised that the only possible connection was the elusive Mr. Norton. He asked me what I knew about your relationship with Bobby."

"What'd you tell him?"

"The truth. That as far as I was concerned you were not Bobby's lawyer and you had no idea what involvement Bobby might have had in the murder. I told him that any interest anyone like Dugre or the mystery couple driving his van might have in you could probably be attributed to Bobby's claiming you're his attorney. If someone was trying to get their hands on Bobby it would only be natural that they would keep an eye on you."

"Was he going to roust Dugre over the van?"

"Given the political realities of enforcing the law in

Berkeley, I doubt it, at least not right away. Dugre has about fifteen so-called public-interest lawyers working for him at any given time and they would doubtless raise holy hell if Malone presumed to even question him." Bernie chuckled. "No, I think he'll wait until he has something more to go on before butting heads with Dugre."

"You wouldn't happen to know Dugre's home address, would you?"

Bernie was suddenly cautious. "What have you got in mind, Claude?"

"Malone may have political considerations to deal with but I don't. I don't like people cruising my neighborhood, upsetting my *wa*. I'm thinking I might pay him a little visit, give him a chance to satisfy his curiosity."

"I don't think that's a very wise thing to do. Keep in mind, he may have had something to do with Hirsch's murder. My advice is to stay away from him, let Malone handle things."

"Yeah, I suppose you're right. Listen, Bernie, thanks for the information." After hanging up Claude walked out to Emma's desk. "Your niece hasn't flunked out of Cal yet, has she?"

Emma snorted with contempt at Claude's impertinent question. Her niece, an honor student throughout high school in Albany's public schools, was a junior at Cal, majoring in molecular biology.

"Good," Claude continued. He wrote Jean-Luc Dugre's name on a piece of scratch paper and handed it to Emma. "This bozo is an assistant professor in the sociology department. Ask her to get me his teaching schedule as well as his office hours on campus, would you?"

Emma fingered the paper with Dugre's name and eyed Claude suspiciously. "Why are you suddenly interested in someone who teaches at Cal?"

"The frustration of having to deal with recalcitrant employees such as yourself has convinced me to give up the wearying practice of law and return to school. I plan to take a degree in sociology and become a county welfare worker." Claude turned to return to his office before Emma could think of something suitably insolent to say. "Oh," he called over his shoulder, "and see if you can locate his home address in the Berkeley phone book. If not, see if your niece can weasel it out of someone in his department at the school."

"Hello, Rocky? It's me, Claude."

Claude lay reclined on his futon, the past week's editions of the daily *San Francisco Chronicle* spread about him. He listened as his friend expressed concern.

"Not to worry, Rocky, everything is just fine." He paused and took a sip out of a bottle of Anchor Steam. "Yeah, the friend I told you about took good care of me. *Si,* a woman. I'll come by for dinner early next week and give you all the details. Oh, and Rocky, I owe you for this. Big-time."

After hanging up, Claude again read the small news item that had appeared in the back pages of the Sunday, March 23, edition of the *Chronicle,* two days after he and Rocky had visited with Ralph Martini.

PAROLED FELON FOUND DEAD

Police reported finding the body of a man identified as Ralph Martini in an apartment on 28th Street in the City yesterday afternoon. A police spokesman, while refusing to divulge any details, stated that Mr. Martini's death appeared to be drug-related. Mr. Martini was convicted of selling drugs to minors in 1988 and was on parole at the time of his death.

He thought briefly about calling Claire Williams and asking about her daughter but decided against it. *Best not,* he thought. *Perhaps next week.* He pushed the papers off the futon and turned off the light.

Claude sipped a cup of coffee as he sat in the truck, looking at Jean-Luc Dugre's house in north Berkeley, just south of the campus. Emma had found his address in the telephone directory, and on the way over that morning Claude had stopped at the Orleans Parish Café for a cup of coffee and chicory and a beignet to go. The beignet had disappeared in two bites and the bitterly strong coffee put him in a bad frame of mind. He got out of the truck and crossed the street, truculently hitching up his jeans after knocking loudly on the front door.

A thin, balding man with the remaining few wisps of his hair tied back in a ridiculous-looking ponytail answered the door. He eyed Claude suspiciously. "What do you want?" he asked, his Quebecois accent identifying him as clearly as a name tag would have done.

"I understand you've been looking for me," Claude responded.

"Who are you?" Jean-Luc demanded in a surprisingly high-pitched voice.

"The name's McCutcheon," Claude said, thrusting his head forward aggressively. He pointed a finger at the academician. "You're Jean-Luc Dugre and I want to know why the sudden interest in me."

"I have no idea what you're talking about," Dugre replied, starting to close the door in Claude's face.

Claude's hand slammed into the door, knocking it from the slighter man's grasp. He took a quick step into the house and grabbed the front of Dugre's shirt, gathering it into his fist. "I don't like people cruising my neighborhood, stalking my house," he snarled, shaking the now-frightened professor, "and I want to know what the fuck's going on."

"Let him go," a voice to Claude's right ordered.

Claude looked and saw the Native American youth with long, greasy hair braided on either side described by his neighbor Sally Pinter. Pointing a short-barreled pistol at him.

"I said let him go," the young man rumbled, thumbing back the pistol's hammer.

"Put that gun away, you fool," Jean-Luc, still in Claude's grasp, hissed. He turned his attention back to Claude. "Let me go and get out of here," he ordered, slapping Claude's hand away from his shirt front.

Claude looked from Dugre to Wolf, contempt on his face. "I don't know who you are, but don't ever let me catch you without that gun."

He looked back to Dugre. "This isn't over," he said, turning abruptly to leave the house.

CHAPTER 13

MARGARET SAW CLAUDE WAITING ON THE TARMAC AT Oakland's general aviation facility as she smoothly taxied the Learjet to a halt.

"Nice landing," Claude said as she walked up to greet him. "Did you do it or did your pilot?"

"Never trust a man with something you can do yourself," she teased in return. "You looked good standing there."

Claude smiled. "You look like the bee's knees yourself."

Margaret nodded her head in acknowledgment, frankly pleased to receive his compliments. She was wearing brown corduroy slacks and a silk blouse under a dark green leather jacket.

"I see you took my advice," Claude added, nodding toward the smallish leather overnight bag she was carrying.

"You said it would be a casual weekend," Margaret replied. "You'd better not tell me now that we're going to the opera."

Claude laughed. "I let my season subscription lapse just last month, otherwise tonight we'd be sitting in a box at the War Memorial Opera House with the Gettys and the rest of San Francisco society, such as it is." He took the bag and opened his truck's passenger door for her. "No, I thought we'd spend a quiet weekend at Casa McCutcheon, discussing art history and drinking beer."

"How's your side?" Margaret asked as they merged onto the freeway.

"Better, much better." He flexed and stretched, wincing a little as the sides of the wound pulled against the staples. "Still a little sore, but healing nicely. Thanks to you and the good Doctor Jenkens."

"Any repercussions?"

"You mean from the authorities? The police?"

Margaret nodded.

Claude shook his head. "And I don't expect any, either. Case closed. How's the lumber business these days?"

"Boring." Margaret smiled at the candid truthfulness of her answer. "My thoughts are elsewhere. How about you? How's the lawyering business?"

"Good question. If truth be told I don't do enough to have an opinion."

"And yet you maintain an office and a secretary." *How do you make a living, even a modest one?* Margaret wondered. Not even Rod Jackson, the ex-FBI private detective she had hired, had been able to tell her that. Although, in the presence of her father, she maintained that Claude knew nothing of Robert Norton's possession and intent to sell the documents, she could not purge her mind of nagging doubt. And far too much time had been allowed to pass—now she had to find out precisely what, if anything, Claude knew, and enlist his cooperation in retrieving the documents. And, if he wouldn't help her voluntarily she would use the knowledge of the murder he committed to force the issue, regardless of the impact on their relationship.

She thought of little else on the short flight down to the Bay Area.

Claude shrugged. "Everybody needs an office for one thing or another, don't you know. As for Emma, well, I do just enough work to pay the rent and her salary. Besides, she believes that I couldn't possibly survive without her sage counsel, so I probably couldn't get rid of her if I wanted to."

Margaret fell silent as Claude deftly maneuvered the truck through traffic. After several more miles they exited the freeway and began winding slowly through Albany's residential neighborhoods.

"Here we are."

Claude turned the engine off and Margaret suddenly found herself nervous at the prospect of spending the weekend with Claude in his home. Not being with him per se, but being with him on his home turf. It represented a loss of control and she felt at once vulnerable and a little frightened. At that instant she did not feel at all like the CEO of a very large natural resources enterprise, nor a graduate of both Stanford and Harvard. The arrhythmic ticking of the truck's engine as it cooled seemed to fill the cab.

"Shall we go in?" Claude asked quietly, taking her left hand in both of his.

Saturday morning took the Bay Area somewhat by surprise. A heavy fog had eased in through the Golden Gate sometime after midnight, catching the weather forecasters, even as late as the eleven o'clock news, completely unawares. It settled confidently onto the land, rolling quietly past the Marin headlands. It consumed Alcatraz Island and continued eastward, gradually obscuring Berkeley, Albany, and El Cerrito, pausing only briefly before stalking up the East Bay hills like a wave of heavily viscous motor oil pushed along by an invisible and irresistible trowel. Towering redwood and blue gum eucalyptus alike resisted futilely, only to disappear each in its turn as the conscienceless fog advanced. In the houses, toward dawn, men and women burrowed unconsciously deeper into their bedding as the temperature dropped a number of degrees lower than they had been led to expect when they retired the previous night. Most people rose later than normal, even for a Saturday, because of the sun's inability to pierce the veil that enshrouded the neighborhoods.

In Berkeley, in a large house three blocks from the campus, Wolf Walks Far stirred inside a filthy sleeping bag. He slept on the floor in a room he was sharing with his mother, Feather, in the home of Jean-Luc Dugre. His bladder was uncomfortably full but he was loath to leave the warmth of the stained and discolored bag he had slept in since he was twelve. As he became more fully awake he could hear, several rooms away, the sound of Jean-Luc engaging in intercourse with one of his students, an eighteen-year-old freshperson from San Diego. Although reported to the Faculty Senate on numerous occasions over the years for engaging in sexual relationships with his female students, Dugre defiantly refused to modify his behavior, knowing, as a veteran educator, that ethics, particularly sexual ethics, was not, despite high-minded pronouncements from administrators to the contrary, a matter with which tenured faculty members need overly concern themselves. For its part, the Faculty Senate, many of whose members had, at one time or another, traded grades for sex, was perfectly willing not to pursue the matter, preferring to think of the young female students involved as willing participants.

Wolf smiled as Jean-Luc's young student made high-pitched sounds she believed would indicate pleasure. Unable to delay longer, he rose from the

floor and walked quietly to the bathroom down the
hall, scratching his behind rather indelicately. Standing over the commode, he was shocked to see a thick,
yellowish discharge oozing from his penis. As he
began to make water the sudden fiery pain confirmed
his first guess as to the pathological origin of the
discharge.

"Goddammit," he cursed as he forced himself to
finish urinating. It was his third dose of gonorrhea in
as many months, this time had from a young woman
who had drifted through Humboldt County the prior
week on her way from Los Angeles, where she had
been supporting herself turning tricks and selling
crack cocaine, to Seattle, where she had heard the
authorities took a more lenient, Christian attitude
toward working women. She and Wolf met at a bar in
Redway that catered to the so-called counterculture
crowd and had fornicated out behind the bar's kitch-
en, on the ground next to the dumpster, observed with
much amusement and critical comment by the bar's
two Mexican busboys. Neither she nor Wolf thought
to ask the other's name. Afterwards, as Wolf was
zipping up his jeans, she made the mistake of asking
him for money. Suddenly enraged, he immediately hit
her in the face with his right fist, closing her left eye
and opening a ragged cut above her eyebrow. The
strength of the blow knocked her to the ground, where
she lay stunned and semiconscious. The two busboys,
even though well aware of Wolf's reputation as a *loco
hombre,* were nonetheless shocked at his explosive
violence, and immediately retreated behind the
dumpster, prepared to run if he came after them. Wolf
kicked the inert young woman several times, cursing
her, before snatching her purse from the ground. He
rifled through it, taking all of her cash and a glass vial
containing several rocks of crack cocaine. He threw
the now-empty purse into the dumpster, kicked the
woman once more almost as an afterthought, and

then, to the vast relief of the busboys, walked content-edly off into the night.

Standing over Jean-Luc's toilet with a fire running through his genitals he cursed her anew, wishing fervently he had done more than merely blacken her eye and cut her face.

"What's wrong with you?"

Feather looked at her son. Although used to his sullen demeanor she could tell that something out of the ordinary was troubling him. The two were seated at a small table in a coffee shop not far from Jean-Luc's house.

"Nothing." Wolf stirred sugar into his coffee and refused to meet his mother's eyes.

"Don't lie to me. There's too much at stake right now for you to be holding something back on me."

"I've got a dose of the clap, okay? It's nothing to worry about. Jean-Luc gave me the name of a free medical clinic here in Berkeley. I'll go down after breakfast and get a shot."

Feather shook her head, a disgusted look on her face. "Haven't I told you countless times to be care-ful? To use a condom?"

"Have you figured out how we're going to get our hands on Norton?" he asked, indicating with a look that his medical problems were of no concern to anyone but himself. "If McCutcheon doesn't have the documents?"

"Yes, I have," Feather responded. "We're going to have someone take us right to him."

"How are we going to do that?"

Feather sighed. There was no question that her son had unfortunately inherited his intellectual capacity, such as it was, from his father. "Think," she admon-ished. "Norton is staying underground, keeping him-self hidden until he can make a deal with the highest bidder. He may or may not have given the documents to the lawyer. If he hasn't, McCutcheon will almost certainly know his whereabouts. Don't you see?" When no response was forthcoming she sighed again, unable to avoid comparisons between her son and the brilliant young college anarchists with whom she had associated when she was Wolf's age. "Why do you think we've been watching McCutcheon's house so carefully the last few days?"

Wolf looked up from his coffee. "So we know when he's home."

Feather shook her head. "That's only partly right. We're also interested in who else might be hiding there—Norton, for example. We haven't seen any sign of him so we're going to pay a visit to Mc-Cutcheon and convince him either to give us the documents if he has them, or to take us to his client if he doesn't."

Wolf smiled for the first time that morning. This was something he could understand, something he could get his thick hands around. He wished he had at least pistol-whipped the attorney when he had confronted him at Dugre's house earlier, and the thought of another opportunity pleased him. "When?"

"Tomorrow morning. Sunday. Before dawn, while all the neighbors are still asleep. McCutcheon will give us the documents or take us to Norton and Norton will give them to us. I don't care which. In either case, by tomorrow evening we'll be back in Redway."

"I understand that you're visiting from Virginia."

Margaret was sitting with A. G. Farrell and Julia in Claude's living room.

"That is correct," A. G. answered in his courtly manner. "Has Mr. McCutcheon, Claude, told you much about our journey?"

"Actually, Claude tells me very little about his private affairs," Margaret answered. She turned and smiled at Julia. "Tell me," she asked the young woman, "are all southern gentlemen so, um, discreet?"

Before Julia could frame a response, Claude entered the room carrying a lacquered tray on which rested three glasses of wine. He presented the wine, with a flourish, first to his guests and then to Margaret.

"Although certainly the odds are greater than for any other region of the country," Claude said, winking at A. G., "one should never assume a priori that all southern men are gentlemen. Having said that, if you will excuse me, I must return to the kitchen and the final preparations for our dinner."

"Let me rephrase my question," Margaret said to Julia. "Is it fair to say, in your experience, that all southern *men* are so secretive?"

"Some are and some aren't," Julia answered rather lamely.

A. G. laughed and the sound brought a scarlet flush of embarrassment to her cheeks and throat. "A Solomon-like response, my dear," he said. He turned to address Margaret. "Miss Morton and I have come to your great state seeking information regarding a certain criminal. I was given to believe that Mr. McCutcheon, Claude, could be of some assistance to me in the matter."

"A criminal? How interesting. Are you, or perhaps I should say, *were* you, a policeman?"

"I was," A. G. said with a smile. "A long time ago I served for some years as the sheriff of Prince George County, in the Commonwealth of Virginia. The particular matter that brought Claude and I together concerns an as-yet unidentified man who committed a crime in my county during the Second World War."

"It must have been quite a crime if you're still actively pursuing the matter."

"As Miss Morton might say"—he paused and smiled at his young lover—"yes and no. The only crimes committed in Prince George County by the man I seek were the rather mundane ones of breaking and entering together with petty larceny. However, subsequent to his leaving my jurisdiction he committed several murders, the circumstances of which continue to attract my interest."

"Dinner is served," Claude called from the kitchen.

"And the man you've been seeking all these years has never been identified?" Margaret asked after they had arranged themselves at table.

"That is correct, although it would be inaccurate to say that I've been actively seeking him for almost fifty years. Not too many years after the war I declined to stand for reelection as sheriff. There was little likelihood that I would ever be able to positively identify, much less assist in the actual apprehension of the man who had become my *bête noire,* and the intellectual challenges of the day-to-day work of law enforcement in a rural southern county were, charitably speaking, minimal at best. So . . ." He paused and took a sip of wine. He reached out and patted Margaret's hand. "Excuse me for changing the subject for a moment, my dear, but"—he turned and looked at Claude—"this is a delightful wine."

Claude acknowledged the compliment and held up the bottle so A. G. could see the label.

"Semper Virens." The old man read the label aloud. "Always living."

Claude indicated Margaret with a nod of his head. "You might be interested to know that Miss Tikkanen has an interest in the winery."

"An interest?" Julia couldn't help asking.

Margaret smiled. "It's a small family business, a labor of love. We struggle to break even." She looked at A. G. "I will pass on your kind compliment to our winemaker. She will be quite pleased to hear it, I'm sure. Now then, you were telling me about not running for reelection as sheriff."

"Ah, yes," A. G. smiled at the memory. "To paraphrase another southern politician, 'If drafted I shall not run, if elected, I will not serve.' However, in point of fact there was nothing but countywide relief when I declared my intention to give up the post. Though I like to believe I was well liked and had done a creditable job, most folks believed I would be better suited in another occupation. Unfortunately, there was no other occupation at hand so I returned to Charlottesville and the halls of academe. And, since all policemen are thumbnail philosophers at heart, I naturally gravitated to that particular discipline."

"A. G. was the head of the philosophy department when he retired," Julia said.

"Indeed," A. G. confirmed. "Professor Farrell. An exalted title for a salt-of-the-earth son of Prince George County, Virginia." He looked speculatively at Claude. "I suspect, Mr. McCutcheon, that you and I are, though separated by a generation, quite alike. I would guess that you, like I, were the first member of your family to attend college, much less law school."

Claude nodded affirmatively.

"And I would further guess that, notwithstanding your university education and urban lifestyle, you remain very much a man of the rural South, a man whose values belong more, shall we say, to the nineteenth century than those of the present."

"What sort of values would you attribute to such a man?" Margaret asked, eyeing Claude speculatively.

"First and foremost a fierce independence," A. G. answered without hesitation. "For example, I doubt that you"—looking at Claude—"have ever worked for another law firm, have you?"

"That's correct," Claude said.

"Furthermore," A. G. continued speaking to Margaret, "since military service is a strong tradition throughout the South, I would say that it is almost a certainty that Mr. McCutcheon is a veteran." He looked at Claude, a look of amusement on his face. "You don't mind us talking about you this way, do you? In the third person?"

"Not at all."

"Good." A. G. looked back at Margaret. "I would even go so far as to guess that your Mr. McCutcheon enlisted in one of the services, probably the army, as soon as he graduated from high school, that he did not attend to his undergraduate education until after being discharged." He turned to Claude. "How am I doing?"

"My life is obviously an open book," Claude answered wryly.

"Not really," A. G. said. "What I've been talking about are the obvious things, assumptions any astute observer with a knowledge of the cultural underpinnings of the old, the rural South, might make. And interestingly, such assumptions probably no longer hold true, for, as with the rest of the country, the South has changed dramatically in the past twenty years."

"For the worse," Claude observed quietly.

"Most assuredly," A. G. agreed.

"How so?" Margaret asked.

"Through a pervasive and debilitating loss of that sense of independence I spoke of a moment ago." A. G. toyed with his wineglass. "There remains, not just in the South but throughout our society, little of what I like to think of as the true spirit of America, the spirit of self-reliance, of responsibility for not only one's successes but one's failures as well. You, Mr. McCutcheon, are of probably the last generation of southerners to be imbued with the notion that your progress through life, the ease or difficulty with which you negotiate your 'four score and ten,' is dependent entirely upon your own initiative."

"I cannot imagine that your views were popular among your fellow academics at the University of Virginia," Margaret said with a smile. "How in the world did you ever obtain tenure?"

"I seriously doubt it could be done today. Fortunately, I began my academic career at a time when the truth was honored above all things." A. G. paused and chuckled. "I fear the lunatics are now in charge of the asylum."

"Well, *I'm* in charge of this asylum," Claude said, "and I say that it's time for dessert." He rose and began clearing the dinner plates and salad bowls from the table.

"Is there no hope for the future?" Margaret asked A. G.

"I admit to a certain degree of pessimism, but there is always hope. Indeed, one might, with some authority, suggest that only a hopeful man, even if perhaps foolishly so, would have persevered as long as I have in my search for the escaped POW." He smiled. "Who knows what facts those two traits, hope and perseverance, may yet turn up?"

CHAPTER 14

"GET UP!"

Feather Rainforest reached out her meaty right hand and shook the formless mass of her son, Wolf Walks Far. Wolf grumbled an unintelligible reply and burrowed deeper into his sleeping bag.

"Get up, I said," Feather hissed, her voice thick with the anger she still felt at what she had witnessed the night before.

"What the fuck?" Wolf, his long, greasy hair matted around his face, emerged from his bag. "I'm up," he mumbled, reaching down into his sleeping bag. He brought out the pistol he slept with and flourished it triumphantly.

Feather shook her head with disgust. "The plan has changed," she said, spitting the words out. "The Tikkanen woman is staying with him this weekend."

"What?" Wolf, still heavy with sleep, couldn't understand what his mother was saying.

"I said, the Tikkanen bitch is staying with him."

Feather had watched the house for an hour last night and had been shocked almost speechless when she saw Margaret Tikkanen, together with Claude, bidding their dinner guests good-night on the front porch. She watched for another hour until all the lights went out and then returned to Jean-Luc Dugre's house to think through the implications of what she had seen.

"I said, get up."

Wolf was still in his sleeping bag and it was all Feather could do not to kick him.

"What do we do now?" Wolf asked, struggling into his filthy blue jeans. "Take them both?"

"No, not right away." Feather had been thinking and she decided that trying to surprise the two of them in Claude's home was too risky. Plus, what she had seen of Claude during her covert observations since he had returned home made her vaguely uneasy. He did not seem anything like the bookish lawyer she had been anticipating. "He may have already given her the documents," she said, more to herself than to Wolf, "but knowing the Tikkanens I doubt she would still be there, sharing his bed, if she already had what she had come for."

"So what do we do?" Wolf asked impatiently, growing tired of trying to follow his mother's train of thought.

"Watch and follow. He probably isn't so stupid as to keep the documents at his house so if he's going to give them to her today they'll have to go get them first. And when they do . . ." Feather's voice trailed off as she pictured the coming confrontation with Margaret and Claude. Her face twisted with hate and Wolf, seeing it, smiled.

Claude was shaving when the telephone rang. He had gotten up some twenty minutes earlier and, after turning on the coffeemaker, had jumped immediately into the tub. Margaret remained in the warm nest the two of them had created under his down comforter, content to drowse until the coffee was ready. His instinctive reaction when he heard the first ring of the telephone was to look at the big Rolex on his left wrist. It was not quite nine o'clock. He thrust his head out the bathroom door and saw that Margaret was still on the futon.

"Would you mind answering that?"

The comforter shifted around and Margaret's head appeared. She yawned and stuck her tongue out at Claude.

"The phone," he repeated, nodding toward the telephone sitting on the floor next to the futon. "I've got shaving cream on my face."

An arm snaked out from beneath the comforter and picked up the telephone.

"Hello?" She made a face at Claude.

There was a slight pause on the line as if the caller had not expected a woman to answer the phone. "Yeah, is Claude there?"

"He's, um, not free to come to the telephone just this minute. May I tell him who's calling?"

"Tell him Bobby Norton wants to talk to him. And that it's important."

Margaret caught her breath when Bobby identified himself. "Just a moment." She put one hand over the receiver. "It's for you," she called out. "Someone by the name of Bobby Norton. He says it's important."

Claude walked out of the bathroom, drying his face with a towel. "Thanks." He took the telephone from Margaret's hand. "This won't take but a minute. Hello, Bobby? Listen, what the hell's going on with you? I thought I made it clear the last time we talked that . . ." He paused and listened, shaking his head occasionally. "I don't care. No. No." He sighed. "Where? All right, in half an hour." Claude hung up without saying good-bye.

"Who was that?"

"A nitwit by the name of Bobby Norton."

"The name sounds vaguely familiar."

Claude nodded. "He was a witness, more or less, to the rather gaudy murder of a locally notorious lawyer, a fellow by the name of Myron Hirsch. You probably read about it in the newspapers." Claude paused for a second, remembering something. "In fact, now that I think about it, we talked about him that first time when we had lunch."

"That's right," Margaret said quickly, "I had forgotten all about him."

"Easy enough to do. In any event, Bobby Norton succeeded in dragging my name into the whole affair by identifying me as his attorney."

"Why would anybody care one way or the other?"

"Normally they wouldn't. However, Mr. Norton neglected to inform the Berkeley police that he took the opportunity provided by Hirsch's violent demise to search through Hirsch's office before the police arrived on the scene."

"And?"

"And, he found a document, probably *the* document the possession of which led to Hirsch's murder. Having found it, Norton, who although certainly no rocket scientist is by no means without street smarts, decided to appropriate it for his own use, to wit, sale to the highest bidder."

"He told you all this?"

Claude nodded as he began dressing. "Eventually. He came to my office and wanted me to assist him in some fashion in the sale of his newly acquired commodity. Before he could tell me anything specific I threw him out."

"Threw him out? You mean you told him you wouldn't help him?"

"Are you kidding?" Claude looked at Margaret as if he couldn't decide whether or not he should be annoyed by her question. "I told him to take the document directly to the police, and that if he did so at once they probably wouldn't prosecute him for withholding evidence in the first place." Claude paused and shook his head with exasperation. "Coming from Bobby Norton, nobody would question a plea of stupidity," he added.

"So you never saw the document?"

"Never. Believe it or not, he actually asked if he could leave it with me for safekeeping. I queered that idea PDQ."

"What did he want just now?"

"He said he wants to talk to me, absolutely, positively *has* to talk to me."

"Did he say why?"

Claude tucked his shirt in and fastened his belt buckle. "No. All he would say over the phone was that he recently came into some information that he thinks I should be aware of. I should probably have my head examined for agreeing to see him, but this will be the last time. As you heard, I agreed to meet him in half an hour."

"Where?"

"A little after-hours club he runs over in Richmond. In fact, the building which houses his club is, or I should say was, owned by the late Mr. Hirsch, and was the nexus which brought the two together the morning Hirsch got himself killed." Claude shook his head, a bemused expression on his face. "It is indeed a strange world we live in."

"May I come with you?"

"I don't think . . ." Claude paused for a second and then shrugged. "Ah, what the hell, why not? It won't take long and afterward we can get a nice Sunday breakfast at Kate's."

Margaret rose from the futon and hurried behind the shoji screens, which provided a modicum of privacy for the toilet. Claude opened a small Oriental chest that sat on the floor next to the futon and took out his Colt .45 automatic, its bluing dulled by years of use and care. He ejected the clip and slid back the action just enough to ensure that a round was securely chambered. In a practiced motion he replaced the clip and thumbed the hammer closed and, standing once again, slid the heavy weapon into his waistband at the small of his back.

"Ready?" Margaret found Claude in the kitchen, a glass of orange juice in his hand.

"Holy cow," Claude said by way of reply. She was wearing a pair of blue jeans with a simple white cotton blouse. "Not many women I know can manage to look that good on so little notice." *I could get used to seeing you in the morning,* he thought but did not say. *Every morning.* "Would you like some juice before we leave?"

"No," she said, "just a sip of yours."

It's nice to see that the city of Richmond is vigorously enforcing the fire safety laws, Claude thought cynically as he noted the steel-barred windows on the front of Bobby Norton's club. The building itself sat uninvitingly at the end of a row of undeveloped, weed- and trash-strewn lots in an industrial section of the appallingly poor city. A large section of the building had recently been restuccoed, and had absorbed moisture unevenly, giving the whole a damp, gray, unfinished look. A sign, hand-lettered by the look of it, over the painted steel door announced to the world that the building was "Bobby's Place." Claude shook his head at the sadness of it all and knocked on the door.

"Claude, my man!" Bobby Norton greeted Claude exuberantly, clapping him on the shoulder as he grasped his right hand. "Come on in," he added, motioning Claude to follow him inside the darkened club.

The interior of the club was darkened, with only the bar lights providing illumination. Claude was surprised to see that the club was in the midst of a major renovation. Several table and radial arm saws sat amidst a tangle of orange electric power cables. Leather and canvas tool belts hung from nails, lumber and sheets of drywall were stacked against one wall, and sawdust covered everything.

"Business must be pretty good," Claude observed. "I'd say you're putting a lot of money into this dump." He looked around the room. "I thought you told me that Myron Hirsch owned this building."

Bobby nodded. "He did. But his brother agreed to sell me the place. It's in escrow right now."

"Aren't you jumping the gun a little, starting construction before you get title? What if something goes wrong?"

Bobby shrugged. "Nobody else is going to buy it. Hirsch's brother was his only relative. From back east somewhere. When he came to town to settle the estate I brought him out here to Richmond to see the place he had inherited." He giggled, an oddly high-pitched sound. "The motherfucker never saw so many niggers in one place in his life. I told him if I moved out the place would be trashed overnight, turned into a shooting gallery, and asked him how much he thought it would be worth then. He agreed to sell it to me right away."

"I can see that you're well on the way to becoming a pillar of respectability in the community," Claude observed dryly. Bobby started to say something and Claude held up a hand. "Wait a minute. I've got a friend with me and I don't want her waiting out on the street." He moved to the open door and waved at Margaret. "She can wait at the bar while you tell me what was so important that we had to meet today."

"Man, I don't know . . ." Bobby's voice trailed off as Margaret joined them at the club's entrance.

"Bobby, this is Miss Margaret Tikkanen," Claude said. "Maggie's a friend of mine," he added unnecessarily.

Bobby took Claude by the arm and pulled him to one corner of the bar. "What'd you bring *her* here for, man?" he hissed, nodding at Margaret.

"What the fuck's wrong with you?" Claude asked. "You act like you know her."

"Man, I *do* know her. Or know of her." Bobby leaned in until his breath was tickling Claude's ear. "She's in the papers, you know what I'm saying? I'm thinking that she and her father's the ones that killed Hirsch."

"What the fuck are you talking about?"

"The papers, man, the goddamned papers, the ones I took from Hirsch's desk after he was killed. The papers were stolen from her father. I don't know how Hirsch got hold of them or what he was going to do with them. I figure they killed him. Anyway, can't you see what's going on here? This bitch has got close to you so she could get to me and the papers."

Claude suddenly remembered his conversation with Emma after first meeting Margaret in his office:

"What does she want?"

"I don't know. Something about wanting to buy commercial property and not trusting the firm they usually use. Didn't make a lot of sense."

Claude looked at Bobby. "How did you know I'd been seeing her?"

"Your secretary, Emma. I tried to reach you at the office last week and when she said you were going to be away for a while I joked and said you must have a new girlfriend. She didn't think it was too funny and finally told me you were seeing some woman from up north. I put two and two together and figured you might be in some trouble."

"What have you done with the documents?" An

anger was brewing up in him, one that he had no immediate intention of turning away from.

"I've got them stashed away." Bobby shrugged his shoulders. "Tell you the truth, I wish now I'd never fucked with them, you know what I'm saying?"

Claude suddenly remembered something. "Goddamn," he said, his voice almost a whisper, his eyes holding Bobby pinned like a butterfly in a collection. "A. G. Farrell." The anger was growing as he realized how he had been set up. "He's a part of this whole thing. You called him."

"Yeah, the old man," Bobby confirmed. "His name and address were in the papers too. I figured he might be interested in buying them so I called him up."

"Was there any indication why his name was mentioned in the papers?"

Bobby shook his head. "No, just some notes about a private detective keeping an eye on his whereabouts over the years. Nothing about why."

"Where have you got the documents stashed?"

"In your office."

"What?"

"I had my cousin go by your office while you was out last week and leave them with your secretary." Bobby smiled. "He told her they were some papers you agreed to look at on a workers' comp deal."

Claude shook his head, pleased in spite of himself, although he did not show it, with Bobby's resourcefulness. "How many other people have you offered the papers to?"

"Besides Tikkanen and the old man from Virginia, just one other, some Indian or something up where she's"—he nodded toward Margaret—"from. Some bitch named Feather Rainforest, if you can believe that."

"How did you know to offer them to her?"

"Hirsch had stapled a note with her name and

phone number to the papers. I figured she . . ." Bobby fell silent when he saw Margaret moving quietly along the bar to where he and Claude stood.

"I'm sorry," she said. "I didn't mean to eavesdrop."

"Not to worry," Claude answered lightly, relishing the anger in him, the feeling that he could explode out of control in a heartbeat, "we were just about finished."

"Good," Margaret said. "I'm hungry. Perhaps Mr. Norton would like to join us for breakfast."

"I don't think so," Claude said before Bobby could respond. "In fact, there may be a slight change in plans based upon what Mr. Norton has just told me."

Margaret raised her eyebrows slightly. "Whatever do you mean?"

Claude smiled and leaned casually against the bar. The smile contained no mirth and the pupils of his eyes, despite the darkness in the bar, had contracted to pinpoints. "Did you kill Myron Hirsch?"

"A Tikkanen soil her own hands?" Feather Rainforest's voice cut through the club's darkness like the sound of a saw blade hitting a nail. She laughed, a short, bitter exclamation point to her rhetorical question. "The Tikkanens hire others to do their filthy work for them."

Feather and Wolf walked up to the bar, both pointing their revolvers. Wolf stopped about three feet in front of Claude and Bobby and pointed his pistol first at one and then the other, his finger caressing the trigger in an almost sexual manner.

"I see you've still got that pistol," Claude observed, recognizing Wolf from his confrontation at Jean-Luc Dugre's house.

"Shut up," Feather warned.

Claude, still leaning against the bar, looked at Bobby. There was a familiar pounding in his ears and he knew that it wouldn't be long before he came unglued. *The dance is over and it's time to pay the band.* "I would say that your auction is going to start a little earlier than you planned."

"She said shut up, white man," Wolf said menacingly, pointing his revolver directly at Claude's face.

"There'll be no auction," Feather said, satisfaction evident in her voice. She looked at Margaret contemptuously. "For once your filthy money's going to do you no good." She turned her attention to Bobby. "As a member of an oppressed race I would have hoped for more from you." She raised her pistol until it was level with Bobby's face. "I'm only going to ask you once. Where are the papers?"

"They're at my home," he lied.

"They better be," Feather said. She looked at her son. "Tie these two up"—she gestured at Claude and Margaret with her pistol—"and stay here and guard them until I get back. You"—she pointed the pistol back at Bobby—"and I are going to take a little ride to get those papers. If they're where you say they are we'll come back here and everything will be fine."

"Turn around, both of you, and put your hands on the bar," Wolf ordered as soon as Feather and Bobby had left the club.

"I'm sorry," Margaret whispered to Claude as they complied with Wolf's order.

"You'll be sorrier if you don't keep your mouth shut," Wolf threatened.

"Fuck you," Claude snarled over his shoulder, anger now rolling over him in waves. Although he did not believe the young Indian had the fortitude to shoot them out of hand, he was feeling reckless and decided to see how far he could push things.

Wolf noticed the bulge under Claude's jacket and pulled the big Colt out with a laugh of triumph. "Turn around," he barked, waving the automatic in the air.

"You're in deep shit, asshole," Claude said, his voice surprisingly calm and even. It had the effect he had hoped for but not exactly the result. Enraged, Wolf abruptly slashed Claude across the face with the barrel of the heavy Colt, breaking his nose and opening a ragged gash along one cheekbone. Claude gasped involuntarily and fell to his knees, his eyes tearing immediately with the sudden intense pain of the broken nose. He heard, as if through gauze, Wolf taunt and curse him. He stayed on his hands and knees and kept his head down to clear his nose of blood. At the very edge of his peripheral vision he could see that Wolf was securing Margaret to one of the redwood beams that was supporting the temporary ceiling. From the sound he deduced that Wolf was using duct tape to do the job, probably from a roll left by one of the construction workers.

"Hey, white man, you're not much of a tough *hombre* at all, are you?" Wolf came back over and lifted Claude's head none too gently with the toe of his boot under Claude's chin.

Claude, still on his hands and knees, blew again through his nostrils, still trying to clear them. A not-so-fine mist of bright red blood spewed forth and fresh pain shot through his sinuses.

Wolf laughed delightedly. "Get up and move over to that post next to the door," he ordered, gesturing with both pistols. "From there you'll have a nice view of me fucking your girlfriend." Wolf half turned to look back at Margaret. "And how much she'll be enjoying it."

The half-turn and gloating look to Margaret was a mistake. A big mistake. While his attention was momentarily diverted Claude rose from the floor and in one fluid motion lashed upward with his right foot, the toe of his elk-hide cowboy boot catching Wolf squarely in the testicles. All the power of Claude's massive thigh propelled his foot, the force of the blow lifting the young man almost six inches off the floor. Wolf crumpled to the floor in a tight fetal position.

The violence of the kick caused a bolt of pain to shoot through Claude's head and he staggered backwards to the bar, catching himself and gasping for breath. A wave of dizziness passed over him and he thought for a brief second that he might pass out. The sound of Wolf vomiting brought him back to the situation at hand.

"Are you all right?" Margaret asked, her voice strangely calm in light of what had just transpired.

"Yeah," Claude mumbled. He straightened up and looked around the room.

"What are you looking for?"

"Something to hold him"—Claude pointed down at Wolf, who was gagging on his own vomit—"until the police can get here," Claude said, his eye caught by a familiar-looking shape in the gloomy darkness.

"Take this tape off me and I'll help you tie him up," Margaret urged.

Claude didn't answer.

"Aren't you going to free me?" she asked again.

Claude waved a hand to silence her. The shape that had attracted his eye was a small air compressor, commonly referred to among the construction trades as a mushroom due to the distinctive conical shape of the compression chamber. He walked over to the compressor and, as he expected, found a large pneumatic nail gun, its slide feeder loaded with 3½-inch, 16-penny galvanized steel nails.

"Sinkers," he said quietly, more to himself than to Margaret.

"What did you say?"

Claude thumbed a nail out of the gun's feeder mechanism and held it up for Margaret to see. "These are framing nails. Framers call them sinkers." He smiled and exhaled once again through his nose, spewing more blood down his shirtfront. "A felicitous nickname, wouldn't you say?"

"Claude, I really don't appreciate the fact that you

haven't taken this tape off my hands. Claude." Her voice became more insistent, and took on a strident tone. "Claude, are you listening to me?"

Ignoring her, Claude searched through the semi-darkness until he found a wall outlet, to which he ran the compressor's power cord. When he turned the compressor on a distinctive chugging sound filled the room. He picked up the nail gun and walked to where Margaret was bound.

"If I remember correctly, these guns can be set so as to adjust the depth to which the nail is driven," he told her. He fumbled with a set screw on the nose of the gun. "I believe this is the adjusting screw." He looked up and into Margaret's eyes. "You've been lying to me from the very first, haven't you?"

"No, Claude—"

He waved a hand, silencing her. "You have and we both know it." He shook his head. "You did a good job, although in all honesty my own stupidity contributed a great deal to your success, didn't it?" He connected the high-pressure hose from the compressor to the handle of the nail gun. The quick-connect fitting on the hose emitted a brief hiss of air during the coupling process, causing Margaret to flinch involuntarily. "And the damndest thing is that all the deception was unnecessary. If you'd have just asked me I'd have told you I didn't have what you were looking for." He looked again at Margaret, his eyes shining in the dim light reflected from behind the bar. "Did you think I'd lie to you about such a thing?" He waved his hand casually in the air. "The question was rhetorical, you needn't answer."

The compressor had ceased chugging, indicating that it had built up sufficient pressure to begin operating the nail gun. Claude bent down and drove three nails in a straight line in rapid succession into the plywood subflooring. He examined the depth to which the nails had been driven and made an adjustment to the gun. He drove two more nails and stood up, satisfied with what he saw.

"One inch," he told Margaret. "I think leaving the nail head one inch above the floor should be about perfect, don't you? That means two and a half inches will have been driven into the subfloor."

"What are you talking about?"

Claude nodded toward Wolf. The young man had not moved from the tight fetal position he had assumed on the club's filthy floor. "I'm going to nail him to the floor."

"What?"

"Just one hand, actually. Unless he's a hell of a lot harder a rock than I think he is, that should nicely hold him until the police get here."

"Where are we going?"

"We aren't going anywhere, darling. I'm going back to my office to retrieve the fatal documents that Bobby stashed there."

"I thought you said you hadn't seen the documents." Margaret's voice took on a distinctly accusatory cast.

"I haven't. Just before dickbrain, there"—Claude nodded in the direction of the supine Wolf Walks Far—"and his porcine mother burst in here Bobby told me he had a cousin leave the documents with Emma, my secretary."

"Won't he be in some danger when Feather finds out that he lied to her about the documents being in his home?"

In spite of the pain from his nose Claude laughed with delight. "Bobby Norton lives in a part of Richmond where white people are generally shot on sight." He chuckled again, delighted with the image of Feather Rainforest encountering Bobby's neighbors. "She'll be lucky if she gets out of there alive."

"What about me?"

Claude shrugged. "What *about* you? You've been playing me for a fool all this time, why should I all of a sudden start worrying about you?"

"Are you going to turn the documents over to the police?"

"I don't know yet."

"Those papers belong to the Northwestern Lumber Company," Margaret said angrily.

"I'll keep that in mind."

Claude, still holding the nail gun in his left hand, reached down with his right, grabbed Wolf by the collar of his shirt, and dragged the semiconscious young man to the center of the floor. He took Wolf's right arm and pulled it away from his body, securing it to the floor, palm up, by stepping on it at the wrist with his cowboy boot. Before Wolf could react to this new circumstance Claude bent down, carefully nestled the nail gun into the center of Wolf's right palm, and pulled the trigger. The explosive report of the nail being driven through Wolf's hand and into the subfloor filled the small club. At impact Wolf's eyes flew open and his mouth contorted soundlessly. He began to flop about spasmodically, his movement all the while constrained by the pain of the nail that secured him to the floor. Claude walked back over to the air compressor and turned it off, dropping the nail gun beside it.

"I'll bet that hurts," he said to Margaret, nodding at Wolf. "Well, my dear, I'd like to stay awhile and chat but I don't have a lot of time. My guess is that as soon as Bobby gets rid of the kid's mother he'll head straight for my office to retrieve the documents, and I plan to beat him to the punch." He examined the duct tape that secured her to the support beam. "I'm not surprised to see that he did a pretty sloppy job of taping," he told her. "You should be able to free yourself within ten or fifteen minutes if you really work at it. In fact, I'll give you a little head start on it." Claude reached into his jeans and pulled out a pocket knife, with which he made a strategically placed cut in the duct tape. "There." He put the knife back into his pocket and walked back around in front of Margaret. "I'm out of here. I figure it'll take me fifteen or twenty minutes to get to my office and then another couple minutes to call the police. I won't say anything about you being here. I advise you to free yourself, get out to the Oakland airport somehow, and head back to New London as quickly as you can."

"What about the documents?" Margaret asked. "Have you forgotten what I did for you in New London? The risk we, my father and I, took when we gave you medical care and shelter when you needed it?" Her voice rose with anger. "Damn you, Claude, you owe me."

Claude paused for a second at the door but did not look back at Margaret. "I'll let you know what I decide."

"Hello, may I speak with Detective Jim Malone? This is Claude McCutcheon calling." Claude lit a Camel as he waited for the woman, presumably Malone's wife, to call the Berkeley police detective to the telephone. He had just taken six aspirins but had no expectations that they would in any way lessen the pounding in his head caused by his recently broken nose. Still, it was worth a try. "Jim? Claude McCutcheon here. Listen, Jim, I hate to bother you at home on a Sunday morning but I think I've got someone connected with Myron Hirsch's murder nailed down for you. No kidding. What's that? No, to tell you the truth, I don't know his name. He's a young kid, maybe twenty or so, at least part Indian. No, American Indian. What? Yeah, right, Native American. I keep forgetting about all the sensitivity training you Berkeley cops get at taxpayer expense. Anyway, he's waiting to be collected at Bobby Norton's club in Richmond. And listen, he had a piece with him. Maybe forensics can match it to the bullet you dug out of Hirsch. And you might want to put out a warrant on this kid's mother. That's right, his mother. White woman, heavy, with long greasy hair. First place I'd look would be around the Hillandale Public Housing complex in Richmond. Right away. I'd consider her armed and dangerous too. Last seen in the company of your friend and mine, Roberto Norton. No, I don't know where he is now, but I doubt he's with the woman anymore. Wait a minute." Claude put his hand over the receiver and listened. Someone, a man by the sound of the footsteps, was coming up the stairs to his office. "Jim, I'll have to talk to you later. Listen, be careful when you pick up the kid. I think he's been pretty well pacified, but you never know." Claude hung up the telephone and leaned back in his chair. "The door's open, Bobby," he called out.

A sheepish-looking Bobby Norton came into the office.

"Claude, my man, it's good to see you." He stopped and did a shocked double-take when he saw Claude's broken nose.

"My ass," Claude said. "You figured I'd still be stuck over at your club with that kid's gun up my ass so you could get over here and collect your little package."

"No way," Bobby objected. "Man, I was heading right over there as soon as I took care of business here, you know what I'm saying?"

"I know. What'd you do with the fat lady?"

Bobby giggled. "I took her over to the Paradise Lounge."

The Paradise Lounge was a notorious pool room, bar, and drug emporium across the street from the Hillandale Public Housing complex. It featured a large gravel parking lot and at least one shooting or knifing a week. The Richmond Police Department never pulled into the parking lot with fewer than two squad cars at a time.

"I pulled into the lot and jumped out of the car before the stupid bitch knew what happened," Bobby continued. "There must've been twenty-five brothers hanging around." He laughed again. "I had the car keys so the bitch couldn't do nothing but walk."

Claude smiled, picturing the scene. "I bet she lost a few pounds by the time she got out of Hillandale."

"If she got out." Bobby paused and looked at Claude. "Are you okay, man? How'd you get over here? Did you kill her son?"

"He wasn't tough enough to need killing," Claude scoffed. "I kicked him in the nuts and left him for Jim Malone to pick up."

"Malone?"

"I was talking to him when I heard you sneaking up the stairs."

"Man, that's cold. What'd you tell him?"

"Not much. Just that the kid was stuck at your place and that his mother was somewhere around Hillandale."

Bobby suddenly remembered something. "What about the Tikkanen woman? Did you bring her back here with you?"

"No. I left her at the club with the kid. My guess is that she's winging it back to Humboldt County by now. I told her I'd give her twenty minutes or so to get clear before I called the cops."

"You not going to tell them about her?"

"No, I'm not." Claude pointed a finger at Bobby. "And that brings us to you, my friend. My advice is that you stick with your original story about not knowing or seeing anything at the Hirsch murder scene. Nothing about the papers you stole from Hirsch's desk after he was killed." Bobby started to protest but Claude waved him to silence. "Goddamn it, shut up and read my lips: Say nothing about what you found. The story about this morning is that you and I were having a friendly drink at your club when the fat woman and her son burst in. Despite your protestations to the contrary, they believed, still believe, that you found something at Hirsch's, something they wanted. In order to split them up, you told them that you had what they were looking for at your apartment. She went with you and left the kid with me. You got rid of her at Hillandale and I took care of the kid. As soon as I got here I called Malone and you joined me here shortly thereafter. And nobody knows anything about anybody else at the club with you and me. Case fucking closed."

"Malone won't believe that shit."

Claude shrugged. "He's got no choice."

"You find the papers my cousin left?"

Claude nodded and pointed to a large envelope on his desk.

Bobby edged toward the desk. "Maybe I'll take them now," he said, looking carefully at Claude.

"Not without a gun you won't," Claude said quietly. "Listen, fool, if Malone even thinks you took something from Hirsch's office after the murder, he'll drop a big-time load on you."

"The woman and her kid will tell Malone that I had the papers and was trying to sell them," Bobby pointed out.

"So what? All Malone's really interested in is finding out who killed Myron Hirsch. It's just your word against those two low-life dickbrains. Malone may not be happy about it but he's got no choice but to believe you. And me."

"What are you going to do with them?" Bobby asked, meaning, of course, the papers.

"I don't know." Claude looked at Bobby, an enigmatic half-smile on his face. "I can assure you, however, that there will be no profit involved, however I dispose of them."

EPILOGUE

CLAUDE AND A. G. FARRELL WERE SEATED IN THE SMALL lobby of the Arlington Arms residence hotel in El Cerrito. A. G. wasted no time in getting to the point.

"I have spoken with Detective Malone at the Berkeley Police Department and he doesn't believe your story."

Malone, in fact, was furious with Claude. By the time a fire department rescue team had freed his hand, a psychologically beaten (not to mention badly injured) Wolf Walks Far had babbled most of what he knew about the stolen documents to Malone. Feather, on the other hand, when arrested in the parking lot of the Paradise Lounge where she had locked herself inside Bobby Norton's car, refused to say or admit to anything. She demanded that Jean-Luc Dugre be notified of her arrest, and he immediately contacted a fellow radical on the faculty of UC's Boalt Hall Law School to represent her. The law professor, a feminist whose strident political agenda interfered greatly with the dean's efforts to solicit contributions for the law school from well-to-do alumni, in turn got in touch with the Berkeley city attorney, a physically challenged lesbian of color. The city attorney, although not technically concerned with criminal matters, felt it politically proper to advise the chief of police that unless Detective Malone was in possession of overwhelming evidence of guilt of some crime, the department would be well advised to release Feather. After a short, unhappy conference between Malone and a very junior assistant district attorney Feather was summarily released from custody. The law professor next arranged a conference with Wolf Walks Far, who remained under arrest in the prison ward at the Alameda County Hospital. Shortly after that conference he informed Malone that he knew nothing about any documents, despite his prior statement to the contrary, and further that he was unsure of the circumstances by which he came to be nailed to the wooden floor of Bobby Norton's nightclub.

"I do not know who killed Myron Hirsch," Claude told an enraged Detective Malone. "As to the existence of alleged stolen documents . . ." He shrugged and refused to discuss the matter further.

Claude nodded in response to A. G.'s statement. "I don't blame him. I wouldn't believe it either. However, he has little choice since there is no one who can, or will, contradict it."

"There is much to contradict it," A. G. pointed out rather sharply, "and you know it. I believe that whatever information Mr. Norton had you now possess, information pertinent not only to my quest but also to the murder of which Mr. Norton was a putative witness. What I do not know, or understand, is why you are refusing to cooperate with the police."

"I would not characterize it as noncooperation— rather, situational cooperation. You might call it the operational version of situational ethics. I determine what is appropriate in any given situation involving legal and moral anomalies. I have absolutely no reason to believe that the police, or the courts, or any other governmental institution would be likely to make better decisions in such matters than I can. The opposite, in fact, is probably true. No." Claude shook his head. "I assure you, I've told Jim Malone everything he needs to know about my involvement in this admittedly sorry affair."

"I can't believe that you, a member of the California Bar Association, would affect such an attitude."

"Believe me, it's no affectation."

"You have a debt to society."

Claude chuckled, a bitter sound. "Spoken like a man who wants something. It has been my unhappy experience that such appeals, if acted upon, invariably cost me a great deal more than the person or organization making the appeal. You may rest assured that any such debt I *might* have owed to this society was paid in full long ago. I owe no one, not you, not Jim Malone, and certainly not your so-called society, an explanation or an apology for any decisions I make or any action I take."

"What about Hirsch's murder?"

"I didn't kill him."

"But you know who did."

Claude shook his head. "No."

"You know the identity of the prisoner of war, the murderer, I'm seeking."

"No, not as a matter of fact."

"But his identity is revealed in the documents held by your client, Mr. Norton."

Again, Claude shook his head. "For the last time, he was never my client. As to matters contained within the alleged documents"—Claude shrugged—"I can't say inasmuch as I haven't read them. And without admitting to their existence," he added, "I don't intend to read them."

"That is an unacceptable response," A. G. said,

seething with anger. "If you persist in this attitude then you are little better than the very man I seek."

Claude stood up. "There are those who would agree with you, although I would not. Nonetheless, I wish you well." He extended his right hand to A. G.

The old man looked at him for several seconds before rising. "You are no gentleman, sir, and I will not shake your hand."

Eureka, California
Monday, April 11, 1994

"Thank you for agreeing to meet with me."

Claude nodded his head in acknowledgment but said nothing. He and Joseph Tikkanen were seated in a sparsely furnished private office at the Stewart Memorial Hospital in Eureka.

"When my daughter informed me that you had made an appointment for a final visit with Dr. Jenkens, I thought that it would provide a convenient opportunity for us, you and I, to meet."

Claude remained silent, content for the moment to watch the old man as one player might watch another in a particularly high-stakes poker game.

"I understand from my daughter that you are returning our documents to us."

Again, Claude nodded. "I plan to stop in New London on my way south this afternoon."

"We, my daughter and I, appreciate your discretion in the matter of our stolen documents. I trust that Detective Malone of the Berkeley Police Department has not caused you too much difficulty."

"Let's just say that he's not one of my bigger fans at the moment."

The old man smiled. "I understand that Malone did all he could to have the district attorney's office indict both you and the foolish Mr. Norton for concealing evidence."

"The formal term, I believe, is misprision of felony, and Jim Malone had neither witnesses nor evidence with which to make his case." *Just like I told Bobby in my office,* Claude thought but did not add to the conversation.

"It also helped that the district attorney was discreetly advised by a member of the state Senate in Sacramento that she could expect considerable support from her party in her reelection bid should she determine that the case Detective Malone and the Berkeley Police Department were trying to make against you and Mr. Norton had no merit."

Claude raised an eyebrow but said nothing in response to Joseph's disclosure. He assumed that the old man was not seeking an overt display of appreciation for taking precautions that clearly benefited him as much as they did Claude and Bobby Norton.

"Did you read through any of the stolen material before returning it?"

Claude shook his head. "As curious as it may seem to you, I have absolutely no interest in the machinations of you or your company. Your daughter did me a great service by caring for me, in confidence, with no questions asked, when I needed such care. In returning your papers I am merely, shall we say, squaring the deal." Claude paused for a moment. "How did such documents come to be in Myron Hirsch's possession?"

"Simply enough as these things go. One of the dangers of absolute authority is the regrettable tendency at times to let one's guard down, to assume an invulnerability that in fact never exists in the real world. Because I foolishly assumed that no one, least of all an employee of the company, would dare steal anything from me, such a person was able to do just that. This person learned of the existence of the documents, cleverly obtained the combination to the safe in which they were secured, stole them, and entered into an agreement with the late Mr. Hirsch for their use in blackmailing not only the company but a number of the, shall we say, public figures identified therein. It seems that Mr. Hirsch, for all his apparent environmental zeal, was not above making a few dollars when the opportunity presented itself. Although one or more of the public figures identified in the documents appeared to be inclined to pay Mr. Hirsch, it has always been my policy to nip such enterprises in the bud."

"So you had him killed." It was more a statement of fact than a question.

"When one decides to enter into criminal activity one occasionally pays a somewhat higher price than anticipated. You, Mr. McCutcheon, of all people, must recognize that."

"And your former employee?"

Joseph steepled his fingers and looked over them at Claude. "Let us just say that now that the papers are once again in my possession there are no loose ends left in the matter." He tugged at his lower lip for a second before continuing. "Let me ask you a question, Mr. McCutcheon. What do you think about me, about a man like me? I ask because frankly I am concerned that perhaps your feelings as regards me might somehow be coloring your feelings toward my daughter."

"I have no feelings one way or the other about you," Claude replied. "In fact, the only thing I know about you, or rather I should say presume to know about you, is what A. G. Farrell told me."

"Ah, yes, the persistent Mr. Farrell." Joseph smiled enigmatically. "Mr. Farrell knows a little and presumes a great deal." He paused for a moment, and when Claude did not respond he continued. "Tell me something. Have you ever heard of the Winter War?"

Claude slowly shook his head. "I don't believe I have."

The old man nodded, clearly not surprised. "Few have outside Finland or Russia. And yet at one time all the world watched as the mighty Soviet army attacked Finland in a vicious war of aggression. For a hundred and five days beginning in December 1939 Finland, with a population of only three million people, defended itself against a nation of almost one hundred and ten million." Joseph paused, his eyes focused on the past. A flush spread across his cheeks and years seemed to drop away from his face as he unconsciously sat up straighter in his chair. Despite his age he was still an extraordinarily handsome man, with sharply chiseled features and cold, blue eyes. "That was a time to be alive, Mr. McCutcheon, to be young. Your American leftists and communist apologists wept bitter tears for Spain but remained strangely silent as Stalin and Molotov bombed innocent women and children in Helsinki. No matter. On skis and bicycles we fought tanks and bombers, and in a hundred and five days it is conservatively estimated that we killed at least two hundred thousand Russian troops while losing less than twenty-five thousand of our own. Almost ten to one, Mr. McCutcheon, men on wooden skis versus tanks and artillery."

"But you lost."

"Even we could not stop the colossus forever. Until the very end both France and England promised aid, men and materiel. All the world saw how they kept their promises, and not only to us, so finally we had no choice but to capitulate. The so-called Treaty of Moscow ceded to the Russians ten percent of our territory, containing some twelve percent of our economic base. A bitter pill to swallow, but we Finns knew it was better than losing all. So we waited. And remembered. And when Hitler invaded Russia in the summer of 1941 we tore up the treaty, declared war on Russia, and took back our territory. Although never formal allies of the Germans we certainly shared their desire to permanently defang the Russian bear, a desire you Americans came to appreciate after 1945."

"Finland's a long way from North Africa," Claude observed.

"It is indeed. As I said, although we were never formal allies of the Germans our countries cooperated in our respective efforts to defeat Stalin. For example, we provided the German general staff with valuable information concerning how to fight an arctic war."

"The information couldn't have been *too* valuable given the defeat the Germans ultimately suffered in Russia."

Joseph smiled. "Not unlike Mr. Farrell you know a little and assume much. I said we gave the Germans valuable advice. They chose not to follow it." He shrugged. "Had they done so, who knows? In any event, our armies cooperated. One of the facets of that cooperation was the posting, in early 1942, of a young Finnish lieutenant as an observer on Rommel's staff in North Africa."

"You."

Joseph nodded. "Me. A long way, as you so aptly put it, from Finland. What I *observed* was the ultimate destruction of the Afrika Korps. As the remnants of the German and Italian armies were pressed inexorably toward the northern coast of Tunisia I knew there was little likelihood I would see my homeland for quite some time, if ever again. When capture became almost certain I destroyed my Finnish army uniform and documents and took the identity of a recently deceased German lieutenant, hoping thereby to spare my country any international embarrassment. Thus it was as a German I was initially captured by the British in northern Tunisia."

"Along with the Italian, Tavecchio."

"The Italian surrendered with his men several days later. His men were sent on to the POW facility at Constantine and he and I, because we also spoke English, were kept as translators." The old man nodded, lost for a second in thought. "He was not so stupid, that one. He deduced, despite the uniform I was wearing, that I wasn't a German national and so, we were released by the British to make our way to Constantine."

"They just released you?"

The old man smiled. "Yes. You must remember, so many units were surrendering, en masse, that the British and American military authorities in the field were overwhelmed. Individuals such as the Italian and I were usually just pointed in the direction of the large Allied facility at Constantine and told to make our own way. On the way, as I said, the Italian deduced that I wasn't a German national, so I killed him. To be honest, I wish I had not done so, but I was young and at war. Only after I killed him did I decide to take his identity." He smiled. "The notion was really quite foolish but of course it worked."

"And the man on the train?"

"Unavoidable." Joseph recounted the killing of the railroad yard bull. Joseph shrugged. "My instincts told me that he was not a good man and in any event I had no choice in the matter."

"What about the farmer? In Mississippi."

"That was a favor for an old black man who fed me."

"Come again?"

Joseph told Claude about the evening he spent with Percy Christmas, and how he decided, quite unbidden, to rid the old man of his racist tormentor.

"It is interesting, is it not," Joseph asked contemplatively, "how things once seemingly clear become less so as one's perspective changes."

"What of the murders in Bonn? After the war."

"I had long since returned to Finland and was living in Helsinki at the time. I learned of them from friends in Germany." Joseph shook his head. "Mr. Farrell was quite foolish to ignore the advice of his superiors. Even had he discovered my identity there is no way my government would have taken any action such as extraditing me. As it was, he succeeded only in ensuring the destruction of records pertaining to my military service in North Africa during the war, not to mention my escape and repatriation, thus allowing me to emigrate to America in 1949." Joseph paused for a second. "Did you tell Mr. Farrell that I am the man he has so diligently sought since 1943?"

"No, but with a little effort I suspect he could find out for himself. Before his mother shut him up the Indian boy told Malone that Myron Hirsch was killed because of documents belonging to your company. Of course Malone can't prove anything but he knows in his gut that the Indian was telling the truth, and so that information is now contained in various Berkeley police reports. It shouldn't be overly difficult for Mr. Farrell to obtain access to those reports and then he only needs to put two and two together to come up with Tikkanen." Claude looked carefully at Joseph. "I would be very unhappy if something were to happen to Mr. Farrell. Very unhappy."

Joseph laughed. "Mr. Farrell has nothing to fear from me, I assure you. He can do me no harm, even if he is successful in learning my name. He would still be unable to prove a thing, and I have many friends, both in Sacramento and Washington, who would be more than happy to characterize him as an old fool, a man obsessed with a fifty-year-old ghost story." He shook his head in dismissal. "Let us forget Mr. Farrell. I have something far more important I wish to discuss with you."

"What?" Claude asked suspiciously.

"My daughter."

Claude's expression hardened. "Your daughter is not a subject I wish to discuss, with you or anyone else." He stood up and started to leave.

"Don't be a fool," the old man hissed, rising and pushing away his chair. He was almost as tall as Claude and retained much of the strength of his youth. "All that I own could be yours. I have built an empire here in Humboldt County, a redwood empire. Marry my daughter and it would be yours together." He placed a strong hand on Claude's forearm. "We are much alike, you and I. I could not have wanted a son to be more a man than you are."

Claude brushed past him without a word and left the office.

"Don't be a fool," Joseph called after him. "Don't be a . . ." As his voice trailed off Joseph, despite his anger, suddenly smiled, seeing more than a little of himself in Claude.

"I'm surprised to see you," Margaret had told him when he handed her the package in her office in New London.

"Why? Did you think I'd not return your property?"

"No, it's just that I was afraid that, you know . . ." She and Claude looked at each other for several seconds. "Is there nothing I can do? Or say?" she asked in a quiet voice.

"Nothing. However, you can accept my apology."

"Apology?"

"For leaving you tied up in Bobby Norton's club in Richmond. I was angry and my judgment was im-

paired by my confrontation with the young man I
secured to the floor, not to mention my concern with
getting to my office and retrieving the documents in
question before Bobby Norton could get there. Nonetheless, I should have freed you before I left. I
apologize."

"I had not expected an apology." Margaret smiled.
"I'm not sure what I expected but certainly not an
apology." She paused and examined the wrapping
Claude had used to package the stolen documents.
"We might actually have been something, you and I."

"I think there's little profit to be had in such
speculation." Claude's tone of voice was not unkindly. "It's interesting, isn't it, how many obvious
clues or signals I ignored in the course of getting to
know you. I suppose I was, as the British might say,
too clever by half. I had no idea that I was as subject
as the next man to the vanity of attraction, the
overconfidence of testosterone."

"I like that," Margaret said, smiling, " 'the overconfidence of testosterone.' "

"I don't think I meant it as a joke." Claude stood
up. "Who knows? Perhaps it helps to keep things in
perspective if one makes a fool of oneself every now
and again."

"Whatever else, I cannot imagine thinking of you as
a fool." Margaret stood up and extended her hand
across the desk. "Might we still be friends?"

"I doubt it." Claude shook his head. "Not for-real
friends, not friends who call each other often, and
worry about each other." He shrugged. "And I was
never much of a once-a-year kind of friend, Christmas
cards with newsletters, that sort of thing."

"Not even another dinner at Carlucci's in Portland
sometime?"

Claude took her hand. "I don't get up to Portland
very often. . . ." His voice trailed off and he turned to
leave the office. At the threshold he stopped and

looked back at Margaret. "I wish . . . ," he started to say and then stopped, knowing he had not the words to tell her what was in his heart, what she had come to mean to him. *Don't let me leave,* he wanted desperately to say, but he could not, so he raised one hand in a pale gesture of farewell and left.

AUTHOR'S NOTE

Cutdown is, first and last, a work of fiction. However, the story of Joseph Tikkanen's capture in North Africa, his transportation to the United States with other Italian prisoners of war, and his subsequent successful escape from a POW camp in Virginia, while fictional, is based on factual data gathered from a variety of sources. The data clearly support the notion that such a story, although at first blush improbable, is nonetheless entirely plausible.

According to the U.S. Army Service Forces, Control Division, *Statistical Review, World War II,* a total of 425,036 enemy prisoners of war were brought to the United States for internment during World War II. The distribution by nationality was as follows:

Germans	–	378,156
Italians	–	41,456
Japanese	–	5,424

An account of the successful escape by Franz von Werra in early 1940 from a train transporting German prisoners of war across Canada can be found in Martin Gilbert, *The Second World War: A Complete History* (New York: Henry Holt and Company, 1989).

A comprehensive account of the Soviet Union's invasion of Finland in December 1939 and the subsequent 105-day war can be found in Richard W. Condon, *The Winter War: Russia Against Finland* (New York: Ballantine Books, 1972).

And, lastly, accounts of the execution of German prisoners of war by American military authorities can be found in the following:

a. Richard Whittingham, *Martial Justice: The Last Mass Execution in the United States* (Chicago: Henry Regnery Company, 1971).
b. Wilma Parnell, *The Killing of Corporal Kunze* (Secaucus, N.J.: Lyle Stuart, 1981).

Author of the *New York Times*
bestsellers *Harvest* and *Life Support*

TESS GERRITSEN

BLOODSTREAM

A NOVEL OF MEDICAL SUSPENSE

Woven with the kind of action and detail
only a doctor could deliver, and propelled by
an expert sense of small-town terror,
Bloodstream is Tess Gerritsen's most unforget-
table thriller yet.

**Now available in hardcover
from Pocket Books**

POCKET BOOKS

2040

**POCKET BOOKS
PROUDLY PRESENTS**

CAUSES OF ACTION

by John A. Miller

**Coming soon in hardcover
from
Pocket Books**

Turn the page for a preview of
Causes of Action. . . .

Dawn eased over the East Bay hills like year-old motor oil draining slowly out of a crankcase. A heavy fog, drawn in through the Golden Gate by the summer heat bottled up in the Sacramento Valley, grudgingly gave way before the rising sun as early-morning commuters fortified themselves with hot coffee and a glance at the headlines.

The darkness in Claude McCutcheon's house was resolving itself into shades of gray when Claude woke up. He lay absolutely still on the futon, aware that something was wrong but unable to pinpoint the source or even define exactly what "wrong" meant. He had gotten in late the night before, sometime after 1 A.M., and was a little groggy from too few hours of sleep. He could have stayed in the City but didn't much care, as a general rule, for waking up in someone else's bedroom. Spending the night with a woman was a clear statement of intent, one that Claude seldom felt comfortable making. And anyway, the drive across the Bay Bridge after midnight was always a pleasant one, the traffic light and the feeling of leaving the darkened City behind, even for the dubious charms of the East Bay, strangely liberating.

He had no idea what had woken him up, but again there was an overwhelming feeling, an undeniable sense, that something was wrong in the little California bungalow. Keeping his eyes closed, Claude stilled his breathing, his ears straining for the slightest sound. The big Colt automatic was tucked away in the small Korean chest next to the futon, a round in the chamber, but for all the good it did him there, it might as well have been on the dark side of the moon.

He put the weapon out of his mind and concentrated on identifying everything in the house with his eyes closed. Almost immediately he felt the presence and heard the calm breathing of the cat, reassuring by its very regularity. Then, behind and above the familiar purring of the cat, what sounded oddly enough like a child whimpering registered on his consciousness. He slowly raised his eyelids. Standing next to the futon, not three feet away from him, was a young boy.

Relief washed over him.

"How did you get in here?"

The boy, perhaps four years old, didn't answer. Claude could see the tracks of dried tears on his face and a small envelope pinned to his sweater.

"What's your name?"

Still no answer.

Claude sat up on the futon. "Who brought you here?"

The boy pointed to the cat, sprawled on the comforter next to Claude. "Kitty."

Claude nodded. "Well, it's a start." He reached out and dragged the reluctant cat over. Oscar was a large, muscular female cat of indeterminate breed that Claude had adopted from the Alameda County SPCA. She had a short temper and a generally surly disposition and, in all the world, loved only Claude.

Oscar took one look at the boy and shrank back. Her experience with children was limited and informed by a healthy skepticism toward all humans, even small ones.

Claude scratched behind Oscar's ears and felt the cat

relax. "The kitty's name is Oscar. Would you like to pet her?"

The boy, wide-eyed, nodded.

Claude patted the futon next to him. "Sit down here and I'll put her in your lap."

The boy sat as directed and a second later was cradling the cat, who was purring madly.

Claude carefully unpinned the envelope. "First time you've ever held a cat?"

The boy nodded, raptly devoted to the cat in his lap.

Claude got up and slipped on a pair of cotton trousers. "You just sit there quietly and tell her you love her while I go make the three of us a cup of coffee."

The boy bent down and clumsily kissed the cat on the head. Quite to Claude's surprise and amusement, Oscar was positively cross-eyed with pleasure.

"You now have a friend for life," Claude told the child.

In the kitchen he started a pot of water boiling and took a container of coffee beans from the freezer. After grinding the beans he leaned against the counter and tore open the envelope that had been pinned to the boy's sweater.

Dear Claude:

I'm sure you never expected to hear from me after all these years, although to be honest with you it often seems like just yesterday that we were at Ft. Bragg together, messing with the Hawk, or in the Nam. Remember Ft. Lewis? Man, we were something back then, weren't we? Artie Gibson put me onto JoJo Watson, over at the VA hospital in the City, and JoJo told me where to find you.

I'm afraid I'm going to have to leave my boy Earl with you for a few days. His mother died two years ago and it's been just me and Earl since then. Earl's got no other family besides me so I'm trusting you to do right by him if it comes to that.

To tell you the truth, I'm not sure how things got so bad so fast. I won't try to tell you what all's going on since I hope to have things straightened out in the next couple of days and I can come get Earl off your hands.

I can't tell you what it means to me knowing that Earl's in your hands. I know it isn't fair to just leave him with you, not after all this time, but I got nowhere else to turn.

                                             Jesse Hamilton

Jesse Hamilton? Claude thought, glancing back at the futon where the boy sat, still entranced by the purring cat on his lap. An image came instantly to mind: three young men, two of them barely out of their teens, sitting on top of a sandbagged bunker, drinking lukewarm coffee out of canteen cups. They had been in Vietnam only a couple of months: Claude, an OCS second lieutenant; Jesse Hamilton, the platoon sergeant, a brand-new E-6 no older nor more experienced than Claude, and Artie Gibson, a squad leader with the rank of corporal. They were the platoon's ruling triumvirate: Claude and Jesse by virtue of their rank; Artie because he was four years older than either of them, the oldest, most experienced man in the platoon.

Claude smiled, seeing in his mind's eye the three of them smoking cigarettes and strategizing. In base camp they sat together every morning after Claude met with the company commander, talking about what the platoon was expected to do, trying to translate theory into reality. The platoon was chronically understrength, whether from disease, casualties, R and R, or whatever creative excuse a soldier could come up with to avoid leaving base camp, and they were constantly shifting men between squads to fill gaps. General Westmoreland most certainly would not have approved of the exceedingly casual relationship—indeed, the friendship—that developed between the three of them, but then again neither did he nor any member of his West Point-educated staff provide an alternative, workable model for use by junior officers in the field. Claude could hear their voices, now bantering, now serious, without even closing his eyes.

That afternoon, after three days in base camp, they had been alerted they were going back out on patrol.

"Cohen reported for sick call this morning," Jesse said, looking up from the small notebook in which he kept the platoon duty roster. "Mac"—the platoon medic—"said it looks like malaria. That puts us nine men"—almost a full squad—"under TO and E."

Jesse was tall and slender, almost elegant, if a man could be said to look elegant in jungle fatigues and boots, with piercing black eyes and startlingly white teeth. He carried himself, whether in base camp or in the field with a full rucksack on his back and an M16 in one hand, with a formal demeanor that made him seem a good deal older than he was. He demanded, and received, respect from not only the men in the platoon but his fellow NCOs in the company's other platoons. Only twenty, he took his responsibilities as platoon sergeant quite seriously, determined to take full advantage of every opportunity the army was prepared to offer him.

"What about all those replacements from brigade we supposed to be getting?" Artie asked, a broad smile on his face. "The last issue of the *Stars and Stripes* I saw said that President Johnson was every day saying what a fine job we're doing fighting the hated Cong." He paused to snag a cigarette from Jesse, lighting it with a flourish with Claude's Zippo. "I expect we'll see thousands of volunteers filling up the ranks any day now."

While both Jesse and Claude tended to be serious, Jesse by nature and Claude by virtue of his position as platoon leader, Artie was the leavening in the mix. Shorter than both Claude and Jesse, Artie was deceptively slight, a powerful young man who stabbed at the earth with his feet when he walked. Not afraid to speak his mind, Artie was by far the smartest of the three of them, gifted with both a keen, if unschooled, intellect and a streetwise cynicism that let him see things Claude and Jesse might have missed. That intellect and cynicism ultimately saved Artie, for while Claude and Jesse became hardened and, to some extent, damaged in Vietnam, Artie retained a perspective that recognized, amidst the horror, the comic futility of what they were doing.

"No replacements," Claude responded, shaking his head. "Zimmerman"—their company commander, a first lieutenant—"told me this morning to quit asking."

"Kitty."

The sound of Earl cooing to the cat brought Claude back to the present. *Don't suppose you know what your dad's gotten himself into, do you, Earl?* he wondered, stifling a yawn. Claude caught sight of himself in the mirror, seeing an unlined, comfortable face looking back at him. Although gray was beginning to show in his dark blond hair, his broad shoulders and trim, athletic body caused most people to underestimate his age by at least ten years.

A gurgling sound announced that the coffee had finished brewing. It was a dark Sulawesi-Kalosi, roasted by a small coffee importer in Berkeley's gourmet ghetto, and it smelled as exotic as it sounded.

Through the window he could see his next-door neighbor, Sally Pinter, in her kitchen. He waved and motioned for her to come over. She smiled and nodded. He was wondering what he had to feed a boy for breakfast when Sally let herself in the back door.

"Where's Bud?"

"He had to drive over to Modesto yesterday. His mother fell and broke her hip, of all things, and he's going to be over there for a few days getting her set up with a home health-care service."

"Sorry to hear it," Claude said.

"Better there than here." Sally laughed and then looked a little sheepish. "I guess that didn't sound very nice, did it?"

"Little Pete doing okay?" Claude asked, ignoring her last comment.

Pete was Bud and Sally's two-year-old.

"Doing great. He's sound asleep."

"Come here a minute."

Claude stepped back and motioned for her to follow him. At the edge of the large shoji screen that marked the slightly raised sleeping alcove, he stopped and pointed. The boy was still cradling the cat.

Sally's eyes widened. "Who is that?"

Claude nodded his head back toward the kitchen. There, his voice low enough so the boy couldn't hear him, he told her the gist of what the letter contained.

"You mean you just woke up this morning and he was here?" Sally asked incredulously.

Claude poured two cups of coffee. "You got it."

"What are you going to do?"

"I'm not sure yet." Claude took a sip of his coffee.

"You mean you're not going to call the police?" Sally shook her head, incredulous. "Or the child-welfare people?"

Claude frowned. "Are you kidding? The county social workers? They're the last people I'd want to turn a young boy over to. Look." He jerked his thumb in the direction of the sleeping alcove. "This boy's father left him here, for what reason I'm not exactly sure. But until I find out, I'm sure as hell not just going to turn him over to a bunch of hard-hearted bureaucrats." Claude finished his coffee. "I need to ask you to do me a favor. Let me leave the boy with you for a couple of hours this morning while I check into a few things."

Sally took a sip of her coffee. "I suppose."

"I'd truly appreciate it. Lord knows I don't have the faintest idea what to feed a boy for breakfast."

"I don't guess you would."

Claude smiled. "Why don't you take him home now, give him something to eat, and I'll pick him up later."

Claude walked back to the futon and knelt down next to the child. "Okay, sport, time to get a move on. You're going to spend the morning with a neighbor lady of mine, Mrs. Pinter, while I try to find your daddy."

The boy looked up at Claude. "Kitty," he said, still clutching the cat in his lap.

Claude sighed. "Well, nobody said life was going to be easy." He winked up at Sally and looked back at the boy. "Tell you what, you be good for Mrs. Pinter, do everything she tells you to do, and you and the kitty can sleep together tonight."

The boy smiled. "Okay."

He got up, Oscar jumping safely off his lap just in time, and reached for Sally's hand.

"Oh, Claude, he's precious." A worried look crossed Sally's face. "Are you sure it's okay? I mean, isn't it illegal not to notify *someone?*"

Claude laid a hand on her shoulder and smiled. "Trust me. I'm a lawyer."

The old-fashioned gold-leaf lettering on the door read CLAUDE MCCUTCHEON, ATTORNEY AT LAW. Beneath the bold print, in smaller letters, were the words CONTRACTS, WILLS AND CODICILS, ALL CAUSES OF ACTION. As little law as Claude practiced, it still pleased him inordinately to see the words on the door.

His office was on the second floor of a small, two-story stuccoed building on Solano Avenue in the city of Albany, a stone's throw from El Cerrito and Berkeley. Originally a single-family residence, the building had been converted to two office flats in the late 1970s when Solano Avenue was metamorphosing gradually from a residential to a commercial street. Within two or three blocks of his office Claude could buy a cup of coffee made from freshly roasted and ground beans, a baguette still warm from the oven, and food or clothing representative of a myriad of cultures. His immediate neighbors spoke English, Spanish, Lao, Persian, and several dialects of Chinese.

Walking up the stairs to his office, Claude guessed that Jesse had found out he was a lawyer now, but somehow doubted that that was the reason he had left Earl with him. Claude paused for a second on the top step. *Christ,* he thought, *how in the hell am I going to find a man I*

haven't seen in thirty years if he doesn't want to be found?
Opening the office door, he smiled grimly, knowing that at least Artie Gibson, two years into an eight-year stretch at San Quentin, and JoJo Watson, obviously in detox once again at the VA hospital, wouldn't be too difficult to find.

"Mornin', Emma. How old is that coffee?"

"Good morning, Claude. I thought you were going straight over to Felix Mackie's this morning." Emma Fujikawa, Claude's part-time secretary, did not bother to respond to Claude's question about the coffee, which she knew he'd asked only to annoy her.

"A little something came up," Claude said. "Besides, I forgot to take the papers home with me yesterday. I must be getting feebleminded in my old age."

"I think the doe-eyed Ms. Ann Abbott has more to do with it than your age." Emma regarded her boss with a chastising look. "I thought you and she were no longer seeing each other."

"How do you know we're . . ." Claude paused, knowing that mere denial was useless in the face of Emma's at times seemingly psychic knowledge of his personal life. He poured himself a cup of coffee. "She has proven to be rather, um, shall we say per*sist*ent, a trait she doubtless inherited from her father the oil baron."

"Humph." Emma had no intention of letting Claude off the hook. "I told you she was going to be trouble the first time she came to the office. If you had—"

"Yeah, yeah," Claude cut her off, thinking that it was just a little too early in the day to get into a discussion of his moral shortcomings with Emma. "'If ifs and ands were pots and pans, beggars would ride.'"

Emma laughed. "Tell that to Ann Abbott. Maybe *she* can make sense out of it." She handed Claude a large manila envelope. "Here are the bank documents for Felix to sign." The telephone rang. "Law offices of Claude McCutcheon." Emma listened for a second, a broad smile playing across her face. She covered the receiver with her hand and looked up at Claude. " 'Is Mistuh McCutcheon theah?' " she mimicked in her not-too-close approximation of a heavy Texas accent. "The first call of the day from the Yellow Rose of Texas," she gratuitously informed Claude.

"Jesus," Claude replied sotto voce, drawing a finger across his throat to indicate that he did not wish to take the call.

"I'm sorry, Miss Abbott, Mr. McCutcheon just left the office. . . . Yes, I'll tell him you called." Emma hung up and smiled sweetly at Claude. "Mark my words, that young woman is going to have your head mounted over the fireplace back home in Dallas for all her University of Texas sorority sisters to see."

"It's Houston—"

"Whatever."

"—and don't count on it."

"Oh, wait," Emma said suddenly as Claude turned to leave the office. "You got a telephone call late yesterday afternoon while you were in the City, uh, 'counseling' the Yellow Rose. He wouldn't leave a number. Said he'd call back."

"Who was it? Anyone we know?"

Emma looked down at her message pad. "A gentleman by the name of Jesse Hamilton."

Bingo. "What'd he say?"

Emma shrugged. "Nothing. Just that he'd call you back. Who is he?"

"He's an old army buddy, a guy I haven't heard from or even thought of for . . . let's see now"—Claude calculated quickly—"it must be thirty years." He shook his head. "If he calls again and I'm out, be sure and give him my home number."

"What do you suppose he wants?"

"Don't know," Claude said over his shoulder as he walked out the door. As much as he hated doing nothing, he'd already decided that he had little choice but to give Jesse at least a day or two to get back in touch with him.

He doubted that either Artie or JoJo would know exactly where Jesse had gone to earth, although Artie might have some idea as to why.

He shook his head.

What the hell am I going to do with a four-year-old kid?

Earl Hamilton was still very much on Claude's mind as he walked into Felix Mackie's gym, which was in the final stages of construction.

"I think we've finally got all the paperwork in order," he said.

"Just tell me where to sign," Felix rumbled.

"Don't you want to know what you're signing?"

Felix shook his head, his immense San Quentin arms folded impassively across his chest. "Don't mean shit to me." Anyone listening would have believed him without a doubt. "This place is either going to make it or it isn't, no matter what those papers say. If it makes it, I'll pay the money back. If it don't . . ." He shrugged. "Not even a bank can't get no blood out of a turnip."

Claude began laying documents on the counter, thinking that anyone so foolish as to try to get blood out of Felix would be in for a long day indeed. When the papers were signed, Claude stuffed them back into his small, leather briefcase. "I'll drop the originals off at the bank and keep your copies with the file in my office."

Felix nodded. "I'll pay *your* money back as soon as I get the check from the bank."

"Whenever," Claude said casually. He had lent Felix enough money to keep operating while the application documents worked their tortuous way through the numerous bureaucratic levels of a minority-lending program. That Felix was a paroled murderer hadn't helped, although Claude had gone to some length to point out to a number of the bank's employees that the crime for which Felix had been convicted and incarcerated did not, in and of itself, necessarily reflect negatively on his fiscal responsibility.

"Nonetheless," Claude had, only half-jokingly, told the bank's minority lending officer, a young Stanford MBA with a new Porsche and little sympathy for people of color who needed to borrow money, "he's not a man I'd want to gratuitously piss off, if you get my point."

The young MBA had indeed gotten Claude's point.

"How come you never had me to sign a note or anything?" Felix asked, still referring to Claude's loan.

"Well, like you just said, I figured you'd either pay it back or you wouldn't. If I'd been worried about it, I would have never lent you the money in the first place."

Felix nodded. "Be a different place in here when I get my hands on that loan. How long will it take?"

"Probably another week or ten days, no more."

"You think it's safe for me to go ahead and order some stuff?"

"Yeah, it's a done deal. I don't doubt the bank's already scheduled a press conference to inform a disbelieving and incredulous world that it's actually going to lend money to a working man, and an African-American one at that."

A hint of a smile passed across Felix's hard face, come and gone so quickly few would have noticed it.

"What's so funny?" Claude asked.

"I was just thinking that they's lots of folks wouldn't believe it if they was to hear that a bank was lending money to Felix Mackie." Felix shook his head at the wonder of it.

"Have you thought of a name for gym yet?"

Felix shook his head.

"You need a good, solid name. How about Felix's Place?"

"I'll let you know," Felix responded, clearly unimpressed. "You workin' out today?"

"No, I don't think so. I've got to get these papers"—he held up his briefcase—"to the bank and then . . ." Claude hesitated, not wanting to say too much. "Something's come up."

"Something always does," Felix rumbled from deep in his throat. "You better be careful."

"Sit right here," Claude said, putting Earl up on one of his kitchen chairs. "You can tell me all about your day while I prepare dinner."

"Kitty," Earl said, looking about the kitchen. He maintained a firm grip on a somewhat bedraggled teddy bear that Sally Pinter had given him that afternoon.

"What are you going to fix him for dinner?" she had asked when Claude picked him up.

"Something simple but nutritious," Claude assured her with a wink.

"Kitty's outside, no doubt looking for a rat to catch," Claude informed the child while filling a saucepan with a couple inches of water. "I thought that for dinner tonight we would try a little oatmeal."

"Oatmeal," the boy repeated, the beginnings of a smile appearing at the corners of his mouth.

"Do you like oatmeal?" Claude asked hopefully.

The boy shook his head vigorously.

"Too bad, 'cause that's what we're having. That and some raisin toast with strawberry jam. What sorts of things does your daddy fix for dinner?"

"Oatmeal."

"I thought as much. Do you know where your daddy is right now?"

"Kitty."

Claude took a quart of chocolate milk out of the refrigerator and poured a glass for Earl. "Can you use *oatmeal* and *kitty* in the same sentence?"

Earl drank half the glass immediately and looked up at Claude expectantly.

"Save the rest for dinner," Claude advised, busy with the bubbling oatmeal and the toaster. "Voilá." He placed a bowl in front of Earl with a flourish. "First, we put a pat of butter in it, to give you a head start on the road to cardiovascular disease, then we sprinkle brown sugar all over it, like so. Then, a little . . ." Claude paused, suddenly remembering he had forgotten to buy whole milk when he picked up the quart of chocolate and the raisin bread. "Oh, well, I always perferred my oatmeal with chocolate milk anyway. How about you?"

Earl, wide-eyed, looked from the bowl to Claude. He nodded yes.

Claude smiled, charmed by the absence of guile in Earl's face. *You better come get this boy quick, Jesse,* he thought, *before I start getting used to having him around.*

"We're going to do just fine," he assured Earl with a wink as the two of them began to eat. "Just fine."